PROMISES TO KEEP

"Until I know you are safe, you will remain with me," Wolf declared.

"That is unnecessary," Isobel replied.

"Perhaps. But until I am convinced otherwise, we are bedfellows in a very real sense of the word."

Her eyes went wide and wild color stained her cheeks. "I will not...you promised..."

"I have never had to force a woman to my will before." Nay, in the past he had wooed them slowly until they came to him with their own burning desires. A primitive jolt of satisfaction moved through him at the thought of Isobel coming to him in the heat of her passion.

It was a challenge worth taking, but that challenge was not for him. He'd made her a promise—marriage in name only. It was a promise he would have to keep, unless *she* changed her mind.

Other *Leisure* books by Gerri Russell:

THE WARRIOR TRAINER

GERRI RUSSELL

WARRIOR'S BRIDE

LEISURE BOOKS   NEW YORK CITY

A LEISURE BOOK®

October 2007

Published by

Dorchester Publishing Co., Inc.
200 Madison Avenue
New York, NY 10016

ISBN-10: 0-8439-5984-3
ISBN-13: 978-0-8439-5984-0

Visit us on the web at www.dorchesterpub.com.

DEDICATION

People are like stained-glass windows. They sparkle and shine when the sun is out, but when the darkness sets in, their true beauty is revealed only if there is a light from within.

—*Elizabeth Kubler-Ross*

For Kathy Jacobs, my sister, and Andrea Heuston, my should-have-been sister, two strong, compassionate women I am proud to call my dearest friends.

I would also like to express my thanks to the eminently talented Trish Knowles, for sharing her passion for and knowledge of blowing glass. You brought Wolf's need to create alive. For that, I am forever grateful.

WARRIOR'S BRIDE

Prologue

Isle of St. Kilda, Scotland, 1353

She hated the darkness.

Lady Grisel Grange tensed against the iron manacles that held her imprisoned. Night would be upon her any moment. With a hitch of her breath, she clung to the slivers of apricot light still visible through the arrow slit in the tower wall.

Icy fear pulsed through her as the slivers became threads, shifting from orange to red. She knew the progression of her nightly terror as intimately as she knew the grooves in the cold stone at her back.

She'd had four months to memorize the nuances of each stone. Four months to consider why her husband had cruelly confined her to this place—a place so isolated and remote she knew after the first week of her imprisonment that the people who brought her food would not rescue her, nor would anyone else.

Once that realization had set in, she wondered why he had not killed her instead of exiling her here in the cold stone tower on the remote isle of St. Kilda. But she already knew the answer: He feared her powerful family. He feared what they would do to him if she turned up dead. Instead, he had kidnapped her and forcibly taken from her everything she held dear. Everything except what he did not know she had.

With trembling fingers she struggled against the heavy iron manacles that encircled her wrists until she found what she sought. Her abdomen bulged beneath her touch. He had not known she was pregnant when he'd locked her in this tower. A soft thump beat against her fingers, easing the fear of the dark that consumed her each night.

If he had known of the baby, he would have used the child as ruthlessly as he had used her, trying to gain access to a throne that was not rightfully his. He wanted the lineage her bloodline and her abilities as a seer could lend him. And when she'd failed to give him a child, he'd tossed her away like damaged goods. It was ironic that what he wanted so desperately he'd never known he had attained.

She smoothed her fingers over her ever-increasing belly. Was the babe she carried a blessing or a curse? The life growing inside her kept her from loneliness each night as darkness fell. But would her child soon share her imprisonment in this nightmare?

The last rays of light slipped from purple to black, and she found herself plunged into darkness. No moon hung in the sky tonight to offer even the slightest hint of light. And despite the child who pulsed beneath her fingers, a sob escaped her.

Another night of haunting emptiness lay before her—relentless, unfailing, unforgivable. Unforgivable because of what the darkness forced her to do.

She slipped her fingers from her abdomen to her neck, to the small white stone with its one rounded edge and one jagged edge nestled in a web of delicate leather cords. Another secret her husband had not known she possessed. If he had, he would have stripped it from her. She clutched the necklace like a lifeline, knowing it was the one thing that quieted her fear.

The Seer's Stone and the visions it provided offered her a way to escape. She gripped the Stone all the harder until the smooth surface warmed against her palm. She knew she should not give in, allow the visions to sweep her away, but she had no choice. She'd succumbed to the light of the visions months ago.

She lifted the Stone away from her neck and brought her forehead down to meet it. Only then could she see into the future.

Whose future? She did not care anymore, not as long as the visions brought light. Captured by the lure of the Stone, her eyes drifted closed. Instantly her mind filled with a myriad of swirling colors: red, blue, green, orange. The colors blended together in a wash of light.

She clung to the image, held it in her mind, relaxing against the cold stone wall until her knees went weak. She slid to the floor, the clink of the chains filling the silence of the night, as the vision engulfed her in temporary respite.

Yet each nightly escape came with a price. That price: a slow spiral toward insanity. She could feel the fibers of her mind snapping, releasing her from her grip with the real world. And each night she vowed the journey would be her last, until the sun set and the Stone beckoned once more.

Beyond turning back now, she pushed into the vision until the tangy scent of sea salt hung in the air, replacing the foul stench of the tower. An image appeared, and white, frothy waves curled toward a beach in end-less progression.

The waves hypnotized her. She let them. She focused her thoughts on the waves rolling toward the shore, grateful for the lack of anything more. Perhaps she'd es-cape further damage to her mind this time. Perhaps she would not become totally lost to madness before she de-livered her child.

As the thought fully formed, so too did the image of a willowy blonde. The young woman stood on the beach. Foamy white waves glistened at her feet. Each surge and retreat of the waves beckoned the girl to join them. The young woman stared out into the distance as though searching for something, someone.

The image shifted from the shoreline to farther be-yond. To a ship with its sails stretched taut against the wind. On the deck of the ship stood a dark-haired man, his body tense with determination. And as if he knew Lady Grange was watching him, his gaze snapped in her direction, his face hardened into a mask of anger, his eyes turning from a rich dark brown to an icy metallic black.

She gasped.

"How did you get aboard my ship?" he asked, his gaze piercing hers.

He could see her. How? No one ever had before.

She tried to pull away from the vision, but it refused to let her go. She would prefer the darkness to facing this angry man. Who was he? Why did the vision bring her here?

"Answer me," he demanded, coming toward her. He reached for her shoulder. Her breath caught as he touched her, his grip firm but not cruel, even as the vision shifted. The man faded from view, and she saw the night sky.

An endless sea of blackness broken only by the moon. Except the moon was split in two. The two equal halves, with jagged edges facing each other, hung in the sky a great distance apart. They drifted slowly together, in an attempt to become whole.

In an attempt to become whole . . .

A shrill scream tore through the void of the night sky, a long, raw sound that seemed to go on and on, straining until it broke on a hoarse note.

With an effort, she ripped the Seer's Stone away from her forehead as that last thought echoed in her mind. *In an attempt to become whole . . .*

The necklace, and the stone it held, thumped against her chest as she stuffed her hand in her mouth to keep another scream from escaping. She would never be whole again as long as she used the Seer's Stone to escape the darkness.

Insanity was her future now. Tonight's vision had proven that. Never before had she imagined the people in her visions could see her in return.

A muffled sob escaped into the silence of the dark, dank tower. How many more days, weeks—or, heaven help, her—years would she have to endure this misery?

As long as it takes, an answering voice from deep within her replied. Her child was all that mattered now.

She slipped her fingers from her mouth and stretched them toward her belly. She had to be strong for her child.

She lifted her quivering chin to stare out into the night. The slight haze of dawn appeared. Relief filled her. She'd made it through the worst of the night.

This night . . . a voice in her head challenged. But she pushed the thought away.

She refused to let fear take hold. All that mattered was freedom for her child. From her womb and from this tower prison. And, with luck, from this isolated isle.

She would continue to be strong for her child.

Chapter One

Isle of St. Kilda, Scotland, 1372

Isobel Grange felt an ominous tingle race across the back of her neck. A portent of doom. Her mother had always warned her of such things. But what could harm her at the crofter's cottage she called home on the remote isle of St. Kilda? The locals paid her no heed, and her foster family only cared about how quickly she did her chores.

Izzy shook off the odd sensation. She had just set a basket of eggs on the wooden table in the center of the room when the door thumped closed behind her.

She turned toward the sound and gasped. A tall, broad-shouldered man stood in front of the door. He was dressed in the style of their countrymen, in a saffron shirt and dark woolen tartan.

"Lady Isobel?"

The breath stilled in her chest. He knew her name—her real name. The stone walls of the cottage seemed to close in around her.

His dark eyes examined her. "Are you Lady Isobel?" His words were short and sharp.

A thick, heavy silence settled over the room until the only sounds that remained were the pop and hiss of the fire and the stuttering of her own controlled breathing. Izzy nervously flexed then clenched her hands at her sides, resisting panic. "I am Izzy . . . Isobel."

He continued his cool assessment of her with eyes that were jet black and framed with even darker lashes—dark as the night sky and as emotionless as the blackest soul. She tried not to flinch as his gaze moved from her face to her unkempt hair, her tattered skirt, and her dusty slippers.

A hint of displeasure crept into the dark shadows of his eyes, and she bristled in response. He would judge her as all the rest did, by her looks and nothing more. Izzy boldly met his gaze despite the gnawing fear that grew with each passing heartbeat. "Who are you?" she said slowly, the words helping her regain control of her emotions. Her curiosity grounded her when nothing else could.

When he did not answer, she stepped up to him, closer to the door and the openness she knew existed beyond. "Remove yourself at once and let me out," she commanded, surprised at the haughty tone in her voice. Never had she spoken to anyone that way. Such behavior might land her back in the tower—a place she vowed never to return to.

He shook his head and kept his hand firmly against the door latch. "I will release the door if you promise to sit down and listen. I have come to make you an offer."

Izzy swallowed against the sudden dryness in her throat. "An offer?"

His angular features became hard. "For your hand in marriage."

Marriage? Izzy blinked, stunned. For a moment she could only gape at him. "Never."

"I am afraid the offer I give you is no better than the one given me." A flicker of compassion reflected in his eyes before it vanished. "You will marry, and you will leave this isle right now."

"Nay—"

"I am offering you a new life."

A new life? New hope? How long had it been since she had allowed herself such a fantasy? Did he truly offer her a chance to escape this isle and her nightmare of being returned to the tower where she'd spent the first seven years of her life? Her mother's death had released her from that torment only to be enslaved by the MacDonalds as their servant. Izzy's gaze fastened on his. A twitch of impatience pulsed in his jaw.

"You have no choice. My men await me at the shore. Come."

"Who you are, and why—" The frantic rattle of the door latch broke off her words.

"Izzy! Izzy!" her foster father called out as he rapped a fist against the closed door. "There is a boat at the shoreline. A stranger was reported headed this way. Is he with you? Izzy, answer me."

The tension in her muscles only increased at the sound of her foster father's voice. "Aldous MacDonald will never let you take me away." Frantic pounding sounded against the wooden portal, echoing through the room.

"Do not be so certain of that." A steely resolve settled in the stranger's gaze. Large and intimidating, he towered over her. If he wanted to, he could make her go anywhere by brute force. Could he force her foster father to release her as well?

He dropped his hand from the door latch. It flew

open. Her foster father filled the doorway with his bulk. "What do ye want with Izzy?" His startled gaze flew between her and the stranger, his eyes revealing first fear, then anger.

"The Lady Isobel?" The stranger's face remained shadowed as he withdrew a folded sheet of parchment from inside his tartan and handed it to her foster father. "She is to be my bride."

Alarm flashed on Aldous's face as he scanned the document. Isobel edged closer until she could see the document clearly herself. It bore the bold seal of Robert II of Scotland, grandson of Robert the Bruce.

"Did my father send you here?" Aldous demanded.

"The king sent me."

Aldous frowned. "How could anyone know of her existence, especially the king?"

"The king knows a great many things." The stranger towered over her foster father like a dark, immovable force. "And he will not be disobeyed without retribution."

A tendril of fear shivered up her spine, not at the veiled threat but as she read her true name, *Lady Isobel,* on the parchment that bore the king's seal.

"No one knew our secret," Aldous mumbled to himself as he examined the papers before him. His skin was pasty, and fear glittered in his eyes. "If the king knows about her, then so does *he.*"

The stranger frowned. "Who do you speak of?"

Izzy knew that he spoke of her own father. That Aldous MacDonald feared the man as much as she did sent a chill to her very core. Her mother had warned that if her father ever found her, her life would be in danger.

Did Aldous fear some danger as well? His gaze darted about the room as though searching for something in the darkest shadows. "If he and the king both know the truth . . ." He returned his gaze to Izzy. "To lose the girl will be difficult . . . She's become quite important to our household."

The stranger's gaze took in her bedraggled clothing and hair, her well-worn slippers. "I can see that." The soft lilt of his words contrasted sharply with the flash of steel in his eyes.

The fear in Aldous's eyes faded, replaced by hopeful appraisal. She had seen that look on her foster father's face when he bartered over goods. He was calculating just how much she might be worth to this man. With a sense of growing irritation, she watched the two men bargain.

"I've spent years training her," her foster father said. "She's quite valuable in that she is strong, biddable, and of childbearing age. Those things canna be ignored or given over without some sort of fee."

"It is usually the groom who is compensated with a dowry." The stranger's face grew shadowed again as he reached for the brown leather bag tied to his belt. He tossed the bag on the table, and the coins inside clinked against each other. "Twenty-five gold pieces should offset your loss."

At the sight of the coins, Izzy frowned. She might not know much about the world, but something did not seem quite right here. "Why would you pay a fortune in gold to take me away from here?"

"Quiet!" Aldous thundered. "Yer future is to be decided between myself and the gentleman."

Izzy raised her chin and stared at the stranger, silently demanding an answer. Before they could comment she continued. "And why should I go with you? I don't even know your name, let alone where you plan to take me."

The stubborn look in the stranger's eyes said she would leave with him no matter the obstacle. "My name is . . ." He hesitated. "My name is . . . Douglas." The word sounded difficult for him to say. "I am taking you to the Black Isle. And you *will* come with me." He turned away from her, putting an end to any further protests. "Now," he addressed Aldous, "do you agree to my terms?"

Aldous reached for the bag of coins. " 'Tis done. Izzy, go peacefully with the man, and make of yer future what ye can. The MacDonalds never meant to hold you captive. We were forced to do so by the secrets of yer life. Now that those secrets are revealed, yer future is up to you."

His words sounded like he did not expect her to have a future at all. In her mind's eye she saw her mother, frail and discarded, among the shadows of the tower room, heard her warning: *Beware of those who know your past, Isobel. For they are a danger and cannot be trusted.*

Izzy shook her head, forcing the memory away. Her mother had been half mad when she'd said those things. Pain-filled ravings, that's what they had been. And memories best left untouched. The only dangers that awaited her were those she brought on herself by putting too much trust in those around her.

Regardless of why the stranger had offered a fortune in gold for her to come with him, she would grasp this opportunity. He provided her a way off the isle. As for his offer of marriage . . . There had to be a way out of that trap. Marriage for her mother had only brought isolation, starvation, and death.

Izzy wanted more from her life, even if she'd never pursued such hopes before. Her dreams of freedom had kept her alive during the most difficult times of her life. And they would give her strength now.

"If your business is done here, then let us be away." She reached for the threadbare wool shawl that hung across the back of a chair, then wrapped it about her shoulders.

The stranger's features softened before he dipped his head in assent. She thought she saw a flicker of admiration in his eyes, but then it was gone. "Get your things, Lady Isobel."

"I am wearing all that I own." She straightened her shoulders with pride despite her embarrassment.

The stranger cursed softly beneath his breath. "Then let us go."

More out of courtesy than thanks, she said good-bye to her foster father and stepped through the doorway. The stranger followed her across the yard beyond the crofthouse and into the heather-scented air of early spring.

Despite her brave words about leaving, her legs quivered as she headed over the ridge that led to the shoreline below. When a three-masted ship came into view, her footsteps faltered. Once she boarded that ship she would leave behind the only place she had ever known.

What was the rest of the world like? She had often wondered. Now she would have the opportunity to find out for herself. Her throat tightened with both fear and excitement. She had waited her whole life for this moment. Why was it suddenly so hard to take the next step toward the shore? She drew a deep breath, as though it would bolster her bravado. If only she did not suddenly feel so alone.

The stranger paused beside her. "Come. We must hurry before the tide shifts and we find ourselves stranded."

"I almost forgot." Pivoting, she ran back toward the house. She gained three steps of freedom before the stranger's hands grasped her waist. Before she could draw a breath, he swept her off the ground and draped her over his shoulder.

"Put me down," she gasped, and kicked sharply at his gut.

The stranger barely broke stride and only tightened his grip. She could feel the heat of his hands through her skirts on the back of her calves and across her bottom. A shiver coursed through her. "Please put me down." Her words came out as a whisper.

He slowed but did not loosen his hold. "So I can have you run away again?"

"I will not run. You have my word."

He stopped and set her down. Annoyance snapped in his eyes. "You have nothing to fear from me."

"It is madness to trust you." A desperate laugh bubbled up. "I don't even know you."

"We will be acquainted soon enough when we are wed." He reached out and encircled her wrist, drawing her toward the shoreline once more. "We've a long journey ahead."

She dug her heels into the loamy soil, forcing him to stop as she cast a glance back at the house.

He tugged at her arm.

"Wait."

"What?"

"I'd like to bring a small piece of this place with me."

He frowned. "I thought you said you owned nothing."

"I don't . . ." She hesitated. "I mean, there is only this one small thing."

Once again, his jaw tightened, and she wished that momentary compassion she'd seen in his eyes would return instead. "Can it be retrieved quickly?" he asked.

At his words, her spirits lightened. "Oh, aye."

"Fine." He turned back toward the yard.

She stayed him with her hand. "Let me go alone. I will be quick."

After a slight hesitation, he nodded.

Izzy raced across the open grass. One small item, it was all she needed to make the journey to her new life feel less uncertain. She disappeared around the side of the crofthouse. No one on the isle would ever know she'd taken it with her.

At least she hoped not.

Chapter Two

Douglas Moraer Stewart, called the Black Wolf of Scotland by his enemies and Wolf by his friends, frowned as the girl disappeared around the back of the house. The woman was annoying, inconvenient, irritating, and more vulnerable than he ever imagined a woman could be. Damn his father and his royal ultimatums. As the king he had every right to demand his subjects do his bidding. As a father he misused that power, asking his sons—even his bastard sons—to perform tasks that went far beyond duty and into abuse.

The man, be he father or king, had abused Walter and himself for years. At first, Wolf had believed it was because of his father's increasing bouts of dementia, but that theory became harder to hold on to as the years passed.

As he and Walter had matured, and fought back, their father's manipulations had only grown worse. It was almost as if the more control he lost over his body and his mind, the tighter his grip became on his sons—

merciless and unrelenting as it was this day. An ultimatum had been issued: Marry the girl or Walter would die for treason.

A false charge, but that mattered not to their father as long as it got him what he wanted: the power to play puppet master over his sons. Wolf clenched, then released, his fists at his sides in an attempt to control his frustration.

In order to save Walter from the hangman's noose, Wolf had come to St. Kilda prepared to retrieve the girl, marry her, then stash her away in some desolate location. His commitment to his father would be fulfilled, and Walter would remain free. Everyone would win— everyone except the girl.

He had seen the shadows that lingered in her eyes— shadows he recognized from the challenges of his own life. It didn't take much looking to see she had been abandoned long ago. Could he, in good conscience, abandon her again?

He forced the thought away before it had time to sway his resolve. He would do what he had to in order to keep Walter out of their father's dungeon. If it meant adding further anxiety to the ill-used waif's life, so be it. She deserved no sympathy from him, not after all it had cost him to graft her into his own life. Marriage to the girl would at least get her off this isle and away from the people who abused her.

He narrowed his gaze on the isolated area near the cottage. What was taking her so long? She had promised not to run away, but could he trust her to be true to her word? Impatient to be on his way, he strode toward the cottage. Suddenly she reappeared. With one hand, she clutched her shawl around her thin shoulders. In the other hand she held a woolen sack. Her steps were quick. "Now I will go peacefully," she said, moving past him, down the hill toward the shoreline.

Wolf followed her to the water. He opened his mouth to ask what she had hidden in the bag, but his attention moved to the gentle sway of her hips beneath her ragged clothes, and he forgot the question. Her movements were graceful, even somewhat refined. Even so, his future bride looked more like a scrawny, underfed bird than a desirable noblewoman. He turned his thoughts away from the girl as they approached his men. Brahan, Giric, Kenneth, and Fergus all stood watch around the small boat that would take them into the harbor and onto the *Ategenos*.

"Is Walter aboard the ship?" Wolf asked when he did not see his brother among the men. He had demanded Walter be returned to his care before he retrieved, then married the girl. He'd been surprised at how easily his father had agreed to Wolf's terms. He still was not sure why his father had done something so uncharacteristic, but Wolf was willing to worry about that later.

"Aye, Walter is aboard. He returned to the ship to prepare for our departure. Is this the girl?" Brahan MacGregor asked, his gaze running over their new shipmate with surprise. Silky brown hair brushed Brahan's temples, adding a touch of rakishness to his otherwise lean and elegant face. "My lord Wolf, are you certain you want to do this?"

Wolf frowned at his friend, his confidant, the captain of his guard. A chill morning wind swept across the land dotted with patches of gorse and heather. An omen of change, his mother had always claimed. Wolf stifled a shiver as he held firm to his resolve. "The king has commanded me. Like it or not, it is an order I cannot ignore."

"And what of my vision?" Brahan glanced at the leather pouch tied to the waist of his red and green tartan. Inside, he carried a small white stone, no larger than his thumb. One side was rounded, the other jagged, and an alpha symbol had been etched across the top. "I have seen it all—your acceptance of his request, your journey, and your death."

"About my death, you are wrong." Despite his denial, a ripple of unease coursed through Wolf.

"You would take that chance?" Brahan's voice turned hard, but concern weighed heavy on his face.

"If it spares my brother's life, aye. I must do whatever it takes to keep Walter safe, to see him freed from our father's manipulative grasp."

Brahan's frown deepened. "She is not at all like the woman the Stone revealed—"

"Enough," Wolf interrupted as he grasped Lady Isobel's thin arm and guided her into the small boat that would carry them to the ship. When he released her, she moved to the bow of the craft and huddled down, hugging the sack to her chest.

The men pushed off, then jumped inside the boat, rowing toward the larger ship in the distance.

"Something's not right here." Brahan studied the girl with a frown. "The woman in my vision was more refined. Less—" Brahan broke off as he met the full force of Wolf's annoyed gaze.

He held out his hand. "Give me that stone. I am done with its magic and its curse."

Brahan drew back. "Nay."

Wolf frowned, knowing that Brahan never went anywhere without the Seer's Stone. "Leave well enough alone, my friend, or I will take that Stone and toss it into the sea."

"You would do no such thing." A touch of humor lifted Brahan's lips as he folded his arms over his chest and gazed at Wolf. "The Seer's Stone and my sight have been far too helpful to you."

Wolf's gaze moved to the splash of white hair at Brahan's temple. Each use of the Stone increased the size of the pale streak in his friend's brown locks. "Then do not tempt me," Wolf murmured with a stab of guilt as he turned his gaze back to the girl. An undeniable sadness shadowed her eyes as she gazed out at the water. He closed himself off to the compassion that threatened. His duty called for marriage, nothing more.

Silence hovered over the small boat as they approached the *Ategenos*. They pulled up alongside the ship. From this perspective, the three tall masts of the large carrack seemed to reach toward the heavens. A gentle breeze tugged at the unfurled sails and sent soft green waves to lap in an unending rhythm against the sides of the ship.

Wolf grasped the rope ladder with one hand as it thumped against the wooden hull and reached for the girl with his other hand. "Give me your bag," he ordered more harshly than he had intended.

She clasped the dirty brown sack tight against her chest. "It stays with me."

Stubborn and innocent. He frowned. "How do you intend to climb the ladder with that bag in your hands?" Could she not follow even the most simple of instructions? "Give me the bag."

"I won't give it up." A subtle challenge rang in her tone.

He grasped her hand, rejecting her dare. "Keep the bag if you must."

Before she could resist, he pulled her over his shoulder for the second time that day.

She gasped but did not fight him as he'd expected. He climbed to the deck above, her weight barely tugging at his shoulder, giving evidence of just how thin she was beneath her well-worn gown. He released her as suddenly as he'd swept her up.

The girl steadied herself against the ship's railing.

"Captain on deck," Walter shouted. The crew snapped to attention as Wolf strode past them to Walter's side. His brother's face had grown thin, his body gaunt, signs of his stay in the pits of their father's dungeon. What kind of father would do that to a son? One who would do anything to get what he wanted, Wolf reminded himself.

He'd been a boy of eleven and his father not yet the king. Yet even then the man had many enemies, and he'd used his sons for his own purposes.

A memory formed before he could stop it. He saw himself and Walter, hiding in the shadowed hallway of their mother's cottage. Wolf held his breath for fear of discovery. He listened in silence for a hint as to why their father had come to visit their mother. He had abandoned her as his mistress long ago, and yet today he had come back. Why?

Cloistered inside the bedchamber, Wolf had his suspicions. This was not a conjugal visit. Nay, he'd seen that look in his father's eyes before—on the day he'd forced Walter and himself to steal horses from the Chattan clan. He gazed through the darkness at his mother's closed door. Something dark and dangerous was about to unfold.

A heartbeat later, the chamber door flew open and their father strode out, turning his back on his mother's soft sobs. Wolf froze, knowing he should flee, get himself and Walter to safety. Yet he could not wrench his gaze away from his mother's sorrowful face. She sat in a chair, her shoulders slumped. Tears fell from her cheeks onto the hand she held before her—a hand that clutched a small white stone.

"Come out where I can see you, boys. I know you are there." The man stopped an arm's length from them.

Wolf stepped out of the shadows, into the light, placing himself between his father and Walter. "What do you want?"

"You will come with me."

"Our place is here with our mother," Wolf challenged him boldly. "She needs someone to protect her now that you've abandoned her."

"You have no choice in the matter," his father said with a touch of irritation. "The deal has been made. My sons for the Seer's Stone."

"Our mother would never make such a deal."

"She had no choice either. The Stone is merely a way for her to see her sons, to see how you are faring while you work for me." He shrugged. "Although I doubt she will find the visions peaceful."

"Why today?" Wolf's anger flared. "What do you need us for this time?"

"So many questions." His father smiled faintly. "That is good. Your inquisitive nature will serve you well as my mercenary."

A shiver ran through Wolf. He met his father's gaze. "We are your sons."

"Aye. 'Tis every son's obligation to protect their father from his enemies."

He wouldn't. He couldn't. "We are too young."

"You are old enough," his father replied. His hand snaked out and grasped Wolf.

"Run, Walter! Go hide and don't come out until Father is gone." Wolf forced Walter out from behind him, sending him flying toward the door. The man moved to catch the younger boy, but Wolf brought his booted foot down hard on his father's instep.

The man howled in pain. His grip tightened on Wolf's arm mercilessly. "I'll get that boy yet."

"Not while I still breathe." Wolf straightened, pushing back his own shock and disbelief. His father would take him away. Turn him into a killer. But he would never touch Walter. Not innocent, softhearted Walter.

"You've cost me dear, boy," his father's voice held steely menace. "You'll pay for that misdeed for the rest of your life."

His father had been true to his word. Wolf had paid dearly, sacrificing his very soul. Forced to play the strong arm of his father's rule by reigning terror across the Highlands, imprisoning and murdering those who offended or opposed him, and pillaging the countryside, he'd earned his name as the Black Wolf of Scotland. For years he had done his father's irrational bidding in an attempt to keep Walter safe, until Wolf could no longer silence in his own mind the mournful cries of those whose lives he destroyed.

He'd extricated himself from his father's grasp by building his own army of faithful warriors. With troops that outnumbered the king's, he'd gained his own freedom.

And that was when the man had gone after Walter.

When would it all end? Would this marriage truly put a stop to his father's machinations?

Wolf allowed his gaze to drift back to the girl. She stood clutching her bag, her gaze connecting with his. A spark of determination flared in the depths of her dark brown eyes. Her gaze said without words that she might be defeated for now, but she was certainly not done with him or having a say in her future.

Instead of irritation, Wolf felt the corner of his mouth pull up in amusement. She had spirit, at least. He acknowledged her challenge with a nod, then turned back to greet his brother with a clap on the shoulder. "Are we ready to sail?"

Walter nodded, his expression relieved until he faced the girl. "She gained my freedom?" Walter's gaze hardened. "If I were you, I'd risk Father's wrath and leave her here."

Wolf frowned. More than anyone, Walter should understand his choice. "I made a promise. A promise that released you from Father's dungeon."

"I do appreciate all that you have had to endure on my behalf, Wolf. But why further your own pain? Promise or not, do you truly have to marry the girl?" Walter grimaced with distaste as a shadow moved across his face. "Through her, you will connect yourself to Father again. She's hardly worth it. Such a scrawny little thing."

Her chin came up as they all appraised her, weighing her against Walter's ill comments. Even so, she remained silent.

"Enough, Walter. She gained your freedom, that's what's important." Wolf turned the full extent of his irritation upon his brother. "No more comments. And no more excuses. You've been given a new start. Make the most of it."

Walter's face went pale a moment before he straightened his shoulders. "Thank you for giving me command of the *Ategenos*. I won't fail you this time. I promise."

Wolf had heard those words many times before. Perhaps this time Walter would follow through without getting himself into trouble. "I would not have allowed you to act as first mate if I didn't think you could perform the task." Wolf scanned the deck, taking account of what needed doing in order to set sail. "The head winds are picking up. I want to get underway immediately."

Walter nodded, then began barking orders to winch the small boat to the deck and hoist the anchor. Away from St. Kilda, Wolf would be free to . . . His gaze sought out the girl. His thoughts vanished at the look of both awe and fear etched on her angular face. She watched the crew as they raised the lateen sails. Once extended, the sails caught the cold rush of wind and the *Ategenos* eased out of the harbor.

Tangy salt air brushed Wolf's face, and for a moment he tasted his freedom. He always did in that first rush of sea air. There were no demands he must live up to, no expectations from anyone else, merely the sea and himself, together as one.

The sails flapped, then filled out as the force of the wind worked upon them. The *Ategenos* leapt, climbing one swell, falling softly down toward the next. He welcomed again the experience of the ship's rhythms, the creaking of the hull, the rustling of the sails, the humming of the rigging. He drew a deep breath of air, relishing the dewy spray of white water as it broke over the lee rail to caress the deck.

"Excuse me." The girl brushed past him. Her face had lost all its color. She lurched toward the rail.

He followed her to the railing as she hung over the starboard side. "Have you never been on a ship before?" he asked with irritation.

"I have never been off the isle," she moaned.

His gaze moved over her. In any other situation he would have allowed himself to feel some compassion for the girl, but this time he could not. To feel anything toward her would only give his father more leverage against him. Why else would the king have insisted on this marriage? As Walter had knowingly pointed out, their father intended to use Wolf's connection to the girl to bend him to his kingly will. Wolf straightened. He would never allow that to happen.

The same breeze that had cleansed his soul only moments before now felt heavy and cold. Wolf reached for the cloak he had left draped across the railing. He shrugged the heavy wool about his shoulders, then turned back to the girl. Shivers racked her body. He frowned as he watched her lean against the railing, her arms crossed over her chest, trying to gather whatever warmth she could to her frail body. Her threadbare clothing offered little defense against the wind's gathering force.

He shouldn't care about her comfort, and yet with each shudder of her body his resolve faltered. He groaned. As a future husband it was his duty to provide his bride with at least simple comforts. He moved beside her and slipped his cloak about her thin shoulders. "This should help."

She turned to him, her eyes reflecting a challenge. "Thank you for the cloak. I may need your protection right now, but I do not have to like it." The words caught him off guard. He had never met a woman more in need of help, and yet she refused to give him any advantage. Intriguing.

Wolf turned abruptly away at the unwanted thought, searching the receding shoreline of St. Kilda. He could not afford to connect himself to this woman emotionally. Danger lay down that path for both of them. Neither had any choice but to play the game the king had set in motion with as much distance between them as possible.

"How long until we reach this Black Isle?" she asked.

He turned back to her. "We have one day of hard sail ahead of us, then two more over land."

"And when will we be forced to marry?"

If it were possible, he swore her skin turned even paler. He had no reason to lie to her, and yet he hesitated.

"I have a right to know my future." Her voice grew stronger as she pushed herself away from the railing.

"As soon as we reach the Black Isle we shall marry."

"I see," she replied, her tone mournful.

Was she that repulsed by him? "It is a fate neither of us can avoid."

Her gaze moved from the deck to the sea beyond, at the receding shoreline that was barely visible now. "Perhaps." She sounded resigned, but the set of her chin warned of something more.

He stared at her without speaking, snared by her image, both vulnerable and strong. Again, an intriguing mix.

He allowed his gaze to linger on her full lips, the soft skin of her neck and shoulders that gleamed with beads of sea spray. A hint of fullness peeked out above her bodice, and Wolf imagined the sculpted breasts that lay beneath. What he could not see, what he imagined, enticed him.

"My lord Wolf." Brahan's shout broke into his thoughts, jerking him back to the moment.

He turned abruptly away from the source of his speculation. "What?"

"Another vision." Brahan clutched the small white stone in his hand. At Wolf's frown he stuffed the Stone back into its protective pouch.

"I told you not to—"

"I had to know more about the girl," Brahan said in a rush. "But I saw a ship in the vision just as the men sighted it in the distance."

From the railing, Walter turned to face Wolf, deep lines of worry etched into his already haggard face.

"Pirates?" Wolf shouted above the wind.

Walter nodded. "She's a square-rigged ship, and she's flying no flag."

"Load the cannon," Wolf called to the crew, who scrambled to do his bidding. Brahan and Walter stood nearby, awaiting their orders. "With square rigging, they will have to tack more often. That should allow us to outsail them, but we must be ready, regardless."

"And the girl?" Brahan asked. "What do we do with her?"

Her gaze clung to Wolf's. A spark of challenge reflected there.

He had no time to battle her. "Take her to my cabin," he ordered Brahan, the words barely audible as a loud boom filled the air, followed by a slow, keening whine. "Cannonball," Brahan yelled as he moved toward the railing. The sound rose in pitch, growing closer and closer until a thunderous splash sounded next to the starboard side.

The *Ategenos* pitched wildly to port. A wall of water

cascaded over the deck, drenching them in a chill ocean bath. Brahan lost his footing.

Wolf caught Brahan's arm with one hand. With his other, he scooped the girl against his chest, holding her tight until the ship leveled. A warmth tingled through him despite the bitter cold.

A light flush came to her cheeks as if she felt it too. She looked away. "My bag," she cried, reaching past him for the brown bag and the object inside that wiggled against its sodden prison.

Brahan regained his footing. "We are under attack. Did I not warn you of such a thing when we set off on this journey? Did the Stone not predict this would be our demise?"

"Not now, Brahan." Wolf scooped the girl into his arms. Through her wet clothing he felt her tremble. He thrust her at Brahan. "Take her below."

"My bag." She struggled against Brahan's grasp.

"I will see to that." Wolf twisted away, turning his attention to the battle ahead. "Ready the cannon," he shouted, prepared to pummel the scoundrels who had fired upon them. No one attacked the Black Wolf of Scotland and lived to tell the tale.

Chapter Three

"All hands into position," Walter cried. "If they have more than one cannon they could fire on us at any time." Under Walter's leadership, the crew loaded the cannon. The weapon was small and light, but sufficient to blow a hole through their enemy's hull.

Wolf scooped the girl's wet bag off the deck. A loud squawk issued from inside. "What the devil?"

He opened the sack and stared, incredulous. A chicken? A protest came from within, followed by a flurry of brown feathers. He clamped the bag shut, but the chicken had seen the way to freedom. Through the fabric, it pecked at his hand. He held the sack away from himself, but that did nothing to spare his fingers from the bird's assault. Just then another cannonball slammed the water, this time off the port side.

"Fire when ready," he shouted as he lurched toward a barrel that had once been filled with grain. He shoved the chicken inside, then turned back to his men. "If our attackers want a battle, let's give them one they won't soon forget."

He studied the enemy ship. Who were they? Had his father sent someone after them? Or was this one of his own enemies come to pay retribution?

His ship's cannon launched with a deafening roar. The acrid scent of gunpowder hung in the air. Wolf watched the ball sail toward the other ship. With a satisfying crack, it pierced the port bow. Shouts of euphoria from his ship mixed with anguished cries from the other as the pursuing vessel slowed behind them.

"Should we prepare to board?" Walter questioned.

"Nay." Through a haze of gray smoke Wolf watched as the other ship listed, sinking lower in the water. "We must continue on to the shores of Torridon. Speed is of the essence."

Walter turned to call out orders to the crew.

Anger churned inside Wolf. Whoever their attackers had been, they would not be following them anytime soon. His ship was secure for now. But could they continue their journey as planned? He had originally planned their passage from St. Kilda to the North Channel. Then, from the port at Torridon, they would begin their two-day trek over land. Only behind his own castle walls could he guarantee the safety of his men. The girl would be safe there as well.

"Captain, sir." A flush-faced sailor hurried toward Wolf.

"What is it?" He set down his sextant, annoyed that he had allowed his thoughts to return to the waif in his care.

The sailor skidded to a stop. His breath came in short gasps. "The Lady Isobel . . . your quarters."

Wolf frowned. "What about her?"

The sailor swallowed hard. "I think . . . you had better see for yourself."

What could have happened now? Wolf held his irrita-

tion in check as he descended into the bowels of the
Ategenos.

"In here, sir." The sailor motioned toward the door.

Wolf strode into the room, then stopped short. "My
God, what has happened here?"

His quarters were in shambles. Charts, maps, books,
and clothing were tossed all over the room as if blown
by gale force winds. Brahan's shirt hung loose at the
waist of his tartan and sported a tear from his shoulder
to his chest. His brown hair stuck up at odd angles, and
beads of sweat dotted his brow.

"Set me free!" Isobel writhed against the ropes that
bound her to a chair in the center of the cabin. When
Wolf entered, her gaze flew to his. "I beg of you, do not
lock me in here." Her brown eyes blazed.

Fury shot through him as he took in the purple welt
at her temple. "What happened? Why is she restrained?"

"It was the only thing I could think of to calm her
down." Brahan's breath came in gasping bursts. "I
brought her in here. I set her on the bed." He ran a
hand through his disheveled hair, only bringing more
chaos to the jumbled mass. "One minute she was as
docile as a kitten. The next she turned wild, like something inside her snapped."

"And the bump on her head?"

Brahan shrugged. "She must have hit it on something."

Wolf looked back to the girl. The fury in her eyes receded and he saw fear, cold and stark. Her skin paled
and a slight tremor raced through her. He stepped
toward her, then stopped. He had seen that look in the
eyes of some of his men before they entered a battle
where their lives were at stake. It was not anger but terror that drove this woman's actions. "Untie her."

Brahan shook his head. "She will only—"

"Untie her now." His words were short and brittle.

Brahan moved behind her and tugged at the ropes. A moment later she was free of her temporary bonds. She attempted to stand but collapsed back in the chair. Tension curled her hands into fists, and her face took on a sickly pallor. "Please," she said. "I must go on deck."

She tried to stand once more, but again sank back into the chair. "I must . . . have air. Please."

Wolf moved to her side and scooped her into his arms. Quickly, before he could reason with himself about what he was doing, he carried her up into the open sea air.

As soon as the chill air abovedeck touched her face some color returned to her cheeks. She gulped in several deep breaths, each one lessening the fear in her eyes. "Thank you," she whispered. "Don't take me back down there. Not down there. Want to stay . . . on deck. In the . . . open." Her eyelids flickered closed as she drew in deep breaths of air.

Slowly, he could feel the tension leave her body. His gaze dropped to her face. An air of innocence hung about her, made all the more dramatic by the sweep of long, dark lashes against her cheek. Sea air caught tendrils of her golden hair, teasing her cheeks and neck with their whisper-soft touch.

Women like her complicated a man's life. Fiona was a very different sort. All that mattered to his mistress was the size of a man's purse. As long as the man had funds to keep her happy, she would stay in his bed, yet out of his way.

Wolf shifted his gaze from Isobel's face to the inky depths of the sea. The expanse of water stretched out before him, silent, calm, icy. So very different from the riot of heat emanating from his body where it pressed against hers. A purely sensual hunger gripped him, and he tightened his arms around her, bringing her close enough to smell the light scent of heather that lingered in her hair.

"Damn the man," Wolf muttered, even though the usual hatred that followed such a curse did not spring forward this time.

Her eyes snapped open. "I am feeling much better." She tensed in his arms. "You may put me down." The commanding tone had returned to her voice.

Wolf slid her down the length of his body, gently setting her on the deck. She was breathing heavily, her chest rising and falling beneath the thin fabric of her gown as she took a step away from him. "Thank you," she said, continuing to gaze at him . . . with what? Fascination? Wariness? Desire?

He held his breath, waiting. For what, he did not know.

"My lord Wolf." Brahan's voice broke through the moment.

Wolf turned to see that Brahan and the young sailor who had beckoned him to his quarters had returned to the deck. Wolf shook off the strange sensations that gripped him. He turned to the sailor. "Bring the bedding from my own bed up here."

"You mean to have her sleep on deck?" Brahan asked.

"It is what she requested," Wolf replied. "And *you* are going to watch over her."

Brahan frowned. "Me?"

Wolf was spared from further questioning when the young sailor returned with the heather mattress and down ticking. "Where do you want these?"

"Place them over here," Wolf said, motioning to the dry corner positioned beneath the aft deck. When the mattress found its temporary home, Wolf waved her toward her new resting spot. "Your room."

Brahan frowned. "So I am to play nursemaid to our guest?"

"Someone must."

"That someone should be you, since you are to be her groom." Brahan's brow arched in question.

"I have a ship to run and a new course to set. We have no choice but to risk the narrow passage of the Moray Firth in order to reach the Black Isle. Someone obviously knows where we are headed and might have set further traps for us along the way." Wolf turned away and took the stairs up to the aft deck in two strides. His duty was to his ship and his men, not to a woman—any woman. At the table that held his charts, he clutched the sextant in his hand. To sail by sea would add an additional day to their journey, but it would be time well spent if it kept them all safe.

He forced himself to study the map, but his gaze wandered to the edge of the table and beyond, to the woman who now sat on the edge of the mattress, alone. Her forlorn expression hid nothing—not her seasickness, not her exhaustion, not even the fact that she'd lost everything she had ever known.

Who was this girl to gain the attention of a king? What about her was worth risking the lives of seamen and a ship? Because he knew the ship that pursued them had been after her. His own enemies would not have been so bold as to attack him in full daylight. Nay, they were more the sort to slink in the shadows, using darkness to their advantage. So who was after the girl?

She lay curled with her knees against her chest. Every ounce of decency inside him cried out to champion her, to protect her from whatever secrets she carried.

But protecting her meant caring what happened. And that would be a deadly mistake, for all of them.

When fools are summoned into service at the promise of great gains, death will surely follow, Brahan's latest vision taunted from the edge of his thoughts. Perhaps the vision had been correct after all.

Wolf tossed the sextant onto the desktop, giving vent to the feeling of doom. Whose death did Brahan's prediction foretell? Wolf's? The girl's? Brahan's? Or were they all at risk as fools summoned into service in a king's manipulative game?

Eldon MacDonald scrambled from the bow of the sinking ship into the last lifeboat the crew had managed to salvage as the hull dipped slowly into the icy black waters below. His cry of despair hung like a death knell in the salty sea air as the girl and her rescuer sailed into the distance. His family would be forever doomed without her.

Eldon shivered against a sudden chill that invaded his aged bones. Lord Henry Grange would punish all the MacDonalds for this. Why hadn't he told the man of his child's birth from the very first moment?

Instead, he'd let Lady Grange convince him that her husband would not be pleased to know he'd sired a daughter instead of a son. From the few times he had met Grange previously, he knew the man was capable of dispatching the bearer of such ill news.

They'd done as the mother had asked, keeping her secret and allowing the child to remain with her while she still lived. For years, the child had quieted her mother's cries. They'd all been grateful for that small blessing. But any blessing had since faded, replaced by danger because of their deceit.

Desperation had driven them to betray the girl, revealing her existence to her father. They'd needed funds to replenish the stores that the harsh winter had damaged. Without food and the means to grow new crops in the season ahead, his clan would not survive. Damn his son, Aldous, for not waiting until he'd returned to the isle before releasing the girl to the wrong man.

How the king had learned of and acted upon that information had surprised them all. And because of that mistake, the clan would suffer more unless they did something else, something even more dreadful than betraying an innocent girl.

A shiver of doom wracked Eldon's body as the crew set the oars and, with coordinated strokes, propelled the small boat back toward the Isle of St. Kilda.

They had no choice but to bargain with Grange for their lives. They might have lost the girl, but they still had one thing Lord Grange coveted: the secret of the Seer's Stone.

Chapter Four

The crofthouse moved, listed, then fell. Izzy moaned softly and hugged the old, threadbare blanket that was her bed, trying to keep herself still. Her efforts were in vain as the cottage shifted yet again.

"Fear not, little one. It is only a squall."

Izzy tried to force one eye open at the sound of that familiar voice, without success. "A squall? But squalls are at sea."

A soft chuckle came from beside her. "You *are* at sea. Or have you forgot?" Her eyelids fluttered open and she stared up into a sky of white canvas framed by the gray clouds beyond. It took her a moment before she could make out the edges of a sail that had been secured above her makeshift bed to protect her from the rain. Tiny pings of sound hit the cloth in a steady rhythm that matched the tilt and lift of the ship.

"It is about time you awoke."

The ship. The man. Izzy turned toward the sound of his voice. He sat on a wooden stool across from her, one leg propped atop the other. He sank his teeth into a hunk of meat.

At the sight of the meat her stomach clenched. Despite her sudden nausea, she tried to sit up, but the ship dipped crazily.

"Lie still. You will only make yourself ill once more."

She sank back against the heather mattress, defeated for now. She brought her fingers up to press against the lump at her forehead. She remembered it all—the ship, the cannonballs, her own confinement and panic. An overwhelming sense of suffocation, bringing back memories of the dark, dank tower, and her many years of imprisonment alongside her mother, had broken her restraint. In her panic to escape, she had struck her head on a low-slung beam. Then, once abovedeck, she'd fallen asleep, exhausted. Izzy closed her eyes, pushing the memory of her panic deep inside herself with other painful memories from the tower.

This man, this stranger, had freed her from the dank quarters belowdeck.

"Are you hungry?" he asked, his tone gruff. She heard a soft shuffling. A moment later, the mattress dipped beneath his weight and the savory scent of roasted chicken touched her senses.

Roasted chicken.

Her eyes flew open and she stared at the platter of meat he had set near her bedside. She sat up, ignoring her queasy stomach. "You didn't . . ." she tried to talk, but her throat felt suddenly dry and thick. "Mistress Henny—"

"Is perfectly safe." He scowled at her then, no doubt offended by her unspoken accusation. He motioned toward a nearby barrel. "Your *belonging* is not pleased with her accommodations."

Izzy turned her gaze to the wooden barrel. "Mistress Henny?"

He nodded and took another bite of his chicken, regarding her through narrowed eyes that were framed by thick, dark lashes. "You have very little trust in people."

"I've had little reason to trust anyone in my life." The thumping of a soft body followed by the rustling of feathers sounded against the wooden slats of the barrel. Izzy knew the sound well. The chicken was irritated by her confinement, but safe. Just as Izzy was now.

"Interesting." He reached out and lightly traced the curve of her cheek. Warm little tendrils of sensation danced beneath the brief touch. His fingertips were callused, his hands large, but his touch was soft as gossamer silk.

She tensed to pull away, expecting his touch to turn harsh as it always did when Aldous MacDonald touched her. But Wolf's fingers remained light, his eyes searching her own.

Seconds clicked by before his gaze clouded and he pulled his hand away. In the silence that followed she realized the rain had stopped and the ship had settled into a slow, rhythmic dip and heave. "How long have I been asleep?"

"Only a few hours this round, but you've been fading in and out of sleep for the last three days," he answered. "How is your head?"

"Three days?" She brought her fingers up to gently examine the lump that throbbed at her temple. "It hurts."

He continued to appraise her, but his expression shifted to something darker, more dangerous. "Why would someone send a ship full of men to harm you?"

Her fingers froze. "Harm me?"

"Why else would the king send me to keep you safe?"

Izzy brought her fingers to her lap, fighting the tension that threatened to overwhelm her. "Marriage is no guarantee of safety." Her mother's experience had taught her that much.

A crooked, bitter smile curved his lips. "Marriage has worked to protect women and trap men for ages."

Izzy had expected a certain arrogance in his words. Instead they sounded hollow, an echo of a deed that must be done, not something he chose to do. "You do not wish to marry me?"

"Because of the king's decree, neither of us has a choice in this matter."

Feeling suddenly confined, Izzy pushed at the down ticking that covered her legs, then struggled to her feet, ignoring the dizziness the motion brought.

"Where are you going?" he asked, a dark frown pulling down the corners of his mouth.

She did not answer. She needed space, needed to feel the wind in her face. Only then could she think clearly. On leaden legs she made her way to the railing of the ship. She drew a slow, steady breath, allowing the sharp air to fill her lungs. She closed her eyes and relaxed into the stiff wind as it buffeted her body, tugged at her skirts, and whipped her hair into wild disarray.

Only in moments filled with sensation did she find release from all her fears. A moment's peace. That's what she experienced now. Yet even as she tried to hold on to the feeling of the wind brushing past her cheeks, Wolf's words about neither of them having a choice crept into her thoughts, weighing her down.

Her ankles were no longer bound by shackles as they

had been while locked away in the tower. At times she found it hard to remember that. Times such as now.

Izzy planted her feet firmly upon the deck. Her chains were gone. She was free, and would remain that way no matter what she had to do. Nothing or no one would restrain her again. Away from the isle and the threat of being returned to the tower, away from the MacDonalds, she would decide the course of her own life.

Bolstered by the thought, Izzy leaned farther over the rail, catching the breeze fully in her face.

"Can you swim?"

She snapped her eyes open and turned to find him standing beside her. Anger and fear reflected in the obsidian depths of his eyes.

"Nay," she replied, watching as he shuttered his emotions once more.

"Then I do not have to fear you throwing yourself overboard."

Izzy frowned not at his words but at the relief that sounded in his words. She could almost believe he cared what happened to her. Almost. "I value life more than that."

"Good." He took a step back, putting some distance between them. "Because nothing short of death can spare us from our fate as husband and wife."

Husband and wife. This was not a course she chose.

"When do we arrive at your home?" she asked with what she hoped sounded like nonchalance.

"Tomorrow evening."

"And the marriage?"

"Will proceed that night." He paused, and a shadow passed once again across his face. Had she imagined a reflection of uncertainty there? "Are you disappointed in your bridegroom?"

"I had hoped for a man who might . . ." She let her words fade away as his gaze returned to her face. What was wrong with her? What had possessed her to give voice to something so personal? She never exposed herself like that. Had her early years not taught her that others would only use her dreams against her?

"Love? Is that what you speak of?" A flicker of amusement brought a spark of life to his cold, unyielding eyes. "Is that what you speak of? Such a sentiment plays no role in marriage."

A stab of disappointment seized her, but she willed it away. He was right. That romantic sentiment was no more than a fantasy created from the fairy stories she'd overheard as a young girl. Love had never been part of any marriage she'd ever witnessed.

She turned away to stare at the sea, ignoring him. Her reward came a moment later when she heard the soft tread of his footfalls retreat belowdeck.

He was gone. But her problem remained. He did not want to marry her any more than she wanted to marry him. If he would not do anything to spare them, then she would. If they would arrive at his castle tomorrow, then that gave her tonight to free herself from a matrimonial trap worse than any tower prison.

The tower . . .

A feeling of foreboding crept through her. Confinement, darkness, death. Her breath hitched and a familiar panic crept along her nerves until she heard the soft shuffle of feathers from the barrel beside her. Mistress Henny. Izzy shook off the overwhelming sensations and moved to the barrel that confined her friend. She removed the wooden lid and scooped the chicken into her arms. It responded with a soft squawk.

Izzy nestled against the hen's soft, downy feathers, letting her pet's soft coo settle her nerves. There had to be some way to escape this ship. She stared out at the water and frowned.

She could hide. She'd seen his quarters belowdeck and the stores the hull contained. Several hammocks hung at various angles alongside the crates and barrels of supplies, and most likely filled with dozing men between their watches on deck. If she tried to conceal herself aboard the ship, the men would surely see her. Besides, belowdeck would be the first place the man, the Black Wolf of Scotland, would look if she turned up missing. Nay, she had to be far cleverer than that.

The silence on the deck gave way to the soft caress of the water against the hull as she searched for a solution. Her gaze moved across the deck to the dory winched near the ship's railing. A boat.

And just as she took two steps forward, two sailors brushed past her on their way to the mizzen deck. As they arrived, the two sailors who were already there departed. A change in the watch.

She continued walking slowly along the railing, her eyes never leaving the men. Could she use the change in the watch to her advantage? Her stroll down the deck brought her to a second dory. She examined the rigging and saw that it could be easily released should an emergency arise and the crew had to abandon the ship.

Izzy tried to contain a smile when she noted that this dory was beyond the watchmen's line of sight. Her hand moved to the winch handle. Could she launch the boat and escape?

Then, as quickly as it had come, her smile faltered. Not in the daylight she couldn't. She would be easy to spot as she rowed away. But perhaps when the watch changed at night . . . Darkness could cover her escape.

As casually as possible so as not to arouse suspicion, she searched the sea beyond the boat for any signs of land. The coastline had to be out there somewhere. Izzy bit down on her lip. To put out to sea without knowing of any refuge would be foolhardy. She continued to look for a glimmer of land as she retraced her steps back to her mattress, awaiting the perfect time to act.

It seemed to take forever for night to fall. Izzy lay awake, staring at the white canopy overhead, listening to the soft creaks and groans of the ship as it glided through the open water. When the final streaks of orange and red vanished into the sea, a soft whistle cut through the fragile darkness signaling the change in the watch.

Shuffling footsteps sounded from behind her before heading belowdeck. The crew that had served the evening watch would wake their nighttime replacements.

Hushed voices came from inside the ship, followed by the soft thumping of the men rolling from their hammocks. She must be quick.

Her heart racing, Izzy returned Mistress Henny to the brown sack and crossed to the railing, racing to the dory in the back of the ship. She carefully placed Mistress Henny in the boat, then moved to the winch and froze as she gazed into the sea of blackness beyond the railing.

A familiar panic seized her muscles and stole her breath. Could she do it? Willingly launch herself into that void of black? She staggered backward with the force of her fears. No matter how much time had passed since her imprisonment in the tower, the darkness always transported her back, crippling her body as well as her thoughts. She sucked in a painful breath, forcing a calmness she did not feel. Could she willingly thrust herself into that eternal darkness?

Footsteps sounded on the ladder coming up to the deck. Not knowing what else to do, she scrambled inside the boat and pulled the sack containing Mistress Henny to her side. She could wait until dawn, until a gray haze could blanket her escape.

At least then when they discovered she was gone she'd be far enough away. She could contain her fear of darkness as long as she knew the dawn would come shortly after.

Until night fell once more.

Izzy stifled a groan. If only she weren't so afraid of the dark.

Chapter Five

Time passed slowly as Izzy lay silent beneath her blanket of dark, cold night. Her muscles ached from her confinement in the small boat. Just when she could stand the strain no longer, a hazy gray dawn lightened the horizon.

Careful not to make a sound, she climbed out of the boat. Grasping the winch with both hands, she prepared to launch the vessel into the water.

"Remove your hand," Wolf threatened from behind her, making no effort to disguise his annoyance.

Izzy spun to face him. A soft cry escaped her as the force of her motion set her off balance.

Wolf lunged for her, but too late.

With no one and nothing to stop her, Izzy fell over the side of the ship.

Water slammed into her back like the lash of a switch. Pain streaked across her flesh with red-hot intensity, driving the breath from her lungs and blackening the edges of her vision.

Icy water surged around her, sucking her down. She flailed her arms, trying to fight her way out of the void, but the barrier was too solid, too strong. Pain seared her chest as the need for air became all-consuming. She tensed, every muscle becoming rigid. She could not give in—giving in would bring certain death. She could endure the pain, she had done so before and survived, but fear of the darkness threatened her where even pain could not.

She had to relax, had to force away the despair that trapped her. Izzy closed her eyes, allowing her muscles to go limp. Her life could not end this way. After all she had gone through, all she'd endured, to drown now seemed so unfair.

The words had barely formed as thought when weightlessness replaced the heaviness of her limbs. A warm arm snaked about her waist and pulled her up. Buoyant and free, she broke through the surface of the water. Wind touched her face, and despite her desperate need for air, she could not breathe.

Wolf held her cocooned in his arms, his warmth, his strength as the water rippled around their bodies. Dark, angry eyes searched her own. "Isobel! For mercy's sake, breathe." He shook her. "Breathe, damn you. Breathe!"

At his command she dragged in a shallow breath. Her lungs clenched, then spasmed. Pain radiated across her back as she tried to force more air into her lungs.

He turned her in his arms, then pulled her against the solid wall of his chest. "You are safe," he whispered from behind her, his tone surprisingly calm. "Take another breath."

Shouts from the ship carried back to them across the water. "Man overboard!" Beneath her back she could feel the steady rhythm of Wolf's chest as it rose and fell with each breath. "Drop the sails!" The beat of his heart punctuated each shout from aboard the ship. "Launch the dory. Quick!"

She drew in a slow, deep breath this time, then another, until the pain in her back receded, replaced by something else—something even more unsettling. Warmth fluttered inside her, underneath her skin like a burst of radiant sunshine surrounded by a sea of ice. She tensed at the contrasting sensations, determined to hide her reaction. A wave rolled past, sliding against her chest and into her face. She turned her head to avoid the full force, only to press her cheek into the sodden fabric of Wolf's clothes. "Relax or you will drown the both of us." His tone was firm, yet not unkind.

"I have no wish to die . . ." Her teeth chattered with each word. "I only want . . ." She let her words trail off. How could she explain what it was she wanted? How could she describe the need that burned inside her to make her own choices, to have a say in the way her life unfolded? Only one word came to mind. "I want freedom."

The sky overhead continued to lighten around them. The ship sat still in the water not far in the distance. Wolf shifted her to face him, holding her by the arms. Any warmth she'd gained from his nearness dissipated, an icy chill taking its place. Dark, cool eyes searched her face. "Do you realize what it is you ask for? Or are you so young and naïve that you have no understanding of what freedom might mean to you?"

"I know what . . . I want."

"Do you truly?"

She bristled at his harsh tone.

"How will you survive without a protector, with no money, with no food?"

"I . . ." She had survived worse, but she would not tell

him that. She had nothing of value that she could trade for money—nothing except one last remnant from her mother's own life. Izzy felt the weight of her mother's necklace against her chest. It was the only thing she possessed except her own will to survive. And that will brought a lie to her tongue. "You are right . . . I have nothing," she forced the words out through chattering teeth.

The slapping of oars in the water filled the silence that fell between them. She felt the heat of his midnight eyes rake over her. "You have me."

Saying nothing more, he pulled her hard against his body. She swallowed roughly as all her senses became centered on the feel of his steely muscle against her breasts. Time seemed to stop. She smelled the salt on his skin, saw the beads of water glittering in his hair, dropping onto the sodden linen covering his broad shoulders. This close to him, she felt small and insignificant and vulnerable and cold.

As though reading her thoughts, he drew her even closer, sharing the last vestiges of his own warmth with her. "Thank you," she said, knowing the word did not express all she felt, though she would not give him anything more.

Something reckless and sinful reflected in his gaze. "You are welcome," he replied.

The sound of the oars cutting the water grew closer and the muffled voices of the men became more distinct with each beat of her heart.

Wolf shifted her body slightly, bringing one hand up to toy with loose strands of her hair as he softly kicked his legs, keeping them both afloat. She tried to pull away, but he held her tight in the lee of his arm. He curled a delicate strand about his finger, brushing the edge of her jaw before he cupped her chin, tilting her face up to his. "I shall make you a promise if you will make me one in return."

"What promise is that?" she asked, unable to keep the breathlessness from her voice.

His gaze moved to her lips. A mindless drumming filled her ears, her blood, as she brought her gaze to rest on the sensual curve of his lips. "Remain in my care with no further attempts to escape and I promise to protect you by marriage and only marriage. Anything beyond that will be up to you."

He slid his hand from her chin to encompass her waist. The pressure of his hands increased as he lifted her closer to his mouth. The air was suddenly too still, the bird too silent, even the rhythm of the sea had settled into stillness as though the waves were afraid to interrupt.

"Are we agreed?" he asked.

Her body trembled. Her thoughts grew faint, aware only of his mouth hovering above her own. A simple nod would bring her lips in contact with his. Afraid to do anything more, she released a breathy, "Aye."

Never had she felt so sharply in tune with the world around her, yet dazed and disoriented at the same moment. Slowly, she brought her hands up to rest upon the bunched muscle of his chest. His heart beat thickly beneath her palm.

His hands tightened at her waist and he lifted her toward his mouth. Her eyelids fluttered closed and she held her breath, waiting for the brush of his lips against her own.

He lifted her higher, then higher. She snapped her eyes open to find herself suspended, her head above his. In the next instant she was swept from his grasp and unceremoniously dumped into the boat that had come to rescue them.

Her cheeks flamed and she dipped her head to avoid Walter's curious gaze. "You are a lucky woman," he said with a scowl as he tossed her a thick woolen blanket, then turned back to the others, who hauled Wolf into the boat.

The world around her resumed. And with it a bone-chilling cold weighed down her limbs, making her feel heavy and weak. The soft pulse of the waves caressed the hull of the boat. A bird screeched overhead. The breeze stirred, plucking away the last vestiges of madness. Her lips tingled with unfulfilled promise. She bit down, fighting the sensation, and brought her gaze to his.

His face was still, his dark eyes shuttered. He reached for the blanket Walter had tossed at her and settled it about her, brushing her shoulder with his hand. Izzy flinched as if touched by fire.

He reached for a second blanket and wrapped it around himself. "I hold you to your promise."

"As I hold . . . you to yours," she said through chattering teeth.

He studied her face as though searching for something, then bowed his head politely and moved away toward the back of the boat.

Moments later they reboarded the *Ategenos*, and Wolf kept his distance. He occupied himself with shipboard tasks, from checking the maps and charts on the aft deck to barking orders to his crew. Whenever he happened to be near her, he offered her a civil nod but nothing more.

Izzy leaned against the port railing, staring at the outline of the shore just beginning to emerge on the horizon. It was almost as if that one moment in the water where barely a breath had separated their lips had never happened. Heat came to her cheeks at the memory. She had wanted to kiss him.

Had her mother not warned her of such things? Marriage was just the beginning of a long, tormented path to madness. Izzy pressed her hands against her heated cheeks. She should heed her mother's warnings. If her reaction to Wolf's nearness were any indication, she would find herself trapped as her own mother had been, with no hope of release.

Was her freedom gone forever? Izzy had made a promise not to escape. She squared her shoulders and brought her hands down to grip the railing. A Highlander was nothing if not true to her word. Her mind, her body, her senses might be confused about what she wanted, but her soul knew. Her soul yearned to find a life that would not be shadowed in darkness or hidden behind walls.

She would find a way toward that end. One way or another, she would be free.

From out of the shadows of another castle not far away, two men appeared. "Milord." They bowed their heads and waited for him to address them. Lord Grange clenched his jaw. Milord. The word grated on him like a thistle against his flesh. They should address him as Your Grace. They would address him as such before the season turned. As consort to the Balliol heiress, he had every right to the throne. If only the Stewarts did not stand in his way.

He growled his frustration as he addressed the men

before him. "The girl. Where is she? Why isn't your father here to return her to me himself?"

Aldous MacDonald paled. "She's gone."

"Where?"

He shifted from one foot to the other, his discomfort obvious. "A man came to the isle with papers that claimed his right to her as his bride. Papers from the king."

"The *king!*" Grange clutched the man's throat, his grip ruthless.

"We followed his ship," the man rasped out. "We tried to overtake them. When we couldn't, we—"

Grange clenched his grip until the man's face turned purple. "One helpless girl is too hard for an entire contingent of men to apprehend?"

"She has a protector," the second man offered. "A warrior. He's headed to the Black Isle with her, milord."

Grange released his death grip on Aldous's neck. "And you think that excuses your failure?"

"Nay, milord." Aldous massaged his neck, his expression filled with fear.

"We haven't failed you entirely," the younger man said.

Grange narrowed his gaze. "Tell me."

"Eldon sent us with information about the Seer's Stone. 'Tis a story your wife passed on to us to tell to her daughter—*your* daughter—when the time was right." The man trembled as he continued. Served him right to be so afraid. "She told us the Seer's Stone was broken in anger years ago, when the feud over the throne began. One half of the Stone was given to each of the battling descendants in the hope that they would find a peaceful way to unite themselves again."

"So it is true," Grange snarled at the men. They took a step back. "She deceived me. She knew about the Stone.

She might have even possessed half, and yet she never revealed its whereabouts to me, her own husband."

Hot rage pulsed through him. He curled his fists at his sides, fighting the urge to strangle both men. "Where is the Stone?"

"We always assumed the girl had it, even though we've never seen it."

Grange flexed his fingers. "Bring me the girl *and* that Stone or every member of your clan will suffer my wrath."

Both men flinched. The younger man's eyes glittered with desperation. "She is well protected, milord. How are we supposed to enter the warrior's castle and bring the girl out without being seen?"

"I don't care how you do it," he growled. "I want what is mine."

The Stone. The girl. The crown.

Chapter Six

They arrived at the cliffs of the Black Isle at sunset. Izzy found it entirely appropriate that the sky was awash with a fiery red glow, making the enormous fortress at the top of the cliffs appear as if it were surrounded by flames. It was a potent reminder that she was entering hell.

Gold pennants bearing the symbol of a black wolf topped each corner of the castle, leaving no doubt about who resided within. "Duthus Castle," Wolf said from behind her, putting a name to the structure that would be her new prison. And a prison it was. Sentries patrolled the turrets and the walkway at the top of the outer bailey. Armed with arrows, these men would keep enemies out as effectively as they would keep the castle's inhabitants in.

She shivered.

"The boat is ready to take us ashore." He grasped her arm and gently led her toward the rope ladder they had used to board the ship.

She hesitated, not ready to surrender to the inevitable. "Mistress Henny?"

"Your pet is in the boat already with Brahan." A spark

of challenge flickered in his bottomless black eyes. He would allow her no leeway. And he had taken her chicken to make certain she followed his command. "The beast will be returned to you once we are safely behind the castle's walls," he said, as though reading her mind.

Izzy kept her back straight, digging into new depths of strength and resolve she hadn't known she possessed to march forward with Wolf and allow him to lead her down the ladder.

Brahan sat in the stern of the boat, clutching a writhing brown sack. "Your hen does not take kindly to confinement."

She cast a dark look at her future husband. "Would you if you were in her place?"

"I suppose not," Wolf said with a soft chuckle.

"And our wedding?" she asked.

"I grant you a reprieve until tomorrow morning."

Until tomorrow morning. Izzy let the words echo in her head as she sank back into the boat. Her marriage to this man was inevitable, but for the small reprieve she was grateful. It gave her time to adjust to the fact that tomorrow she would be his bride.

The trip across the small inlet from the ship to the shore at the base of the castle seemed to take but a moment's time. Too soon she found herself escorted up the sea cliff on foot, across the surrounding approach to the gate, then through the massive gatehouse and its protective portcullis.

Brahan and the other men followed Izzy and Wolf into the outer bailey. The hum of voices, blending with the clanging of metal upon metal, filled the wide, open space. All around her mailed men trained in pairs with their weapons of war. With each group they passed, the men stopped their battling, their weapons sometimes arrested in mid-blow, their gazes assessing her as she marched past, feeling very much like the prisoner she was.

"Welcome home, milord." A dark-haired knight sheathed his sword and offered the man beside her a bow.

Wolf stopped. A smile came to his lips. "It is good to be back, Fenwick."

"Milady." Fenwick greeted her with a hesitant nod. His gaze shifted from her to Wolf, then back again, in a decidedly uncomfortable manner. "Ah, milord, I doona know how tae tell ye—"

"My love, you are finally arrived," a feminine voice squealed from the far side of the courtyard. "I could hardly believe my eyes when I saw the *Ategenos* approach."

A female drifted toward them dressed in tawny silk that molded snugly to her narrow waist and pushed her breasts high enough to mound impressively over the bodice. Her soft brown eyes narrowed suspiciously when they lit on Izzy, and her perfectly sculpted lips turned down in a pout. "Do not tell me you've brought more servants into this already overly staffed household. Whatever shall I do with them all?"

Her cloying perfume overwhelmed Izzy's senses and turned her stomach with its suffocating sweetness. The scent reminded her of standing in the heather patch with no breeze to draw the fragrance across the isle.

Brahan handed the sack imprisoning Mistress Henny to an older woman. "Take this to the keep. Mark the chicken in some fashion so others know not to harm it in any way. Anyone who tries will have to answer to me." The woman nodded and took the hen away.

Brahan tossed Wolf a look Izzy did not understand before he strode forward to greet the flawless beauty. "Fiona Kincaid, how good to see you again."

The woman stopped moving forward to accept Brahan's greeting as he bent over to offer her hand an airy kiss.

Izzy felt Wolf's hand slide from her arm. "This day could want for nothing more," he muttered just beneath his breath. His gaze traveled slowly over the woman's hourglass form, coming to rest on the swell of her breasts.

Izzy smoothed a hand over her old brown gown. No wonder the woman thought her a servant. She looked the part and had played the role for years now.

The woman's sharp gaze traveled over Izzy from her face, down the length of her willowy form, to her work-worn slippers. She was every bit as much a lady as the woman before her, yet she felt more like a dusty moth in the presence of an exotic butterfly.

Izzy nodded a greeting, which was met with a spark of fury in Lady Fiona's eyes. "You've been gone far too long, my love." She stepped around Brahan with a laugh that tinkled a bit too brightly.

"Fiona," Wolf said with a touch of irritation, "we need to talk."

"We can talk later." The woman wriggled closer until the curve of her hip nestled against Wolf's muscular thigh and pressed up on her toes to kiss his mouth.

A multitude of wild emotions stirred inside Izzy, taking her completely off guard. Those moments in the water, alone with Wolf, had brought a strange, unreasonable yearning to her soul. What kind of woman was she to long for freedom one moment, then crave a man's kiss the next?

Regardless of her own confusion, this woman's presence proved Wolf would be true to his word and never want anything more from her besides marriage. Izzy pressed a hand to her stomach, then turned away from the sight of her soon-to-be husband and his mistress. "Brahan, please take me inside. I wish to rest."

The sound of the surf filled Izzy's ears. She reached out, hoping to connect with something solid. Then Wolf was there, drawing her against his side, sheltered within the curl of his arm. Without so much as a word between them, hope for something more blossomed inside.

Fiona gasped.

Izzy turned her gaze to the sky, to the shimmer of nightfall that hung there like a veil, ready to drop at a moment's notice. Wolf's powerful hands gripped her body, holding her almost possessively. "This woman is no servant, Fiona. She is—" He stopped when Izzy brought her gaze back to his face.

"She is what?" Fiona asked dryly.

Despite Izzy's best intentions not to, she looked into his eyes—eyes as dark as midnight. The possession she saw there warmed the core of her in a way she didn't comprehend and certainly couldn't explain. Her breath stilled as she waited for his answer. How would he explain her presence here to this woman? The sound of the surf faded and the night grew silent.

"She is a visitor here. Lady Fiona, may I present Lady Isobel of the Isle of St. Kilda?"

Something inside Izzy twisted, and pain centered in her chest. He would not claim her. The very thought made her . . . she hesitated, not wanting to put a name to the emotion. Her legs felt weak beneath her. She found herself pulled even more tightly against Wolf's side, yet it was Fiona he looked at with the same enchanting smile he had given her upon their first meeting.

The pain in her chest tightened as she struggled to

breathe. Oh dear heavens, what was wrong with her? She was actually jealous of the woman before her.

Izzy brought her hands up to hide the blush that suffused her cheeks. She pulled out of Wolf's grasp. "If you will excuse me . . ." She took two steps toward the keep when she heard Wolf curse, grasp her arm, and shove her forward into Brahan's arms.

"Brahan," he shouted, his voice sounding unlike his own.

Startled, Izzy half twisted, turning back toward Wolf. Instead of the anger she expected to see written on his face, pain was reflected there. Her gaze dropped to his chest, to the splash of crimson that stretched across his saffron-colored shirt beneath his long, strong fingers. The bolt of a crossbow protruded from his chest.

Izzy gasped. The sound was swallowed up in a cacophony of sound. "Up on the castle wall!"

"A lone archer!"

"Call to arms!"

Beneath the dying sun, Wolf's warriors flooded the bailey like the rushing of the tide. In an instant motion, every hand grasped a weapon—claymores, dirks, targes, and axes—surging to defend. A group of warriors formed a ring of protection around herself, Wolf, Fiona, and Brahan, while his men stormed the interior castle wall in pursuit of the traitor who had somehow secreted himself inside the castle.

Wolf staggered toward her, knocking her fully into Brahan's arms. "Keep her safe," Wolf bit out as he stumbled backward, then fell, hitting the ground hard.

"Get down, milady," Brahan cried.

The next moment she was crushed beneath Brahan's big body. Izzy clawed at the dirt, pulling herself free until she made her way to Wolf's side. Her breath became trapped somewhere between her lungs and her throat as she stared in horror at the crossbow bolt piercing his chest.

Despair welled up, nearly choking her with its intensity. "He is dead."

Chapter Seven

Over a maelstrom of shouts and thundering footsteps, Izzy crouched beside Wolf's body. Gray darkness shadowed his face. It was the same look that had settled across her mother's face at the moment of her earthly release— a release from the torment her marriage had brought her.

He was dead. With his death came her own release from marital commitment. The thought left her a little hollow and sad. Because she had never reached out to him in life, she reached out now in death as a show of her regret.

He lay so still, his face a pale reflection in the golden torchlight that lit the outer bailey. He did not seem so dark or villainous now. She brought trembling fingers up to his brow to brush aside an errant lock of his dark hair. "I am so sorry you had to die."

Wolf's eyes snapped open, his gaze unfocused, wild. Then something shifted. He turned his head to stare at her with uncanny intent, his look calculated and in control. "Do not count your blessings so fast. It will take . . . more than a bolt to slay me."

Izzy snatched away her hand, as unsettled by his miraculous recovery as she was by the army of warriors flooding the bailey. "But . . ."

He gained his feet with the bolt still protruding from his chest.

"But how?" The words were a mere whisper of sound.

He grasped the crossbow bolt and yanked it from his chest. The iron tip bent unnaturally to the left and was covered with a smattering of bright red blood. "Scottish mail is like its warriors—strong and unyielding. It hurts like the bloody blazes to be shot, but I will live." Silence descended around them despite the chaos in the outer bailey as his men continued their hunt for the lone archer. "As will you." The fierceness faded from his expression as he looked down at her. Possession clearly reflected in the depth of his dark eyes.

Unsettled by that one look even more than his unexpected resurrection, Izzy dropped her gaze to the rapid rise and fall of his chest. A hint of silver glittered through the hole the bolt had created in his linen shirt. He had not been wearing mail on the ship. Why did he think he needed such protection once he returned to his own castle?

"That bolt was meant for you."

With this second attack, no longer could she deny that her father knew she lived. Her identity had been discovered, and this man had almost paid for that secret with his life.

Fiona swept forward, forcing Izzy to step back. "My love, do not be so dramatic. That bolt could not possibly have been meant for either one of you. It was merely a practice shot gone wrong."

Izzy kept her gaze fixed on him. He did not accept Fiona's explanation any more than she did. Her father must want her dead, just as the man had wanted her mother dead. A shiver chased down her spine at the thought. All the years she had spent in the tower with her mother, hearing stories of the man who was her father, she had never expected him to come forward and kill her outright. Nay, she had expected him to use her, manipulate her, and then, once he was finished with his game, offer her a slow and painful end, like the one he had given her mother.

Her mother had told her tales of her father's villainy day after day in the shadows of the tower. She had told her as well of her refusal to use her talents as a seer to help him in his quest to rule Scotland, and how that betrayal had pushed him over the edge of reason.

Izzy had never known how much to believe, what pieces of her mother's tales were fantasy or reality. Her gaze strayed to the bolt in Wolf's hand. The proof lay before her own eyes. Her father was a dangerous man. If she didn't do something to protect the people around her, her father's villainy would reach them as well.

"My lord." Hesitantly, she touched Wolf's arm. Her fingers barely brushed the soft linen of his shirt. Her pulse quickened at the simple touch. "My lord Wolf. Certainly now you must realize how dangerous it is for me to remain here."

"My men will apprehend the assassin."

"Will you stop the next assassin? Or the one after that? The threats will continue until you set me free."

"Who continues to threaten you, Isobel?" He moved closer, nearly forcing Fiona out of the way.

"It is best for you not to know."

"For me, or for you?" Cool, callused fingers touched her cheek.

Izzy swallowed, breathing too hard. "Please, it is not

safe for me to stay." His touch, meant to comfort, did anything but. A ripple of sensation passed across her flesh, warming her skin. She willed herself not to flush. The simple gesture meant nothing to him, yet it stirred her blood with unfamiliar cravings. Cravings she had no right to explore.

The heat of his gaze faded and his fingers fell away, leaving a chill in their wake. "By the king's command, you are in my care. And there you will remain until I release you."

"Heavens, Wolfie." A worried frown puckered Fiona's brow. "If the girl wants to go, release her. We can find another, more amenable servant."

Wolf clenched his hands at his sides. "She is no servant."

"Then just who is she? Who did you bring into our castle?"

Wolf twisted toward Fiona. "This is not your castle. You are here because I let you stay." His gaze sharpened on Fiona with deadly precision. "Who knew the intent behind my trip to St. Kilda?"

Fiona paled. "We knew nothing. Only that you had gone on an errand for the king," Fiona explained, her voice a mournful plea. "Who is she, Wolfie? Why are you so upset?"

He turned away from her to grip Izzy's elbow. "To the keep. We will all be safer inside. Brahan, escort Lady Fiona."

Fiona's protest was lost in the shouts and stomping feet that filled the crowded outer bailey. Izzy allowed Wolf to guide her. She glanced up at the suddenly dark skies. Night had fallen without her noticing. In the past, she always noticed the passing of day into night and the darkness that had cloaked the tower in nightmarish shapes and sounds. The passing of night meant she had to be more aware, alert to every possible danger. Did the same response apply now that she was here in Wolf's care?

Izzy quickened her pace, avoiding the ghostly shapes that came in and out of the torchlight as they passed through the less crowded inner bailey toward the hulking gray shape of the keep.

"What will you have me do now that I am here in your home?" Izzy asked, hoping conversation would help turn her mind from the feeling of enclosure that always came when she entered a room.

"You will do what the other women do." His lips tightened.

He had made it clear their conversation was done. Though it was brief, she had gained the information she needed. She relaxed the tension that had crept into her shoulders. He would expect nothing more of her than the MacDonalds had.

Wolf drew her through the massive wooden door of the keep. Izzy held her breath, fearing the dark. But instead of darkness, golden light filled the enormous chamber, from the clean flagstone floor to the vaulted ceiling. She searched above her for chandeliers that should have held a thousand candles, only to find none.

Instead, giant torches, suspended from the stone walls by curving iron hooks, lined the chamber. The flame from each torch reflected against a small arched window covered with glass the color of springtime ale. The combination of glass and flame cast a yellow-gold light into even the farthest corner of the great hall. Izzy searched the opulent room from the cut blocks of silver-gray stone that made up the walls and high over-head arches to the tapestries of rich, vibrant blues, greens, and reds that covered the walls. The effect was warm and inviting, not cold and enclosed as she had expected.

"It's beautiful." It was an inadequate description, but she knew not how to verbalize the effect the light had over her fears. "I've never seen glass used in that way before." She had overheard tales of such wonders told by Eldon MacDonald after his trips to the mainland.

She searched the room in continued awe as Wolf led her to the massive hearth. He positioned her directly before the roaring fire. Instant heat enveloped her. She shivered convulsively, not realizing until that moment how chilled she had become.

He released her elbow and stood before the fire himself, rubbing his hands together. He was as cold as she was. "You have never seen a window?"

"Never. Nor did I expect to find them in a castle."

"It is one small luxury I allow myself. The windows are strategically placed so they will not make the castle vulnerable to enemy attacks. You will be safe here."

Light from the fire flickered over Wolf's dark hair and stroked the rigid planes of his jaw. He said she would be safe. But could anyone, even Wolf, protect her from her father? Her mother had claimed that only her anonymity protected her from his vile reach.

Izzy gazed into the red-gold flames. What was she supposed to do—stay or leave? Both options held danger for herself and others.

"Whoever threatens you will not succeed while you are in my care," he said, as if reading her thoughts.

"How can you say that?" She glanced at the hole in his shirt. "They already have."

He offered her a tight smile. "They had one shot and only succeeded in drawing blood. Now I am warned. They will never succeed a second time."

Izzy closed her eyes against an unexpected rush of emotion. How she wished his words were the truth. She clasped a hand to her wrist, rubbing the callused scars left by the shackles she'd been forced to wear in the tower after she'd once been caught trying to escape with her mother. She knew from experience the power her father could wield.

She started at a gentle touch on her chin and opened her eyes to find his gaze fixed on her. "I have given you very little reason to trust me, but I beg your indulgence now. Trust me to keep you safe."

He offered her a sincere smile, not the tight-lipped one from moments before. Yet somehow she wished it had been, because this smile did strange things to her insides. It brought a warm, flowering sensation to her core. A smile should not have that kind of power over anyone, not the kind of power that would make her do something so foolish as to endanger others with her presence. She should ignore that smile, turn away from it, tell him she would leave this very night for the sake of them all.

"Thank you for protecting me," she whispered. "No one has ever done that before."

The rush of gratification that moved through Wolf at her words was like nothing he had experienced before. He swallowed, breathing too hard, trying to gather himself against the unwanted emotion. He wanted to protect her. Nothing more. "You are welcome. Now, make yourself at home." He turned to Fiona, and a heaviness descended over him at the dark scowl on her face.

"What is the meaning of all this, Wolfie? I expected a

different sort of greeting from you after your lengthy absence." Fiona tapped her foot against the flagstone floor. A pinched look settled over her delicate features, making her appear more like a displeased shrew than a lover awaiting his return.

He tried to muster the same protectiveness for Fiona that Isobel had brought. Fiona had been in his care for the past two years, and had been almost as helpless and bedraggled as Isobel at first. He'd found her wandering along the shoreline near where he moored his ship—abandoned by her lover, desperate and alone. Wolf allowed his gaze to linger on the low neckline of Fiona's gown, remembering the fullness of her breasts, and their rosy pink nipples.

Nothing.

He frowned. Perhaps the crossbow bolt to his chest had injured him more than he thought. Fiona had always garnered at least a glimmer of lust from him.

A movement at his left brought his gaze around. Isobel stood, statue still, holding a mug of steaming pottage out to him.

"This should warm you and take the chill away."

He accepted the savory stew and took a sip, suddenly realizing that none of those who had arrived on the ship had taken food since the previous night. So intent had he been on returning to the Black Isle that all else but arrival had faded from importance.

Isobel turned back to the hearth to fill another mug, then handed it to Brahan, who accepted the meal with a nod of thanks. Next, Isobel offered a mug to Fiona. Instead of accepting the food, Fiona clenched her fists at her sides, her gaze sliding from Isobel to himself.

"You claim she is no servant, yet here she is serving you." Fiona lashed out, striking the mug from Isobel's grip. It hit the floor with an ominous thump. "You forget I am no naive girl. I can see the deception in your eyes. Tell me who this woman is."

"We will speak of this matter in private, Fiona." Wolf set his mug on a table near the hearth.

"Your silence is more damning than your words. If I were a weaker woman I would fall into a faint at the thought of you bringing your *new* mistress here."

Wolf's expression darkened. "She is not my mistress." He took a step toward Fiona when Isobel once again caught his gaze. She knelt before the discarded mess and began to wipe it up with an apron left near the hearth. He knelt beside her, puzzled by her actions. "What are you doing?"

A worried frown creased her brow. "As you suggested . . . what a woman does."

He lifted her hand from the apron, leaving the mess behind, and pulled her gently to her feet. "That is not what I meant."

She slipped her fingers from his grasp and nervously brushed at the gathers of her dirty brown gown.

His frown deepened at the glint of triumph in Fiona's gaze as she fingered the rich linen of her own kirtle and surcoat. "Do you have any training?" he asked Isobel in a harsher tone than he had intended.

Her brown eyes widened. "Only to serve."

"Did your mother never teach you the ways of a lady?"

"There was no need," she said simply.

"And you never resented that fact?"

"There is very little room for resentment in my life—past or present." Her chin rose a notch.

Anger and pity battled inside him, and he turned abruptly away to the serving girls who had gathered round to clear up the mess. "Find Mistress Rowley to take Isobel upstairs. See that water for a bath is brought up. And for God's sake, someone find her some clothing that befits her station."

Fiona crossed her arms in front of her, her gaze a malicious assault. "What station is that?"

Wolf flexed his hands open and closed. When he felt more in control he turned back to Isobel. The heat from the fire had brought a golden glow to her skin and turned her straw-colored hair to burnished gold. Despite her impoverished state and bedraggled appearance, there was something both innocent and seductive about the way she held herself, like a blade of grass in stormy winds that neither wilted nor bent. A blade of grass that belonged to him.

This woman was his to protect, to own, to bed. His father had bound her to him. At the moment that fate did not seem such a bad thing.

"Answer me, Wolfie. Who is she?" Fiona demanded, interrupting his thoughts.

He allowed his gaze to linger over Isobel's narrow waist, the soft swell of her breasts, the long column of her throat. The woman would be enchanting given the slightest bit of care. "Fiona," he said without taking his gaze from Isobel, "meet my future bride."

Chapter Eight

Silence descended in the great hall like the falling of a gauntlet. All eyes turned to stare at the foursome gathered near the hearth.

"Your bride?" Fiona shrieked.

An expectant lull hung in the air as Wolf's household awaited the acknowledgment of his words.

A series of rapid emotions darted across Isobel's slight features—anger, denial, fear. She moistened her lips with her tongue as if to speak. "I . . ."

"You what?" Fiona challenged.

Isobel's pulse fluttered wildly at her throat. "I . . ." she tried again.

Anticipation hovered over the room. Wolf waited, like everyone else, for her response. Time stretched with agonizing slowness. He leaned forward, awaiting her acceptance.

Bloody hell. What was wrong with him? He wrenched his gaze away, seething with sudden frustration. When would he ever learn that caring what others thought about him only led to great pain? "She needs to rest,"

Wolf cut in. He caught her about the waist and, ignoring her resistance, guided her toward the stairs at the far end of the great hall.

Fiona kept pace. "If she stays here tonight, then I shall not."

Wolf halted. "I don't care for ultimatums."

Fiona's features were hard. "Why, Wolfie? Everything was perfect between us."

Wolf frowned. He hated that name, and she knew it. Yet she persisted. "What the king had ordered cannot be undone, not by you, not by me."

Fiona's dark eyes blazed as she gazed at Isobel. "Perhaps when you tire of her you will return to where you belong. In my bed and by my side." With a flash of tawny skirts, she stormed away.

"You should go after her." Isobel tried to pull out of his grasp. "She needs you." A look of confusion had settled over her face, and he longed to wipe it away.

"Nay," he snapped, irritated by his response. "Fiona will be more reasonable when she has had time to cool down. Besides, you need me more. Until I know you are safe, you will remain with me."

"That is unnecessary."

"Perhaps. But until I am convinced otherwise, we are bedfellows in a very real sense of the word."

Her eyes went wide and wild color stained her cheeks. "I will not . . . you promised . . ."

"I have never had to force a woman to my will before." Nay, in the past he had wooed them slowly until they came to him with their own burning desires. A primitive jolt of satisfaction moved through him at the thought of Isobel coming to him in the heat of her passion.

It was almost a challenge worth taking, but that challenge was not for him. He'd made her a promise—

marriage in name only. It was a promise he would have to keep unless *she* changed her mind.

He loosened his grip about her waist but did not release her. "Come. I shall show you how safe a castle can truly be."

He gave her no choice but to follow as he hurried up the stairs. At the top of the staircase, he continued down the hallway at the same swift pace. To Isobel's credit, she kept up with him without complaint. At the end of the long hallway he stopped before his chamber's door. He had never taken a woman into this room before, not even Fiona. Their dalliances occurred in another chamber two doorways down. A wife or a mistress's room would have adjoined his own, but that was before he had converted the chamber into a solar.

The soft sound of her breathing whispered behind him. "I would be more comfortable in the great hall near the fire." Her voice held a slight tremble. He turned to look at her, noting the glimmer of fear in her eyes. The question was, did she fear him or the enclosed space they would share?

"You need not worry, Isobel. This room will be to your liking. It is a favorite of mine." He lifted the latch and swung the door open, revealing not a darkened chamber but a room filled with prisms of brilliantly colored light.

He stepped back, giving her access. The hitch of her breath as she entered the room brought a curious warmth to his chest.

Her face awash with awe, she glided into the chamber and turned slowly around. "It is even more impressive than belowstairs." Her gaze caressed each tall, thin window that flanked the outer wall of the chamber. Thin plates of glass in a repeating pattern of orange, purple, gold, blue, and green filled the room with dazzling splashes of color. He watched her expression, craving her approval. She moved to the window and reached out with one finger to touch a pane of purple glass. She plucked her finger immediately away, as though expecting the smooth surface to be warm to the touch, not cool.

Wolf allowed his gaze to move from the curiosity on her face to the shadows of the trees to the west that marked the edge of his land. Working glass was not the hobby of a warrior, nor that of a gentleman. Yet the craft brought him pleasure when the responsibilities of his station weighed heavy upon him. As of late he had spent many hours before the clay oven, melting beechwood ash and washed sand into glass as he tried to determine how to deal with his hostile neighbor to the west.

Lord Henry Grange was as vile a man as he was a master. Many of the crofters and servants who lived at Duthus Castle had come seeking shelter from the abusive tyrant. Wolf had offered them asylum, which only angered Grange more.

Wolf's attention returned to Isobel, and he was startled to find her gaze on him.

"Who created such a wonder?"

The reverence in her voice caught him off guard, with his thoughts still centered on his enemy. A sharp rap on the door spared him from answering.

The door swung open and Hiram entered the room, carrying a copper hip bath in his bulky arms. The overly large warrior set the bath near the hearth. "Milady," he greeted in a shy tone, careful at all times to present the unmutilated side of his face to Isobel.

A renewed spark of anger flared inside Wolf at the damage Grange had caused one of his own warriors for failing to win a battle. Hiram looked at him, and his face paled. "Forgive me, my lord. I dinna mean tae displease ye."

Wolf cleared his expression. "It is not you, Hiram, who has me angered. Thank you for your service."

Hiram bowed, turning to leave, when a gasp from Isobel stopped him. He turned fully toward her, then just as quickly hid his face and raced from the room.

Isobel stared after him before her gaze swung to Wolf, her accusation clearly written there. "The man fears you." Her gaze sharpened. "You hurt him."

Wolf clamped his jaw tight, trying to stall the slash of anger that surged through him, opening a wound he thought had long since healed. Why did they always assume the worst about him? He wanted to explain the truth, but he'd learned long ago that his defense often fell on deaf ears. The sins of his past, sins forced upon him long ago by his father, were a curse he would always bear.

Still, he had hoped for something more from her.

He was oddly relieved when Mistress Rowley stepped into the room, bearing a wooden tray laden with smoked meats and crusty brown bread. Four maids followed in her wake, carrying buckets of steaming water. They filled the bath, then left as quickly as they'd come. Only Mistress Rowley remained behind.

"A bath and a meal for master and his bride." Mistress Rowley offered him a knowing smile. " 'Bout time you decided to settle down and start giving me some bairns to chase after. How else am I to keep myself young, don't ye know?"

All the color drained from Isobel's cheeks. She looked utterly terrified. Of him.

He clenched and unclenched his right hand, imagining the solidness of his grozing iron there. His work helped him think, helped him vent his aggressions into something more productive than anger or worry. It was where he needed to go now.

He looked at Isobel, and then Mistress Rowley in the fading light of the evening that forced its way through the colored glass. "Isobel, you will be safe with Mistress Rowley. I shall expect you belowstairs shortly to join me for dinner, and when you do, please see that you smell of something other than seaweed and salt. I'd have my bride smelling of sweet flowers and not the sea."

Alone in the rooftop watchtower of his keep, Wolf rolled the long metal rod in his hands, heating the glass at the end in the clay oven he had built himself.

By day he wielded a sword, by night, a grozing iron. Destroyer and creator. It was the sum of his life thus far.

Twisting motions took the unformed glass in and out of the flame. In the heat, the molten mixture left behind obscurity to become something more. A phoenix rising from the ashes to bathe the world in light.

As the glass heated and changed its shape, Wolf glanced about the enclosed space of the tower. His private lair. No one dared enter here, at least no one who valued his life. The members of his household respected his warnings to stay out. He knew they whispered among themselves, wondering what he did in the darkened space at the edge of the keep, but no one had ever violated his edict in order to find out.

There was a time when he had deserved their fear. He had been the nightmare his father had named him—dark and ravenous. But those days were behind him. He had changed since that first meeting with Master de Joinville in Vienna.

That first glimmer of liquid fire had become for the Black Wolf of Scotland a beacon of light to a brighter future. In the dark and dusty hovel where the master created miracles with glass, Wolf had found the salvation he so desperately sought. He'd risked it all and turned away from his father, gathered his own men, and tried to serve his people as best he could.

Wolf tightened his hands on the warm metal rod, rolling it once more in and out of the flames. Yet nothing had changed. His love for his brother and his misguided compassion for Isobel had shackled him into service once more.

Wolf paused, the rod hanging slightly above the greedy flames. What would happen if he let whoever was after Isobel find her? With her death he'd be free. But even as the thought formed, he knew he could never be so cruel. The nightmarish beast he had once been could have done such a heinous thing. But he was that man no more. He protected life. He did not destroy it. And he would protect her.

Resolved to his fate, Wolf removed from the flames the grozing iron with its liquid ball of blue glass at the end. Carefully, he reached for a second grozing iron and transferred the ball of glass from one rod to the other. Once that task was complete, he drew his dagger and, with a flick of his blade, sliced open the end of the glass ball.

With slow, even movements, he rotated the rod between his hands. The cut glass elongated and stretched, forming a cone with each passing rotation. The weight of the rod pulled at his arms and beads of sweat dotted his brow. The controlled movements worked his arms in ways his sword never did, as well as easing the tension from his shoulders, neck, and soul.

In creation he found peace.

He allowed the sensation to pass through him, to draw away his worries of the day. Even the troubles he had gained along with Isobel no longer seemed as overwhelming or discouraging. Someone had tried to kill her. He had to figure out not only who, but why.

Brahan could help. He could demand Brahan use the Seer's Stone to reveal the culprit. But at what cost to his friend? Each time Brahan used the Stone to predict the future, a piece of his life drained away.

Renewed tension tugged at Wolf's neck. He stepped back to the oven and returned the glass to the flame. He had to keep the glass fluid and supple until he achieved the desired shape.

Once again lost in the process of creation, the tension in his neck eased. Neither Brahan nor the Stone were the answer to this situation. Nay, Isobel knew who was after her; he had seen that knowledge in her eyes after the attack in the courtyard. He did not blame her for withholding the truth. She had very little reason to trust him.

Perhaps once she became more at ease in her surroundings, she would confide in him. Wolf tightened his grip on the grozing iron. Forcing her to marry him would not aid his cause. But what other choice did he have?

None.

Wolf returned his attention to the rod in his hands. Neither of them had a choice about the marriage. Yet perhaps he could make her see it was best for both of them if they peaceably gave in to the king's demands, for he knew all too well what could happen if he disobeyed his father.

Wolf pulled the glass from the oven. Holding the rod

at waist level, he quickly spun the metal between his hands. The elongated cone responded immediately by transforming into a flat, circular shape. He continued to spin the circle until it became a thin, iridescent blue disk from which he would cut the windowpanes. He moved to the oven. With one hand he grabbed a wire brush and dusted the coals into a semicircle around the edges of the oven. Using a metal cutter, he removed the formed glass from the rod and set it on the heated surface to cool along with the coals.

With a sense of satisfaction, he placed the grozing iron against the wall and stepped back to admire his work. The glass piece would be perfect for the window he was creating for the solar—a room he and his bride would share.

His bride. He barely knew anything about Isobel. Yet he could hardly turn his thoughts away from her.

It was abuse he saw in the depth of her eyes, her fear, her trauma. He recognized the shadows that lingered there. Some part of him connected with her, felt sorry for her, wanted to help her. And that was the very reason he should avoid her. She would be nothing but trouble. Had she not been that and more already?

He brought his hand up to massage the bruise on his chest left by the unknown attacker in the courtyard. If he had not heard Brahan's warning replayed in his mind before they'd reached land and dressed in mail, he would be dead. Just as Brahan had predicted.

Once again Brahan's abilities as a seer had given him an edge, a warning, another chance to change the outcome. Wolf was certain Isobel was the reason behind the attack. The girl had secrets, secrets he would glean from her one way or another.

Wolf turned away from the clay oven that held his creation, feeling suddenly eager for the challenge that lay ahead. He knew how to get Isobel to talk. An intimate dinner, a goblet or two of his favorite wine, and he'd have her singing like a nightingale in spring. He felt his lips pull up in a smile. Such wooing had always worked on the women in his life before; why would Isobel be any different?

He'd have her secrets, and his answers, before the night was through.

Chapter Nine

His bride.

Pleasure and terror collided at the thought. Izzy clamped her arms around her waist, trying to contain the turmoil inside her. The action brought neither comfort nor ease.

How could she feel such conflicting emotions for a man who could destroy her life as her father had destroyed her mother's?

Izzy pressed her wrists against her waist. Memories filled her mind of her mother's wild eyes, endless hours of rambling and thrashing at the manacles that bound their arms. Each tug upon the manacles had only pulled the metal encircling Izzy's wrists, cutting into her flesh. Her mother never realized that fact, and Izzy never told her.

It was the sacrifice a seer made. Sanity for the visions, her mother had said. Izzy wanted no part of seeing into the future. What purpose could knowing the future have for her? She preferred to know naught of the torments that awaited her. Dealing with the present was difficult enough.

A gentle touch on her shoulder startled Izzy. "Let us get you into the bath before the water cools."

"I appreciate your help, Mistress Rowley, but I'm so tired. I just want to rest."

"You'll feel more comfortable if you bathe first," she said, her gaze moving to the newly poured bath. "The water is here. 'Twould be a waste of the maidservants' efforts to let it go unused."

Izzy frowned. She detested wastefulness. Still she hesitated.

Mistress Rowley must have taken silence for acquiescence. She bent and grasped the hem of Izzy's dress, intending to help her remove the garment. Izzy stepped to the side, pulling the coarse fabric from the woman's fingers. "What are you doing?"

" 'Tis my job to assist you, my dear." The look she gave Izzy brooked no argument. Mistress Rowley clutched the hem of the tattered dress and with skillful efficiency lifted it up over Izzy's head. A moment later her shift rested on the floor in a pile along with her dress. "That wasn't so hard, now was it?"

Izzy fought to keep from covering her bare self with her hands. "I am not used to having help with my personal needs."

"As lady of the castle you will eventually grow accustomed to such things. Now to the bath," Mistress Rowley directed.

Izzy remained where she stood. "I'm not certain."

"Of the bath, or of the master?" Mistress Rowley asked. "He only wants what is best for you, my dear."

Izzy frowned. Before she could object, the woman scooted her toward the steaming tub. "Get in."

A moment later, Izzy found herself chest deep in water. Instant heat seeped into her, warming her clear to her core.

The older woman knelt beside the tub and gathered Izzy's long hair in her hands before she rubbed the ends with a cake of soap. The scent of evening primrose coiled with the steam of the bath, growing more intense as Mistress Rowley worked her way up the golden strands to Izzy's scalp. "Relax, my dear. Have you never had anyone wash your hair for you before?"

"Nay."

The hands stilled in her hair. "Not even by yer own mother?"

Izzy dropped her gaze to the surface of the steaming water, examining the clear liquid with sudden intensity. "I have no family."

"None at all?"

Tightness filled her throat. She did not want to lie to this woman, yet she could hardly tell her the truth. "I am an orphan and have been for many years." That much at least was the truth.

A loud *tsk* issued from Mistress Rowley, and her hands moved more gently against Izzy's scalp. "Well, my dear, you are here with us now. I'll take good care of you."

Her response was kind, gentle, accepting—and not what Izzy had expected. Not trusting her voice, she simply nodded, hoping the motion communicated her gratitude. A warmth that had nothing to do with the bath centered in her chest. This was what it must feel like to be cared for by a mother. Even though she'd had a mother, Izzy had always offered the comfort, never received any for herself.

Humming a soft tune, Mistress Rowley began rinsing the soap from Izzy's hair. She pressed her eyes tightly together, blocking out the light or anything that could break this moment. She drew in a deep breath and held it—desperate to surround herself with the sensations of being cared for. What harm could there be in imagining she belonged here in this castle and in this room, pretending she could confide in and trust Mistress Rowley with her deepest fears?

For years Izzy had confided in her pet chicken, fully aware that the animal was merely a proxy for the human companionship she wished she had. What would it be like to reveal her fears and her hopes for the future to this compassionate woman?

A hesitant smile came to her lips. What would it be like to have a true friend? But one did not lie to their friends. At the thought her smile faltered and she released her pent-up breath. Fantasy had no place in her life, and it never would.

"Where are you from, my dear? We know so little about you." Mistress Rowley dipped a soft towel into the bathwater and rubbed it with the sweet-smelling soap, then handed it to Izzy.

Izzy scrubbed at the dirt that clung to her body. "The isle of St. Kilda," she admitted. There was no harm in revealing that small truth.

"Then how did you meet the master if you lived so far from here?" Mistress Rowley frowned. "Certainly it wasn't at court." The older woman took the dirty towel from Izzy's hands. "I beg your pardon, my dear, but you are more the sort of woman my lord Wolf brings home to serve in the household, not the sort he would bring home with plans to marry."

"It was the king who decided that fate for us."

A flicker of surprise passed over Mistress Rowley's face. "The king, you say?"

Izzy nodded.

"Heaven help all of us then," Mistress Rowley said in a dire tone as she retrieved a fresh towel and patted Izzy's hair dry.

"I don't want to marry him."

"Truly?" Mistress Rowley arched a brow, her expression skeptical. "How can you hope to defy the king's command? Not even Wolf, his own s—" She cut off her words, a frown once again in place. "Not even my lord Wolf can defy such an order." She draped a fresh towel at the side of the bath, then turned away. "Regardless of how you were brought together, I hope the master gives you a reason to marry him. 'Twould be best for both of you—you'd have a family and there would be one less way for him to be manipulated by his king."

Izzy stood and wrapped the cloth around her body. Her skin tingled at the slight chill in the air. "What do you mean, manipulated?"

Mistress Rowley sighed. "Forgive me, dear. I'm just a rambling old woman." She led Izzy to a chair next to the hearth where she'd laid out clean clothing. She scooped up a kirtle of leaf-green damask and held it to Izzy's face. "You'll be a beauty in this. Despite that 'tis one of Fiona's castoffs, the master will be pleased."

Izzy stared at the luxurious fabric. She could never wear something so exquisite. Doing so would bind her to him. "I do not wish to please him."

"Then wear the dress." Both women turned toward the door at the sound of Fiona's voice. "Wolfie hates green. He will detest you on sight in that rag." She stood inside the doorway, holding a wooden serving platter bearing slices of apple and a wedge of yellow-gold cheese.

"Have a care, Lady Fiona," the older woman said as

she tossed a silken smock over Izzy's head. The sheer undergarment fluttered over her waist and hips until the hem hung just above her ankles. "The master does not want you here in this chamber."

Fiona came forward and set the tray on the table in the center of the room. "I'm not here to make trouble. In fact, I came to make peace." She waved her hand at the food. "And to offer my services, now that I've decided not to leave the castle."

Mistress Rowley frowned.

"What kind of services?" Izzy asked hesitantly, suspicious of the woman's motives.

Fiona plucked a slice of apple from the tray and delicately nibbled on the pale flesh. Her movements were polished, cultured, dramatic, yet quite civilized. And nothing Izzy had ever been taught. "Mistress Rowley might be able to clean you up and make you presentable, but I can teach you things only a well-bred woman knows. When you are ready to learn, you will come to me." Fiona's beautiful features were set with less than attractive hardness.

"Lady Isobel needs no lessons from you." Mistress Rowley picked up the kirtle and gently pulled it down over Izzy's head, then worked her arms into the long sleeves. The older woman ignored Fiona as she set about buttoning the small buttons at the sleeves of Izzy's dress. With that task completed, she moved behind Izzy to grasp the gown's lacings, pulling the garment tight across her ribs and waist.

"We will see about that in time, won't we?" Fiona said tersely. "And, as I suspected, that dress does nothing to augment your looks." Fiona swept back the skirts of her own richly embroidered kirtle and surcoat, then left the room.

"Don't you listen to her, my dear," Mistress Rowley soothed. "You look enchanting." A smile came into the older woman's eyes as she fussed with the fabric that molded itself to Izzy's waist and hips. "Aye, my lord Wolf will definitely approve." She picked up a comb and began working her way through the damp length of Izzy's hair. "Once I plait your hair, you'll be a vision indeed."

Izzy stood perfectly still, feeling like a stranger in her own skin. Her breath hitched in her chest as she spread her fingers open across the rich thickness of the clothing. The fabric embraced every curve of her body, making her feel suddenly exposed. "This gown is not right for me." She could not hide her feminine curves in the folds of this garment as she did in her plain homespun gown. The loose fabric had allowed her a certain amount of obscurity. The silken texture of this new gown draped against her flesh, caressing her in the most intimate of ways. "I want my old dress back."

Mistress Rowley frowned. "Whatever for?"

Izzy released her grip on the cloth and reached behind her back in an attempt to loosen the ties. She had to get the dress off.

"Nay, my dear." Mistress Rowley caught her hands, gently holding them between her own. "Your clothing needs to be washed and mended. Besides, the master asked that you change into something more befitting your station as mistress here. You don't want to disappoint him, do you?"

Izzy pulled out of Mistress Rowley's grasp. A feeling of panic overwhelmed her. She lurched toward the bath and bent to retrieve her old clothing from the floor.

Mistress Rowley scooped it away first and clutched the garment to her chest. "I cannot allow you to do that. My lord Wolf would blame me."

Izzy cringed. She had no desire to get Mistress Rowley in trouble and yet she had to see to her own needs. "It is only a dress." Izzy took two steps toward the older woman. "He will understand."

The woman twisted toward the fire and tossed Izzy's dress into the flames.

"Nay." She lunged forward, but too late, as the hungry flames devoured the one item of clothing she had brought with her from the isle.

Mistress Rowley turned toward Izzy. Tears pooled in her gray eyes. "Forgive me, my dear, but you left me no choice. My lord Wolf will have his orders obeyed one way or another. This is for the best."

Tears sprang into her own eyes as she straightened and turned her back on the fire that consumed the last remnants of her dress. "How do you know what is best for me?" she asked through the tightness that suddenly invaded her throat.

Mistress Rowley lowered her gaze. "Forgive me, milady. I shouldn't have done that. I beg that you be compassionate in your punishment."

Izzy's tears ceased. "I will not punish you." What right had she to punish anyone? As lady of the castle she would soon have every right to see to the discipline of her people. It was a daunting thought. "I am saddened by the loss of my dress. But you need not fear me." She released a soft sigh. "I can understand your reaction. My lord Wolf is more to blame for this situation than you are."

Mistress Rowley's eyes widened. "Oh, no, milady. 'Tis my fault entirely."

Izzy lifted her chin. Nothing the housekeeper could say would change her mind. Wolf was to blame. "Thank you for your care this eve, Mistress Rowley. All I wish to do now is rest. Alone."

"The master bid you to come to dinner."

"The *master* is done making demands on me this eve. Tell him I will not be joining him now, or ever."

Mistress Rowley shook her head, her expression grim. "He won't be pleased."

Izzy smiled her first true smile in what felt like a good long time. "He might have forced me to come here. And I might have no choice about marrying him, but I am still in charge of when I eat and with whom I dine."

The housekeeper hesitated. "He won't like your decision."

Izzy shrugged and crossed the room to the windows. She tripped on the hem of the new gown, catching herself before she fell to the floor.

"Goodness," Mistress Rowley exclaimed, rushing to her side. "The dress is too long. I will have it altered for you."

Izzy gathered herself, lifting the long skirt away from her feet and offered the older woman what she hoped was a grateful smile. "Nay, please, do not fuss on my behalf. If you have a needle and some thread I would like to fix it myself."

"But—"

"Please? Sewing relaxes me. I am quite capable of performing the task."

Mistress Rowley frowned. "The master won't like his new bride doing such menial work."

Izzy straightened. "The master's likes and dislikes do not concern me."

Mistress Rowley released a heavy sigh. "All right, my dear, you win. I'll be back with a needle and thread."

True to her word, the older woman returned a moment later with a small basket of sewing supplies. She handed them to Izzy. "Sew now, but be forewarned that my lord Wolf can be quite"—she paused, as if searching for the right word to describe the man. "He can be persuasive when he wants to be."

"I need no persuasion. I simply want to be alone. The last few days have taken a toll on me. Would the master not want me refreshed in spirit as well as in body?"

She frowned. "I suppose . . ."

Before the woman could change her mind, Izzy ushered her to the door. At the portal, the housekeeper stopped and glanced out into the hallway before turning back into the room. "Rest now, for I have no doubt the master will come calling on you."

Izzy bolted the door when the housekeeper left. What had Mistress Rowley meant? Izzy pressed the heel of her hand against her temple, trying to slow the wild thoughts and emotions racing through her head. So much had changed for her in the last few hours.

Wolf had claimed her as his bride. He'd introduced her to his mistress, and now he had settled her in his bedchamber.

She pushed away from the door and began to pace. It was her own fault this was happening. She should have found a more clever hiding spot on the ship, or taken the risk and launched the boat under the cover of darkness, despite her fears.

Izzy groaned. No matter how hard she tried, she never would have survived the darkness. It was only wishful thinking to believe she could have done anything other than what she'd done.

She stopped pacing. The real problem lay deep within herself. Somehow, at that first meeting on the isle, the man had slipped through her guard. It was that look he had given her—the initial impression of a dark and vulnerable man.

Wolf vulnerable? The idea seemed almost laughable. Yet she could not quite shake the feeling that she had seen through to the real man for just that one brief moment. It was that impression that refused to leave her brain.

She released a heavy sigh. Wolf needed her pity even less than he needed her company belowstairs. Let him dine with his mistress tonight. Izzy's gaze fell upon the table bearing the slices of fresh apple and the sewing basket.

Hemming her gown was the very thing she needed to calm her thoughts. She pulled a chair from near the hearth over to the table, then sat. She selected a slice of apple; then, gathering the bulk of the dress in her hands, she settled back into the chair, ready to focus her attention on something more useful than her own worries.

Even if only for a short while.

Chapter Ten

Wolf paced the length of the great hall, clutching the missive from his father in his fist. *Send me word by messenger when the deed is done.* His father's bold handwriting stared back at him.

The *deed* was not done. Wolf crumpled the parchment, then tossed it into the flames in the hearth. He had sent the messenger away.

Wolf glanced at the table set with an intimate service for two. He had hoped to discuss the matter with Isobel tonight like two civilized beings. He did possess manners, and even a small measure of charm, his mother had often claimed. He had hoped to tap into those reserves tonight with his bride-to-be and perhaps ease her fears, as well as expose her secrets.

He frowned at the empty stairwell. Where was she? How long did it take for one woman to bathe, then change her clothing and present herself for supper?

"Wearing a trench in the flagstones?"

Wolf stopped at the base of the stairs and turned to see Brahan sauntering toward him.

"You look like a man in need of distraction." Brahan's hand moved to the pouch where he kept the Seer's Stone. "I could tell you how all this will play out." He tossed the Stone into the air and deftly caught it in his palm. "Will she or won't she come down to supper?"

"Put that away," Wolf growled. "Where women are concerned, I'd rather not know the future."

Brahan slipped the Stone back into its protective pouch. "Why? Because the Stone might reveal something you don't envision?"

Wolf glared at his friend.

Brahan returned a steady gaze, unaffected by the assault. "You are the only one who believes you deserve to be cursed and alone for the rest of your days because of your past deeds."

The barb echoed his very thoughts. "It is a reality, Brahan, one I cannot escape."

"You've already escaped. Why can't you see that? Walter's release from imprisonment has freed you both from your father's grasp."

"Has it?" Wolf asked. "Who else could be threatening Isobel's life besides my father? He will stop at nothing to bend me to his will. He binds me with the blood of kin and of strangers."

"I could tell you who is behind the attacks." Brahan reached for the Stone.

Wolf stalled Brahan's hand with his own. "Regrettably, I must refuse. Your last prediction still haunts me. I need no further torment."

Brahan shrugged. "As you wish. I only thought to—"

"Beg pardon for interrupting, my lord Wolf." Mistress Rowley attempted a hurried curtsy as she came down the stairs.

Wolf searched the woman's face. "Where is Lady Isobel?"

The older woman stopped at the foot of the stairs and lowered her gaze to the floor. "She refuses to come down."

"She what?" Wolf asked, his voice savage with frustration. He cast a sharp glance between Mistress Rowley and Brahan. The housekeeper paled and took a step back.

"Did she tell you why?" Brahan asked, amusement lighting his eyes.

"Lady Isobel wishes to be alone," Mistress Rowley explained in a faint voice. "She says she is tired from the journey."

Anger stirred within Wolf. Anger at himself for caring whether she joined him or not. Anger at her for refusing him. In the privacy of his lair he had convinced himself that it was only her secrets he'd been after. Had he wanted more?

He clenched his fists. The woman had seeped through his defenses. It wouldn't happen again. He strode toward the stairs. She *would* dine with him tonight. He would see to that. He took the stairs two at a time. His heartbeat thrummed in his ears as he pounded on the locked door of the solar. "Come to supper."

A startled thump sounded from within the chamber. "Nay. I wish to be alone."

"I asked you to join me for supper. Now open this door." He was surprised how calm his words sounded, belying the fury that rippled beneath.

"Nay."

"Damn you, woman, I'll not be disobeyed." His resolve snapped and he heaved himself against the door. The barrier remained unaffected by his assault.

For a long moment there was absolute silence, until

the sound of Brahan and Mistress Rowley's footsteps reached his ears. "My lord Wolf, please, have a care for her feelings."

He heard the words, but they had no effect on him. He hit the door again with his shoulder. Pain radiated through his arm. He clenched his teeth against it.

"My lord Wolf," Mistress Rowley pleaded.

He hit the door again with the full force of his body, once, twice, three times. The wood quivered, then the bolt gave. The frame splintered and the door swung open, then slammed back against the wall. He lunged into the chamber, the heat of his blood pulsing through him. His gaze sought her out—a hunter seeking his prey.

But his prey seemed unimpressed by his attack. She sat in a chair, her feet tucked up under her, with the hem of a leaf-green gown stretched across one hand. Her head was bowed in concentration as a needle dipped in and out of the fabric. She appeared as though she hadn't heard him break through the door. Then he noted the slight tremor of her hands as she pulled the thread through.

Slowly, she raised her gaze to his. "Is there something you wanted?"

He strode toward her. "Don't ever bolt a door against me in my own home. I will not hesitate to show you how much that displeases me if you do." He clenched his fists at his sides.

Fear drained the color from her face.

Sweet Mary! She assumed he meant to strike her. He released an irritated growl and clutched his hands behind his back. "You have nothing to fear from me as long as you do as I say." His voice was still tight with anger.

"I shall not dine with you."

Wolf glared at her.

Isobel's fear receded and hot color crept into her cheeks. She glared back, the gaze an unspoken challenge.

Unsettled by her bold response, he glanced at the half-eaten plate of apples that rested on the table beside her before returning his gaze to her. "I will spare you this eve, but tomorrow you will dine with me or I shall not be so patient."

She stared past him to the shattered and beaten door.

He frowned. All right, so he had not been all that patient this time either. "Do not test me again." He moved past Mistress Rowley and Brahan to the battered door. He turned back to Isobel. "On the morrow, you *will* attend me at supper."

She gazed at him, back straight, cheeks flushed. Her eyes reflected a strength of purpose he had not witnessed before. "I heard you, *my lord.*"

Her words spoke of acceptance, but her gaze still held the hint of a dare. He turned and left the chamber. Once in the hallway, he moved to the darkened staircase to the left of the tapestry.

A passage to his secret lair. Without another word, he vanished into the shadows of the night like the beast he had just been.

Chapter Eleven

Izzy stared at the battered door of Wolf's solar. In his absence, her anger began to fade, replaced by an overwhelming exhaustion she'd been fighting since leaving St. Kilda. A dull throbbing pulsed at her temples. She ignored it, too tired to do anything else at the moment.

"The master's not himself tonight," Mistress Rowley said.

Brahan stood inside the doorway. A dark frown played across his face. "He has not been himself since that last visit to his father. Wolf's burdens grow heavier by the day, thanks to that man. Does he not realize—"

"Brahan." Mistress Rowley shot him a dark look. "Let's not be throwing salt into that festering wound. Please, go belowstairs and check on Lady Fiona. Heaven knows what mischief she may be up to."

Brahan's frown deepened, his reluctance obvious. "That woman is definitely one to find trouble where none exists." He turned, then paused to survey the damaged wood. "I suppose Lady Fiona is not the only one who does not take kindly to change," he added. "I'll see that the woodsmith is sent up immediately."

A pang of remorse stirred within Izzy. None of this would have happened if she had only come down as he had asked. A wave of dizziness swamped her. She closed her eyes, fighting the sensation. It was her guilt that made her feel this way. She had to let it go. Drawing a steadying breath, she opened her eyes and looked at the jagged, splintered wood surrounding the doorway.

She had expected some reaction from the man when she rejected his offer of supper. She knew he would come. Mistress Rowley had even warned her of that fact. What she hadn't anticipated was his violence or his destruction. It was naïve to think of him in any other way than what his name described—dark, untamed, a beast.

At the thought, the splintered wood suddenly became blurred and unfocused. She blinked hard, and her vision cleared. She stared beyond the doorway to the shadows that flickered and twisted in the hallway. Dark and mysterious shapes like those she had conjured out of the shadows while confined to the darkened tower on St. Kilda.

Izzy groaned. Such demons did not exist—not in the shadows and not in the light. It was only her mind's response to what had happened here.

"Are you well, my dear?" Mistress Rowley eyed her with concern.

Izzy pressed her fingers into her aching temples. She was not well. She had not been well for days now. And she very much doubted she would be well while Wolf confined her to the interior of the castle. Only in the open sunlight did she feel as if she could breathe freely. This open and multiwindowed chamber went a long way toward alleviating the feelings of enclosure that sent her heart racing while inside. But nothing compared to the feeling of fresh air upon her skin.

Izzy sighed. "So much has happened. Perhaps after I sleep a while I'll feel more at ease." She brought her hands down to settle at her sides. "Would you mind terribly if I asked to be alone for now?"

Mistress Rowley frowned. "It might not be wise to leave you unprotected now that the door is—"

"This castle is a fortress. Who could harm me here?" At the skeptical look on Mistress Rowley's face, Izzy added, "I promise to remain on guard."

"All right, my dear," Mistress Rowley conceded. "I'll close the door as best I can. No doubt the woodsmith will be here shortly to repair the damage. Rest well."

Izzy waited until Mistress Rowley's shuffling steps carried her from the room before she allowed her shoulders to droop with the weight of her exhaustion. Her claim of tiredness had been no lie. She truly did wish to rest but doubted she would ever sleep in this strange and new place.

Perhaps if she continued sewing for a while she would find it easier to sleep. Izzy retrieved her needle and thread. With a sigh she realized that she did not want to sew anymore. She set the needle aside, then picked up a slice of apple, only to return it to the tray. Her hunger had vanished.

A sudden wave of dizziness swept over her again. She clutched at the table until the odd sensation passed. What was wrong with her? She had lived through worse confrontations. Why did this brief altercation with her future bridegroom bother her so much? She returned her gaze to the doorway as the need for fresh air pressed in all around her, until her chest rose and fell in short, sharp breaths.

The need for air became an all-consuming necessity. She stepped into the hallway and quickly searched the shadows for signs of Wolf. No one lingered about. Moonlight spilled onto the flagstones from a stairwell opposite a large tapestry of men and women engaged in hunting a tiny fox. Terror filled the fox's eyes as he raced across the embroidered canvas. It was how she'd felt tonight—hunted, panicked, terrified.

She'd managed to find the strength to defy Wolf, but inside she had trembled. Just as she trembled now as she gazed up the stairs. A stairway that led to air. It would be much simpler to go down the hallway back to the great hall, then out into the courtyard to find fresh air. Except that it would take too long. She needed air now.

She had defied him once tonight. To do so again could prove foolhardy. Her gaze fell once again on the stairway leading up to the tower room. He had warned her against going up the staircase. But where else could she find the breeze she sought so desperately?

Need overcame reason and before she could stop herself, her feet carried her up the first step, then the second. She had no desire to go into the tower. All the saints in heaven knew she did not want go into an enclosed and darkened space.

Yet, if she wanted to feel the breeze on her face, she would have to brave the tower to reach the battlements and the fresh air beyond. Or would she find something else instead?

Would *he* be in the tower? She paused to listen. No sound came from above. The night air stilled and became heavy, suffocating. She took a step closer, desperate for a breath of fresh air. One more step would take her to the door.

Stagnant, musty air surrounded her, dulling her mind and slurring her thoughts. Only the need for fresh air gave her the strength to thrust her feet forward. A few steps more and she would find what she needed.

It was one fact she knew about towers: They all had either an arrow slit or a doorway that led to a wall walk— an opening to wreak vengeance on anyone who dared to attack. Her own experience had taught her as much. A lurch forward brought her to the door. She grasped the latch and pushed.

Air. She needed air. All thoughts centered on her goal. Her reward came when a wisp of fresh air brushed her cheeks. Izzy latched on to the sensation, allowing it to carry her the rest of the way into the room.

Candlelight flickered about the room from three wall sconces that clearly illuminated two arrow slits cut in the gray stone. Her feet took over, leading her to the arrow slits, and in no time at all she drew a breath of cool, sweet air into her lungs. She sagged against the stone wall and allowed her eyes to drift shut. She drew another deep, reviving breath, suddenly feeling exhaustion overcome her.

Two more breaths and the pounding beat of her heart lessened to a dull thud. She sagged against the stone, allowing her gaze to travel about the room. In addition to the sconces, a fire lapped at peat and logs set inside a round clay structure with an opening at the front. It looked almost like an oven, but what would an oven be doing in a tower room?

Set against the wall near the oven structure were three baskets. One held wood, the next sand, and the last held gray ash. On the opposite side of the room a simple wooden table held various metal rods and a knife, as well as several odd metal objects twisted at different angles.

A sudden chill chased across the nape of her neck. Were these the tools her husband used to conjure up demons from the darkness? To torture his men?

The metal pieces looked more like tools than instruments of the dark arts. More curious than afraid, Izzy reached out to trace the tip of one of the short, thick rods. When she pulled her hand away, a fine crystalline dust covered her fingertips. The fine powder twinkled as it caught the glow of the flickering light.

Her frown deepened as her vision blurred and her own fingers became shapeless spots of color against the yellow-gold light of the room. She shook her head, trying to clear her vision. But that only made the entire room swim before her eyes.

"I told you never to come here." A shape separated itself from the darkness.

Izzy blinked hard. Her vision worsened to the point that she could no longer see where one shape ended and another began. A rhythmic pounding began at her temples. "I needed air," she said thickly.

"There are other places to go besides here."

Heat rose to her cheeks, making the throbbing in her head worse. She tried to push herself away from the wall, to show him she was not afraid, but her stomach roiled and she doubled over instead. A stab of agony shot through her middle.

Instantly he was at her side. "You are not well?"

She tried to speak but could only groan a response. The next thing she knew, he swooped her off her feet. Clutching her tightly against his chest, he raced down the tower stairs. Izzy was grateful when his motion stopped. Her gaze clung to his features, desperate to keep the shapeless image of his face from fading to black. But darkness crept over her. She sucked in a gulp of air, trying to keep the closing tunnel at bay.

Then she was moving once again. A moment later, the fire of her skin was bathed in a blissful breeze. He had taken her belowstairs, to the courtyard beyond the great hall. Whispers of air caressed her face, her arms, her chest, but the darkness lingered at the edges of her vision. Pain speared her stomach. She twisted in his arms.

"You are safe. There is no need to panic," a disembodied voice called from the inky darkness that closed in around her.

Izzy struggled to swallow. "Awaah abbaha," she croaked.

"Isobel?" The voice called out of the darkness. "Isobel!"

Pain seared her middle. This time she didn't fight it. She hurtled down into the waiting darkness.

Chapter Twelve

"*Sweet Mary!*" Wolf thundered as he strode back into the keep, up the stairs, and into his solar with his unconscious bride-to-be draped across his arms. One look at her pale cheeks and wild eyes had been enough for him to know that something was terribly wrong. Something more than her fear of enclosed spaces. Wolf tightened his arms around her.

He stood at the battered doorway to his solar. A sense of hopelessness swamped him as he frowned down at Isobel's lifeless body. "What do I do now?" he muttered to himself.

"My lord Wolf." Mistress Rowley's panicked voice intruded into his thoughts. He turned to see her racing toward him from the stairway. Her steps faltered when she saw Isobel in his arms. "Nay, not her as well." The older woman placed a hand upon Isobel's cheek. "She's burning up, just like Lady Fiona."

"What did you say?"

"Lady Fiona has been poisoned. And so has our Lady Isobel."

"Poison?" Shock ran through him; whatever he had expected, it had not been that.

"The healer is with Lady Fiona now. He says 'tis wolfsbane that has made her so ill."

"But how? Who?"

Mistress Rowley moved past him into the solar and headed for the small table that Isobel had sat near the last time he had entered. The older woman reached for a slice of apple from the half-empty plate that rested beside a book and brought it to her nose. "Whoever did this knew what they were doing. A tart apple would disguise any bitterness from the poison."

A savage anger pulsed inside him. "She should have been safe within the walls of my castle."

"Whoever wants her dead is determined to succeed, no matter the obstacle."

Wolf forced his anger away. Losing control of his emotions would not help. "No one will succeed in that venture. Not here, and not with her."

Mistress Rowley smiled. "The young miss is fortunate to have you to protect her."

Wolf looked down at his intended bride. "I doubt she would agree." He snapped his gaze back to his housekeeper. "Quickly, bring the healer to Isobel. If anything happens to her . . ."

"Aye." Mistress Rowley turned toward the door. "I shall return shortly. In the meanwhile, place her on the bed and make her as comfortable as you can."

Wolf laid Isobel on the tall four-poster bed at the far end of the chamber. He spread a woolen throw his mother had made for him across her body. She lay so still. So deadly still.

His knees felt suddenly weak as he stared down at her golden hair spilling across the pale gold linens. He refused to give in to the confusion that tangled inside him. He locked his knees and stood rigid beside her. Wolfsbane. A vile and swift poison that would twist her insides into knots until she died from the pain.

Her murderer's choice of weapon was not lost on him. Wolfsbane. A toxin that reflected his own bastardized name. Such a choice of weapon pointed all fingers at his father.

Wolf frowned. That knowledge did more to clear the king of the crime than any other evidence. His father might be manipulative, but he was no dullard.

Which meant only one thing: Someone else was out to harm Isobel. And Fiona now as well. He had to determine who was behind the attacks and stop them before someone died.

Perhaps he was already too late. Against the pale gold linens, Isobel's face appeared a ghostly gray. The darker smudges that hovered beneath her closed eyes gave her a fragility that sent a piercing stab of regret through his gut. How could he have failed her so miserably in such a short period of time?

The sound of footsteps in the hallway ceased his dark thoughts. Mistress Rowley bustled into the chamber, drawing the silver-haired healer along in her wake. "She's over here, Mortimer. Quickly. You must give her the same purgative you administered to Lady Fiona."

Wolf stepped back, away from the bed, and allowed the healer to take his position by Isobel's side. "This antidote will work?"

The healer grunted. "Only time will tell."

Mistress Rowley placed her arm on his sleeve. "She's a fighter, that one. She has a better chance than most of pulling through."

"And Fiona?" Wolf asked Mistress Rowley.

"She had only a small bite of the apple. I watched her eat it myself. Eats like a bird, that one does. And for once it has served to her benefit."

"What else can be done to help Isobel? Name it and it shall be done." He did not bother to disguise the growing desperation in his voice.

Mistress Rowley's brows drew together in thought. " 'Tis not my place to tell you what to do."

"And when has that ever stopped you?"

Her severe expression softened before becoming sullen. "You might not like my suggestion."

He glanced at the bed, at the healer as he forced a cup of milky white liquid past Isobel's unresponsive lips. "If I did not want your opinion, Mistress Rowley, I would not have asked. Pray tell me, what else might I do for her?"

"Foil whoever is trying to harm her. Do the thing they are trying to stop and marry her now, then flee from here together."

Of all the advice he had expected, it had not been that. He clenched his fists. "I will not run from my battles."

Mistress Rowley looked Wolf directly in the eye. "Honor and pride. You and your father carry the same fatal flaws. Neither of you will submit to retreat."

He acknowledged her words with a slight nod. She had never been one to fear his anger. For that he was truly grateful—which was why he listened to her now, why he allowed her to say things to him that no one else would dare. "There is no retreat until I am dead."

"Must it come to that extreme before you heed the warnings?"

Wolf shifted his gaze back to the bed. The healer had rolled Isobel to her side, awaiting the effects of the purgative. "If she makes it through this attempt, no one will get close enough to her to harm her again."

"How can you guarantee such a thing?"

"My men will protect her."

Mistress Rowley frowned. "Only your men?"

Wolf pushed the hair back from his temple in a futile attempt to disguise his frustration. "What more can I do?"

"Protect her with marriage vows. Then you will have no reason to leave her side."

"I cannot argue."

Mistress Rowley's eyes widened. "You agree?"

He nodded.

"Then I suggest you send for the priest as soon as she recovers," the housekeeper said with a note of triumph in her voice.

"There is no need for her to recover in order for us to finish what my father started."

Mistress Rowley nodded her approval. Any further communication was cut short by the retching sounds that filled the chamber. Isobel flailed upon the bed, fighting the effects of the healer's potion. The process seemed to take forever, until finally she settled back against the bed cushions, her eyes closed, her face ashen.

"Who would try to kill her?" Wolf wondered aloud. "She was a recluse on a remote isle. The girl is no one of importance. The threats must stem from her connection to me. But what?"

He rubbed at his temples, as if doing so would clear his thoughts. The idea that formed there took hold, refusing to go away, regardless of the risk. There was one way to find the answers he sought. "Where is Brahan?"

"You sent him to attend Lady Fiona," Mistress Rowley reminded Wolf.

"Bring him back to me. I have need of his services."

Desperation did odd things to desperate men. As little as he liked the idea of using the Seer's Stone, it seemed he had no other choice. Wolf would have his answers by any means available if such knowledge could keep Isobel safe.

His men might think him a beast at times, but he was also known as a fierce defender of the innocent. And Isobel was truly an innocent in all that had happened to her so far.

"Then call for the priest." Just saying the words brought a strange twist to the center of his chest. "He will either perform a marriage or offer extreme unction this eve." Both possibilities existed. At the thought Wolf's emotions veered crazily between hope and despair.

A wedding or a funeral. Only time would reveal which service would prevail.

Chapter Thirteen

"She will survive the poison." Brahan removed the Seer's Stone from his forehead and snapped his eyes open, breaking the connection to the images that danced across his mind.

Wolf stopped pacing, his face a savage mask. "You are certain?"

"Aye. There is no distortion in the image." Brahan glanced at the bed where Isobel lay. The pale and life-less form on the bed would soon shift, and color would once again flood her cheeks. The image had been so clear, more clear than any vision ever before.

He took a step closer to Isobel. The Stone in his hand grew warmer. He took another step, then another, until he found himself at the foot of her bed. The Seer's Stone glowed an iridescent red, yet it did not burn his skin. The warmth brought a certain comfort to his hand and to his soul, as if it was meant to be near this woman.

"What are you doing to the Stone, Brahan?" Wolf asked.

Brahan took a step back from the bed. The Stone

grew cooler. A step closer to the bed made it heat up once again. "I'm not doing anything. It's her."

Wolf's gaze fixed on Isobel's silent form. It was then that he saw something there he had not seen before. Fine leather cording encircled her neck, connected to a small, iridescent red stone nestled within leather-laced net.

He strode to her bedside and gently lifted the glowing stone from where it rested against her warm flesh. The heat of the stone warmed his fingers. "She wears a stone as well. Are there two Seer's Stones? Or is this something else entirely?" He looked to Brahan's temple, to the lock of white hair that increased in size after each use of the Stone. Except this time the patch of white remained the same, no worse, no better. "What does it mean?"

Brahan shook his head. "I've never heard of two Seer's Stones, but her stone responding to mine must mean something. The Seer's Stone has never acted like this before."

"Can you still see the things that have yet to be?"

Brahan nodded. "Her stone is helping to clarify the visions. I wonder how."

Wolf set the stone back against her skin. "We will figure that out later. Right now, I must know who is trying to harm her."

"And so you shall." Brahan closed his eyes and placed the Stone against his forehead. Prisms of light swirled before his mind's eye. Colors mixed and melded through space and time as they tried to form into images of things to come and things that had already been.

"Who is trying to kill her?" Wolf's voice invaded like a breeze rattling the leaves of a tree.

Brahan waited, focusing his energy on the visions, going deeper into the trance, until all sound faded and only the steady beat of his own heart remained. "I see a tall, willowy woman cloaked in black speaking to a younger woman—a serving woman—from your own kitchen. Nay, the image is gone now. The images are clearer than before, but they are moving so quickly, it's hard to hold on to them, to see everything I need to see." Brahan tried to slow down the images without success.

"Just focus on what you can," came Wolf's voice.

"I see two tartans. One is red and green like that of the Stewart clan. The other I do not recognize, but it is blue and green and black." Brahan concentrated harder, trying to pull the meaning from the image. "Both tartans lie in the middle of a clearing—nay, a field of battle. They are coiled together and bathed in blood." His instincts told him to pull back, away from the vision that developed. Instead he forced his vision to go on.

"I see an older man wrapped in the other tartan. He carries something in his hand. I cannot tell what it is—a light, a torch, I don't know."

"That's enough, Brahan. You've told me all I need to know." The words came from outside the cocoon of shadows and light that surrounded him—disjointed, unnatural.

"There is more. I can feel it. I must go on." The light changed, shifted, forming yet another image. "Brilliant lights, of all colors, fill a room. It's like walking into a rainbow. In the center of the room I see a woman. It is Lady Isobel. She's holding a sword. At least I think it is a sword. It is long and pointed and glitters, yet it does not look like steel. There is a man there, too, but I cannot see who it is. His face is in shadow. His side of the chamber is dark, so dark and cold. Something separates the light from the dark . . . a bridge . . . a chasm . . . the image is unclear. But I sense it is that thing that will determine Isobel's destiny. The man isn't trying to kill her; he wants something from her. It is those who get in his way whom he wants to harm."

Brahan could feel his heart pound against the wall of his chest, each pulse more painful than the last, until he found it difficult to breathe. "It is . . . you the man is after. He will kill you . . . just as my last premonition about you revealed."

"Come back, Brahan. Your hair is once again turning white as the visions take their toll. Come back, now."

Brahan concentrated all the harder despite the dangers of using the Stone. He knew the Stone revealed the future by tapping into the life force of the seer. He never minded that sacrifice if it meant helping others. In an effort to go further, he directed all his energy to the Stone. Tranquil white light filled the space in his mind. From within the brilliance, a female figure emerged. A halo of heather wreathed her golden hair. "Lady Isobel . . . She awaits her destiny—that of either a bride . . . or a corpse." Brahan shivered violently at the image, feeling as though ice suddenly flowed in his veins.

"Brahan, enough. Come back. This was a mistake. I will not lose you over this."

Brahan ignored Wolf's urgings and pressed forward into the image. His head throbbed with the effort, but a face appeared . . . that of a man. . . . "I see the dark stranger from before. I do not recognize him." Brahan's shivers became shudders. His whole body trembled at the effort of reaching for this last vision. "So many faces tumble through my mind: your father, the maid in the kitchen, your brother Walter, Fiona, and . . . my own face . . . and there is more. So much more . . ."

Sharp pain lashed through Brahan's mind, matching the pain in his chest. He tried to focus the faces into some sort of order without success. The vision narrowed, like a tunnel of time and space, until only one image remained. "It cannot be." The words tumbled from him in a gasp.

His fingers tingled with numbness. The Seer's Stone cooled and fell away from his forehead. His body tumbled not against the hard floor but into a cushion of softness, instantly cradled in warmth. Darkness filled the inky corridors of his mind. His body went limp. He felt himself falling and let himself go, welcoming the silence.

Wolf caught Brahan as he collapsed. "Fenwick, Gerard," Wolf called to the two men-at-arms he had positioned outside the battered door of the solar.

Instantly, the men appeared. "Milord?"

"Help me take Brahan to his chamber." The warriors grasped an unconscious Brahan by the shoulders and the feet while Wolf bent to retrieve the Seer's Stone from where it had fallen to the floor. The three of them managed to swiftly move the hulking warrior down the long hallway and onto his bed. A torch set against the awaiting wood in the hearth filled the chamber with radiant heat.

Wolf dismissed his men and sat on the bed beside his friend. A slight smile lingered at the corner of Brahan's mouth, and despite his unnatural paleness, he appeared as he usually did at rest. There was one notable difference, however: The small white streak of hair that had graced his temple had turned into a solid white stripe.

The cost of the visions had been great—greater than Wolf had anticipated. Guilt brought an oppressive weight to his chest. "I'm sorry, Brahan. I should have listened to you and turned back from this quest, but my pride wouldn't allow it."

"Are you doubting your destiny?"

Relief filled him. "Are you well?"

"I am. As are you." Brahan reached out and pressed his hand into Wolf's shoulder, lightening the burden that rested there. "Do not doubt the journey you have chosen."

"You doubted my decision not too long ago."

Brahan chuckled. "I was wrong."

Wolf didn't feel the same amusement. His gaze strayed to the white stripe at Brahan's temple.

"That bad, is it?" Brahan asked as he brought his hand up to touch the affected white strands of hair.

Wolf attempted a nonchalant shrug. "The women will no doubt find it quite heroic."

Brahan's smile increased. "Then all is not lost." He struggled to push himself up in bed.

Wolf resisted the urge to assist him, knowing Brahan would not appreciate it. "Are you well enough to talk about what happened?"

A thoughtful expression replaced Brahan's smile. "I saw his face."

"The stranger's?"

"Aye. At first I was not certain, then something shifted, and his face became bright and clear."

"Who?" Wolf tensed, expecting to hear his father's name.

"Lord Grange."

"Grange?" Wolf heard the rage tremble in his own voice. "That he wants to kill me, I understand. But why Isobel? She's an innocent."

"Is she?"

Wolf stood, unsettled by the mixture of anger and surprise that raced beneath the surface of his emotions. Why would Brahan say such a thing about someone he knew so little about? "Did you see such in your vision?"

Brahan shook his head. "Nay. It is just that she is *so* innocent—too innocent. I sense something about her that I did not upon first meeting her."

"Such as?"

Brahan reached for the pouch where he kept the Seer's Stone. "For one, why did the Stone respond to her proximity as it did?" He tensed when he felt nothing. "It is gone."

"It is safe." Wolf held out the Stone to Brahan. "You dropped it when the visions ended."

He tucked the Stone back into its protective pouch as he struggled to sit at the side of the bed. "It's answers we need. Lady Isobel can enlighten us."

"Impossible. She is still caught in the grip of the poison."

Brahan pursed his lips and nodded. "What do we do until she recovers?"

"When you can stand, you've a marriage ceremony to attend."

Brahan arched his brow. "You're serious?"

"Deadly serious. Your vision identified two assassins. If Grange objects to my marriage, then going through with it will stop the attacks on Isobel's life."

Brahan frowned. "Either that or intensify them."

"The men and this castle will keep her safe."

"Does Isobel have anything to say about this?"

"Not one single thing," Wolf said bluntly.

Brahan stood, a little uncertainly at first, then with more stability. "Then let us go get this over with."

Wolf nodded and proceeded toward the door. The sooner this whole business was over, the better. In the hallway, Wolf hesitated. "Go see to the preparations," he said. "I have something I must do first."

Brahan's brow shot up in question, but he made no comment. Instead, he gave a brief nod and headed down the hallway toward the stairs. Wolf remained where he was until Brahan vanished from sight. Then he headed back to the solar, back to Isobel. In the room, he sank down on the bed beside her. She looked peaceful in her drug-induced slumber. The tension in his body eased. The assassin's attempt to take her from him had failed.

Take her from him. He frowned. When had he started thinking of her as his own? A virtual stranger. Compassion engulfed him and he reached out to her, gently caressing her pale cheek with his rough finger.

So soft. So tender. So innocent.

The breath in his chest stilled. Unspoiled and pure. Brahan was wrong. Isobel was not the deceptive sort. Fiona had taught him enough about deception to know the difference. And soon this gentle woman would be his wife.

He allowed his fingers to linger down the roundness of her check, down the angle of her chin to the long line of her throat.

A soft sigh escaped her lips and she turned in to his hand, almost as if she were pleased with his touch and longing for more of the same.

"I will protect you from Grange," he murmured.

Granted, he protected many people from Grange. But somehow this declaration seemed more personal than all the rest. The desire to keep others safe usually motivated him to go against his enemy. But this promise felt like something more. An instinctual need to protect her came out in him whenever she drew near.

Isobel needed protection. Wolf studied her silent form. Is that why his father had sent him to retrieve her? Had he known the way his son would respond? Was all this just more deception on his father's part, or could his intentions be honest for once? It was almost too much to believe.

Wolf sat back, dismissing the thought. His father hadn't done anything worthy of such hope or trust yet. Time would reveal his true intentions. It always did.

In the meanwhile, Wolf had no more doubts about one thing—his marriage. For better or worse, he would wed the woman laying beside him. The sacrifice would be more than worthwhile if it protected her from Grange.

Wolf's gaze moved to Isobel's face and lingered on the delicate curve of her cheek, the long column of her neck. He would protect her. A warmth came to the center of his being. Who was he trying to fool? With Isobel it was more than just a matter of protection or a sense of duty. She made him feel things—things he had no right to feel.

A man might be capable of such curious emotions, but that man was not him. His past indiscretions, his own dark reputation would always be there, a chasm too big to hurdle. His father had seen to that. And no golden-haired maid could change his destiny.

No matter how much he might wish it to be so. Best to focus his attention on the things he could change. "As soon as we are wed, I will go after him," Wolf told her. "I will keep you safe if it is the last thing I do."

Chapter Fourteen

A ring of brass lanterns had been set up around Isobel's bed. Golden tendrils of light flickered about the room, spreading eerie fingers of illumination into the darkened corners of the solar.

Mistress Rowley sat beside a sleeping Isobel, gently combing her hair. The woman had changed her into a crisp white nightrail. Above the bedlinens Wolf could see the delicate curve of Isobel's shoulders. He allowed his gaze to travel lower, to the soft rise of her breasts. With each breath, the outline of her nipples grazed the fabric.

Seductive and innocent.

He allowed himself a rueful smile. So like a bride, and yet he knew Isobel had no idea of the picture she presented. How could she? Unconscious as she was, her participation would be limited to her mere presence. Her mind would be otherwise engaged.

And what did she dream about? he wondered. A blissful peace had settled over her features as the wedding party gathered about her bed. Would she be glad for what he did for her now? Or would there be hell to pay when she awoke? Would she judge him as a man doing what he must to keep her safe, or as a beast forcing his will upon her?

Wolf frowned. What did it matter what she thought? Neither of them had a choice about their marriage. Beast or man, the outcome would be the same.

Unsettled by the direction of his thoughts, Wolf shifted his gaze to the room's other occupants. Walter stood at the foot of the bed, frowning at Isobel. This marriage would secure Walter's freedom, but he didn't look at all pleased. Brahan leaned quietly against the wall, a somber expression on his face. His friend knew what Wolf was capable of and did not judge him.

The worst judge of all stood on the far side of the chamber. Father Alasdair MacMurphy looked both bewildered and uncomfortable as he waited by the hearth, his hands worrying the pages of a Bible. No doubt trying to determine which persona to assume—preacher or savior.

Wolf had no need for either this eve. Once the service was through, he had a different service to perform, and it had nothing to do with being a bridegroom.

His hand strayed to the sword at his side. Blood would be spilled soon, but it would not be Isobel's. Grange would pay for whatever harm he had tried to inflict on his bride. Wolf looked at the company gathered about the bed. This woman was not just an abandoned girl from an isolated isle anymore. Soon she would be his wife, his kin.

He clamped his fingers about the hilt of his sword. The weapon used to bring a sense of comfort. Now it felt cold and destructive. That coldness had been enough for him until *she* was forcibly thrust into his life.

Without thinking about what he was doing for once, he moved to the bedside and sat beside Isobel. He drew her hand into his own. Her touch settled the chaos brewing inside him. It stayed him. In that whisper-soft touch he felt her warmth, her vitality, her essence.

Pure and gentle, and nothing that he deserved, yet she was part of the bargain he'd made with his father. Isobel for Walter. He found a certain peace in the thought that he'd been the winner on both counts.

All eyes in the room settled upon him. He could feel the curious gazes at this back. He did not move away, but neither did he move toward her. He simply stopped, giving in to the moment.

After one last breath, he drew his hand from hers. The warmth faded, leaving only the haunting chill that usually settled about his heart. "Let's get this over with." Intimacy faded, leaving only an empty irritation. Wolf signaled for the priest to come stand near the bedside.

Father MacMurphy trembled at the harshness in Wolf's tone. "Really, my lord Wolf—I don't think—"

"Precisely. Do not think. Simply read the ceremony and say the right words in all the right places."

"But the legality—"

Wolf picked up the leather-encased document that bore his father's seal. "The king has sanctified this union. What further legalities do you need?"

"It . . . it isn't that. It's just . . ."

"What? Speak up."

The priest clutched his Bible until his knuckles turned white. "You cannot force this woman into marriage. I need her consent. Until then it is not morally legal."

"Nonsense." Wolf felt his face harden. "It's been legal, morally and otherwise, for centuries gone by. Why would this instance be any different?"

The priest blanched. "We will need a proxy for the girl."

Wolf's gaze lit on Mistress Rowley. "Will you serve the role?"

She nodded. " 'Tis all right, Father. This marriage may not be the most conventional, but it is what is best for both parties involved."

"Perhaps." The skepticism in his tone hung in the air of the chamber as those in attendance gathered around the bed. "We shall proceed with a recounting of the dowry."

Wolf's gaze moved to his bride. She brought nothing to the marriage except herself, compared to his many holdings and sources of income. Why acknowledge that fact? Even if she would never know the difference, he could save her that embarrassment at least. "There is no need to recount our holdings. Continue."

The contract was laid on a flat stand before him. Wolf gestured to Mistress Rowley to come forth and sign in Isobel's place. He placed the quill in her hand.

She hesitated above the parchment. "What is the mistress's full Christian name? I fear I do not know."

Wolf's father had not revealed that information. It mattered not. "Lady Isobel will have to do."

Father MacMurphy frowned. " 'Tis most unusual."

Wolf took the quill from Mistress Rowley, dipped it into the pot of ink, then signed his name to the document. "Proceed." The deed was almost done.

Father MacMurphy cleared his throat, then began droning the oft-repeated rites and vows of the marriage ceremony. He did not look at Wolf or at Isobel's prone figure. Instead he directed the promises of love, honor, and obedience to the floor. Only once did his gaze stray, to the shattered remnants of the chamber door. His words came to a halt. A scowl of disapproval lent a fleeting touch of animation to his face.

Wolf clenched his jaw. The man's opinion mattered not. "Get on with it." He kept his voice low, deceptively silky.

The priest flinched regardless. "Do you have a ring for the girl?"

Wolf withdrew from his sporran a simple gold band dotted with tiny sapphires. His mother's ring, one of the few pieces of jewelry she owned that had not come from his father. Instead, the ring had been passed down from mother to son for close to four hundred years. A great family heirloom. One that should be given to a bride he loved. And yet, as he gently eased the ring onto Isobel's finger, it seemed to belong there.

He looked back at the priest.

"By the powers vested in me, I now pronounce you husband and wife. You may kiss your bride."

His bride. An unusual sensation tightened his chest. He reached out to brush an errant lock of hair from her brow.

Her eyelids fluttered open, then closed, and she tried to lift her head.

He bent to give her a quick, chaste kiss on the cheek, but her lips called to him instead. Tenderly his mouth molded over hers. At the slight touch, his body weakened, feeling almost drugged. She tasted sweet, like the first nectar of spring. Her breath stirred against his mouth, and he pulled away, despite wanting nothing more than to feel her, taste her, experience all that she was, all she could become beneath his lips.

His heart thundered in his chest as he gave in once more, this time directing his kiss to the side of her cheek near her ear. "You're safe now," he whispered. "Grange will pay for the attacks he's brought upon you. I will see to that."

She stirred. Her head moving toward him, toward his words, toward the warmth of his kiss.

All he had to do was lean forward to take her lips again. He stood, then headed for the door, desperate to escape the odd reaction he'd just had to the woman who was now his wife. "Walter, come with me."

Brahan stepped toward Wolf, blocking his way. "We have to ask her about the Stone when she wakes."

"You can ask her."

Brahan frowned. "Where are you going?"

"Grange obviously has someone working with him here at the castle. I intend to find out who."

"Lady Fiona might have an idea since she oversees the kitchens."

"I will speak with her eventually. For now, I will start with the kitchen maid you saw in your vision. Perhaps she has some answers." Wolf glanced back at the bed that held his bride. "Stay with Isobel. I know she will be safe with you." At Brahan's nod, Wolf and Walter continued toward the door. Stopping, Wolf frowned at the splintered wood of the frame. "And get someone to fix this door."

The shackles had returned to her wrists. The icy chill of the tower seeped deep into her bones. Imprisoned and cold.

Izzy woke with a start, staring blindly into the darkness that surrounded her. She thrashed against her bindings, expecting to feel the tug of metal against her flesh, but her hand sailed easily through the air until it came to rest on the bedding beneath her.

It had only been a dream. She was no longer in the tower. She was in Wolf's castle. Safe for now.

He had told her as much a short while ago. His honeyed voice had whispered those words close to her ear. A shudder ran through her at the memory.

She huddled down into the bed linens in an effort to warm herself. Why had he said that? She closed her eyes again, trying to remember what had happened through the throbbing ache at her temples. She remembered feeling dizzy. Pain had sliced through her stomach. Wolf's arms had closed around her. The physician had forced a vile potion down her throat. Then the wedding . . .

The wedding. Izzy tried to sit up. "It cannot be—"

"You're awake. Excellent."

Izzy opened her eyes to see Brahan lounging in a chair at her bedside, one leg thrown over the arm, his booted foot swinging.

Brahan regarded her critically. "I wanted to talk to you. You've been most unresponsive as of late. Wolf insisted I stay with you until you regained your senses. How do you feel?"

She tried to sit up once more. "What happened?"

"Lie still," Brahan chided. "You were poisoned."

"Poisoned?" Her eyes widened. "How?"

"Poisoned apples. Any idea who would want to harm you? Or why?" Suspicion hung heavy in his words.

Only one person wished her harm, but that was her secret. Izzy shook her head. She was immediately sorry when the room swung in sickening circles before her eyes. She collapsed back against the pillows.

"If I was poisoned, then why do I remember a priest? He said things . . . and there were people gathered around. . . . I vaguely recall seeing your face . . . and Wolf was here. . . ." She brushed her hand across the bedding at her side. "Did I receive the last rites? Am I dead and all this just a dream?"

Brahan laughed. "It is no dream. And nay, you are not dead. You were married, nothing more."

"Married?" The room suddenly seemed as frigid as a crisp January wind. "I never gave my consent."

"Your consent was not needed. Mistress Rowley served as your proxy."

She felt it then—a heaviness on the third finger of her left hand. She glanced down at the brilliant gold band dotted with sapphires that had appeared on her finger while she'd slept. "He cannot . . ."

Brahan's gaze shifted to her hand. "He already has."

Marriage is the evil from which springs insanity. Her mother's voice filled her mind. *Sacrifice your maidenhead and you will know the full power of your gift. Visions from the light will bring you nothing but anguish.* Izzy clamped her hands over her ears. It was happening already—the gradual slide into the abyss of insanity.

"Lady Isobel?" Brahan questioned, his hostility gone. When she didn't respond, he reached for one of her hands, gently lowering it to the coverlet. The look of concern in his eyes startled her. "What is it?"

She dropped her gaze, shielding her face, hiding the secrets she kept locked inside. "Nothing."

He sighed. "Well, since you do not wish to talk about that, perhaps you'll talk about the stone about your neck."

His gaze lit on her necklace—the one her mother had given her. "My necklace?"

"Aye." Brahan scooted closer to the bedside. "Where did you get that stone?"

"From . . . my mother. It was her mother's . . . before that, and her mother's before . . . that." When his frown only deepened, she clamped her lips shut. Why had she revealed such personal information to him? Izzy slipped the necklace inside the bodice of her nightrail, hiding it from his view. "It is just a necklace." She struggled to sit at the edge of the bed.

"What are you doing?" His brows knotted.

Izzy stood despite the fact that her knees felt as though they would buckle at any moment. She could not stay in bed. Lying in bed made her feel vulnerable. Many aspects of her life might at present be out of her control, but she would never be vulnerable again. She straightened her shoulders. "I must speak with my lord Wolf."

Brahan's brow rose in response to her demand. "The last I saw him was this morning, when he stopped by to check on you."

Izzy's cheeks warmed at the unexpected words. "He came to see me?"

"He has come every hour since we knew you would survive the poison."

And yet he did not stay. Izzy took two awkward steps toward the hearth in an effort to hide her disappointment—a disappointment that made no sense. What did she care if he stayed with her or not?

"He's speaking with the tenant farmers this morning about which fields will be sown with what crops," Brahan offered as she continued toward the warmth of the hearth.

Standing before the fireplace, Izzy absently fingered her necklace. Wolf's life had returned to normal, while her existence still spun wildly out of control.

Brahan moved to stand beside her. "Tell me what you know about that stone."

"My mother gave it to me when I was seven, just before she died."

"May I see it?" he asked.

She tucked the Stone deeper inside her bodice. "I haven't taken it off since she died." She had vowed never to remove it. Why was he so interested in her necklace? Her mother had never mentioned anything important about it to her. She has always hoped the Stone was of some value, in case she ever needed money. But apart from that, the necklace was a mere sentimental piece handed down through her mother's line. Or so she thought.

"No more questions." She fixed her gaze boldly on him. "I wish to dress. Please leave."

The irritated set of his face told her their discussion of the necklace was not over, only temporarily forestalled.

Before he could start up again, she hurried across the chamber to the armoire from which Mistress Rowley had taken a gown when she'd first arrived. As she plucked the elegant green gown she'd worn before from a hook, she heard the door softly close behind her. Brahan had gone. She breathed a thankful sigh as she tossed the dress over her head. Izzy quickly buttoned the sleeves and secured the ties at the back of the gown. When she'd finished, she turned toward the newly repaired door.

At the chamber's entrance she paused, running her fingers along the freshly milled wood. She could clearly recall the noise of saws and hammers while the structure was repaired. Changes abounded all around Duthus Castle.

Were those changes for the better, or for the worse? The verdict remained undecided.

Chapter Fifteen

"Where is that woman?" Wolf growled to himself as he searched the great hall for signs of his wife. Brahan had informed Wolf immediately upon his return that Isobel was awake but had left her bedchamber and was somewhere in the castle without an escort. Brahan had explained that he'd thought he'd had time to select two men he trusted to guard her while she changed her clothing. But she'd dressed faster than he thought any woman could.

Wolf stared hard at the men and women in the hall as they went about their chores. A young squire stoked the fire while a kitchen maid turned the spit of meat for the midday meal. Two other servants swept around the others who sat at the trestle tables, discussing the day's events.

No sign of Isobel. He knew that she still remained within the castle walls, for the gates were secured and guards were posted. Even so, no one had seen her for the last several hours. And what originally began as concern and curiosity over where she had gone now approached fear.

Wolf drew in a heavy breath. It was happening again. Despite his determination to remain aloof from yet another needy soul within his castle walls, he was slowly, inexorably being drawn in by an alluring face and a pair of bewitching brown eyes.

Nay, his growing fascination went far beyond what his eyes could see, he admitted to himself. If only she wasn't such a combination of strength and innocence. One moment she would cast him a soulful glance where he could see the emptiness she had learned to live with, the next she would straighten her spine and challenge his beastly behavior with all the skill of a seasoned warrior. Damn, but she fascinated him.

Wolf threw open the heavy wooden door that separated the great hall from the outside. The door jerked back on its hinges, protesting the abuse. He squared his shoulders, ready to do battle with whatever and whoever might stand between him and his bride.

After he searched the interior of the castle for her, he explored outside. As he did he tried to push all fears of foul play from his mind. She had to be out here somewhere.

Then he saw her. Sitting alone at the edge of the fish pond. At her side, a familiar brown puff of feathers pecked at the ground while Isobel absently tossed tiny pebbles into the water that lapped at her bare feet.

The sky above was dotted with clouds and a cool spring breeze curled across the surface of the pond to tease the tendrils of her golden hair as they spilled across her shoulders and tumbled down her back. Despite the slight chill in the air, she appeared every inch the summer nymph—seductive, innocent, tempting . . . and unharmed. Relief filled him only to be replaced in the span of a heartbeat with rampant desire.

As he drew near, Mistress Henny, with a bold red spot painted on her back, stopped her assault upon the ground and stared at him with a hint of reproach in her normally vacant stare.

Isobel, however, paid him no heed. It was almost as if she were so lost in thought that she had not heard his approach.

"Isobel?" he said. A hint of pique lingered in his voice. Why was she so careless with her own safety?

She started. The pebbles she held in her hand scattered on the ground. "My lord?"

He felt his face harden at her formal address. "Need you always address me so?"

Her cheeks flushed pink, only adding to the picture of her sitting beside the water's edge, her bare and delicate feet peeking out from beneath her gown. He swallowed roughly. Something about her feet—long and slender—nearly undid him.

He bent to retrieve the pebbles she had dropped, grateful for the distraction. "I could not find you." He handed her a pebble. She accepted it with hesitation. "Why did you leave the safety of the keep?"

"I am not used to being indoors all the time. I felt . . . restless."

"Someone has tried to kill you twice. Restless or not, you stay inside. Do you hear me?"

She paled at his words. "Another demand?"

Others did as he demanded. Why not her? He turned back to the water and, lining himself up with the shore, sent a pebble skimming across the water. One . . .

two . . . three . . . four. "Why are you restless?" he asked more gently.

"How did you do that?" She jumped down from the rock on which she sat, her pert toes disappearing beneath the hem on her dress.

"Tell me why you are bored and I will show you how."

The animation left her face. "It matters not."

The catch in her voice at the end of her words went through Wolf like the thrust of a sword. He started to reach for her, then thought better of it. Touching her would only muddle his thoughts. "I want to know."

"I . . ." She paused, her eyes filling with trepidation.

"Continue," he urged, keeping his voice calm, encouraging.

"I have no place in this castle. When I awoke, I needed to do something to make myself useful. I went out to rake the chicken yard and was shooed away by the others. I tried to help in the kitchens, but Fiona rules down there. I have tried to assist Mistress Rowley in her chores, only to be told that a lady's place is near her husband." The last word echoed with such sorrow that her pain became almost palpable. "This castle has three mistresses," she continued, "and one of us had to concede."

"I had no idea." He turned back to the pond, and away from the misery that lay heavy on her shoulders. She was his bride and the rightful mistress here. "I will speak to Fiona."

"That will do nothing," she said softly.

She was right. Only one solution could fix this problem: Fiona had to go. "Regardless of Fiona or Mistress Rowley, you are the lady of the castle and the occupants need your care."

The arch of her brow told him she was not convinced.

"I need your help," he said simply.

"You do?" This time her brows arched with concern.

"I could use your assistance with the cook to set the menus. The herbs from last season must be inventoried and new seeds planted. And I've asked the weaver to create a new tartan weave for you. A marriage gift." Her breath hitched at the last comment, but he continued, giving her no time to respond. "And Walter—he is new to the household and needs some direction." He paused. "Will you assist me?"

She nodded, but the heaviness that surrounded her did not ease. His gut twisted in response, suddenly realizing at that moment that he would do anything to see a glimmer of a smile upon her face. He bent to retrieve two stones from the ground, handing one to her. With a slight hesitation, she accepted it. "Watch me." He aligned his body with the edge of the shore and bent slightly at the hips. With a flick of his wrist, he sent the rock hopping across the water's smooth surface . . . five . . . six . . . seven times.

Fascination brightened her face. "What's this called?"

"Skipping rocks."

"May I try?"

The eagerness in her voice made him smile. He waved his hand at the water. "Be my guest."

She followed his earlier example by lining herself up with the water and sent the rock out, only to have it drop with a splash through the water's surface. She frowned. "It is harder than it looks."

"Let me show you." He slipped another stone into her hand and, standing behind her, enveloped her slight body within the shelter of his arms. The cascade of her hair, soft and silky, teased the exposed skin at his neck. Desire stole through him so quickly it robbed him of breath. At a loss for words, he reached for her, wrapping her delicate fingers within his own war-seasoned hands.

The light scent of heather invaded his senses. He pulled her more tightly against him in response. He inhaled deeply, capturing her essence, committing it to memory.

"What do I do now?" she asked, bringing him back to the moment.

"Draw your hand back like this," he managed to say through the thickness that invaded his thoughts. "Then release." With a quick flick, she sent the rock out over the water. She counted each touch of the rock to the water's surface, but he barely registered the words. She half turned in his arms, revealing her face. A delighted smile pulled up the corners of her mouth, illuminating her, chasing all the shadows from her features. She should smile like that all the time.

Wolf's gaze fastened on her lips, and he suddenly was dying for a taste of her mouth.

Her smile shifted. Fascination took its place and the pulse at her temples quickened. She swayed backward as though losing her balance. He shifted her against his side, holding her tightly, unwilling to let her go. In the next beat of his heart, his lips touched hers, filling him with an unexpected thrill as liquid heat spilled through him.

She gasped as he tunneled his fingers through her hair and cupped her head to hold it still. His tongue slipped between her parted lips. All his senses exploded at once, leaving him deaf and blind to anything but the magic of her kiss. He gave himself up to the sensations, allowing the pleasure to build, gathering inside him until he thought he would burst.

"Sweet Mary." Wolf wrenched his mouth away from hers, his breathing ragged and fast, his desire stretched so taut, it felt as though it would rip him apart. He dragged his hands from her hair and allowed them to slide down the length of her arms, stopping at her wrists. He wanted to let her go, yet he could not quite bring himself to release her. "I . . . shouldn't have done that."

"Why not?" she whispered.

Because everything I care about my father uses against me. The reason swam through his senses, grounding him in the here and now. Forestalling an explanation, he feathered his thumbs against her wrists. Instead of soft, delicate flesh, he felt rough and callused skin.

He stepped away from her, her wrist still clasped between his own fingers. He searched her skin. White rings encircled her flesh—scars—deep and many. "Who did this to you?"

Her face turned pale and she tried to shrug the ends of her sleeves down over the marks. "It is nothing."

The marks looked as though they were made by manacles. But how would she have ever been anywhere on St. Kilda to experience such a horror? "Isobel, who did this to you?"

She dropped her gaze to the water lapping against the shore. "My father."

His mind raced. His breath stilled in his chest at the enormity of what she'd confessed. Parents were sometimes cruel to their children—his own father was proof of that—but to keep her in irons? Then, suddenly, something clicked inside him—her fear of dark, enclosed places, her abandonment on St. Kilda, the tower. "Dear God." Emotion flooded him. He didn't know how else to convey what he felt, so he eased her against his body and held her.

She leaned into his embrace, but the tension in her body was palpable. She felt so tiny, so vulnerable in his arms. He wrapped himself around her all the tighter. His own body shook with reaction. Sympathy. Fear. And something else he dared not examine. "How did you deal with such abuse?"

Isobel raised her head from his chest. Her eyes were not filled with the pain he had expected. Instead he saw strength and a renewed resolve. "I learned to survive."

He brought his right hand up. The tips of his fingers brushed the curve of her cheek before he tunneled his fingers into her hair, cradling her head. "So brave." His thumb stroked the sensitive skin below her earlobe.

"Not brave. Only determined."

Her words whispered across his lips, their flavor mysterious and seductive. And he could resist no longer. He brought his lips to her mouth, the touch light, fleeting, and yet it made them both shudder. He could feel the tension building inside her as though she held herself back. He felt the sensation as well—the hot, needful hunger that coiled ever tighter until he could scarcely breathe.

"Wolfie." The shriek came from behind. Wolf's head snapped in the direction of the sound. Fiona stood not three feet away, her eyes narrowed, her color high, her nostrils flared.

"What?" He could not keep the annoyance from his voice. His irritation only increased when Isobel stepped away, her long lashes coming down to veil the emotion in her eyes.

Fiona rushed forward and placed her beringed fingers upon his arm. "You are needed in the keep."

"Why?" He kept his gaze on his bride. She turned away from him now, moving back to the water's edge. She drew one bared toe through the water in an almost mournful movement. And he nearly smiled. She grieved their interruption as much as he did.

"There are half a dozen people in the hall who all wish to speak with you. The mason wants to know about the addition of the east wing of the castle. Three traders have arrived from Orkney and wish to show their goods. Cook has a new tart that needs your approval. And the weaver needs your input about the new tartan you asked her to create."

Wolf's eyes narrowed suspiciously. "What are you at, Fiona? Brahan can deal with the mason and the traders. Mistress Rowley can speak with Cook and the weaver."

"They will have none but you. After all, you are the lord here," she said with a bland smile.

"I must go." Wolf turned away and strode toward Isobel.

"Where?" Fiona's tone sharpened.

"I am taking Isobel for a ride. It is time that the new mistress of this castle saw the land she must now govern along with her husband."

Isobel's head came up. She stared at him in surprise.

"You are needed here," Fiona said through gritted teeth.

"Isobel, will you ride with me today, outside the castle walls?" He had scouted his land earlier for signs of Grange or his henchmen and had found none. "My men and I shall keep you safe."

Fiona tried to interrupt. He darted her a cold glance. "I wish to show you my land, Isobel. Come with me." His expression softened as he looked back at his wife.

"You are asking me?" Stunned disbelief lingered in her voice.

He smiled, touched by the surprise that widened her eyes. "I have been too demanding of late, and aye, I am asking for the pleasure of your company."

She hesitated, then gave a slight nod. Surprise shifted to pleasure in her gaze, and an answering smile came to her lips.

"Wolfie, you must come to the castle," Fiona protested.

Her words faded into the background as he held out his hand to Isobel. Deep inside he felt something pull tight. He knew he had a responsibility here, but suddenly he didn't care. Her fingers stretched out to meet his. Only a heartbeat separated him from turning away from a lifetime of doing what others asked of him instead of what he wanted to do. Her fingers came around his, steady and strong. He clung to her grip, finding strength in the warmth of her touch.

He needed this time with her more than he needed his next breath. He wasn't abandoning his duties forever. He only needed a short while to revel in Isobel's presence, to replace the sadness he'd seen in her eyes when she spoke of her father with joy.

He did not have much to share with her, but he could share his love of this land. He wanted her to experience the scent of the rain, of the damp earth, of the gorse and the heather and the granite. The sweet scent of the thistle and the way it prickled against a bare leg. He wanted to surround her in the tang of the pine, the fir, the cattle—the shaggy red-coated beasts with wicked horns upon their heads. Together they would sit on the hillside and listen to the call of the eagle and the babble of the brook. And he would speak to her in Gaelic . . .

about the things he wished he had time to do, to see, and experience. . . .

He held her hand and strode with her in the direction of the stables. As he passed Fiona, he paused. "We will speak when I return."

Isobel fell in step beside him, seeming as eager as he to leave behind the castle and all who lived there.

A quiet peacefulness stole over Wolf with each footstep he put between himself, Fiona, and the castle. He had made the right decision to get away for a time.

Nothing would go wrong if he ignored his duties for just a short while.

She had lost him.

"Nay," Fiona vowed as Wolf and Isobel walked away. "I will *never* lose him."

She thought about the lies she'd told, the evil she'd done to win him, to share his bed, the things she still did to try to keep him there. She hated herself for what she'd allowed her previous protector to do to her—and she almost hated Wolf for making her want him enough to do it.

She watched as he slipped an arm around the scrawny girl's waist and drew her against his side. She did not miss the tenderness of the motion, nor the intensity of his gaze as he turned to look down upon the girl as they disappeared inside the stable.

Rage, hot and hard, erupted inside her. He'd never spared such a look for her. Never.

Yes, he'd cared for her every need and given her the kind of freedom she'd never dreamed of having. But she yearned for his touch. His presence near her, beside hers was a kind of salve that eased away the vileness she'd allowed to overtake her life. Without him, the poison of her actions would kill her.

She needed him. And by God, she'd have him. He might be done with her, but she most certainly was not done with him.

Chapter Sixteen

Izzy had never experienced anything like it. The day had been pure bliss. She and Wolf had ridden alone together to a place not far from his castle, yet looking at the ancient beauty of the green hills and craggy mountains, it felt as though they'd slipped into a private domain.

Izzy curled up upon the grass near the brook that gurgled quietly beside her and soaked up the sunshine like a sleepy cat. It was a moment of blissful ignorance—time apart from all the deceptions, the pain of the past, the uncertainty of the future.

Dappled sunshine filtered through the shrubbery at the water's edge, sending glimmers of light to dance upon the surface like twinkling jewels. To Izzy, it was a gift more precious than real stones. As the light glittered and faded, she felt a sense of peace, of security, and even happiness that chased the shadows from her mind.

The moment might be fleeting—but it was hers for now. She drew a deep breath of the heather-scented air and tried to etch this moment on her memory.

"You look happy," Wolf said as he sat down beside her, his hard, muscular thighs resting against her hip. The clean, spicy scent of him stirred her senses in ways she couldn't comprehend. Her heart hammered in her chest and her awareness of the beauty around her faded away until there was only him.

She tried to force herself to remember the past—the darkness of the tower, the decaying scent of her own flesh, the pain of her bindings, her mother's insanity, yet none of it seemed to pierce the sensual warmth he created with his presence.

What was happening to her? "Why are we here?" she asked, even though her tongue felt heavy and slow.

His mouth curved into a devastating smile. "We are both going to leave it *all* behind. Just for a moment."

"But why me and not Fiona?" she blurted. She dropped her gaze from his, no longer able or willing to see what she would read in his eyes.

He placed a finger beneath her chin and tilted up her head until she looked in his eyes. "Fiona is not my bride. You are." His smile shifted to a grin of satisfaction.

"Are you happy with this arrangement?" Again, she flinched, wondering what possessed her to speak so honestly with him. She had everything to lose by such forthright talk. Upon their arrival, she had wanted nothing more than to be freed. Now she wasn't so certain leaving was the answer.

"I've grown accustomed to the thought." He offered her a teasing grin this time.

Her stomach fluttered in response. He was melting her, disarming her defenses, and with a start she realized she didn't mind at all.

He swayed forward, and she felt the brush of his lips skim her cheek, an unspoken pact between them. He extended his hand. "Walk with me. I want to show you something."

Izzy swallowed and slipped her hand into his. His strong fingers closed around hers as he drew her to her feet and steered her toward a path that followed the water's edge. "Where are we going?"

"Do you trust me?" he asked.

"Aye," she replied without thinking. Her next step faltered and she nearly tripped.

"Steady there." His hands snaked out to grasp her waist.

She nodded her thanks and eased out of his grasp. "It must have been a rock."

He smiled, but said no more, simply took her hand and continued down the path. The sound of the water as it flowed over the rocky creek bed filled the silence that had fallen between them.

They walked in companionable silence for several minutes until they came to a widening in the path made even more defined by the hedging that cropped up beside the pebbled pathway. The road continued to widen until a small house appeared in the distance.

"A house?" Izzy said, her voice filled with surprise.

"Come." Wolf tugged her arm gently as he increased his pace to a brisk walk—nearly running. A soft smile broke out across his face, illuminating his features with almost boyish glee.

"What is this place?" she asked when they reached the front walkway.

He stopped, forcing her to do the same. "Where I grew up. It is my home."

Pride laced his words. The small but neatly trimmed house was neither as elegant nor as noble as Duthus

Castle, yet she felt the warmth of his pride flow through her. He'd had a happy childhood here. "Who lives here now?"

"No one. My mother used to, but she died nearly five years ago." Before she could respond, he steered her around the side of the house to where the trees sprang up alongside the brook. "This is what I wanted to show you." He stopped before the sturdy trunk of a rowan tree.

A tree? "Oh, it's very . . . big."

He laughed richly. "Not the tree. The ladder and more." He motioned toward a series of wood slats attached to the tree's trunk. Her gaze followed along the muscled curve of his arm and over his strong hand to the structure that hovered overhead. Built into the branches of the tree, it appeared like an extension of it—made more by nature than by man.

"I built this myself when I was only a lad."

Izzy could feel the walls of her defenses tumbling down with each new revelation. He was sharing his life, his past with her. Why? They were already married. He did not have to woo her. She was already his. And yet, he was. He had made every attempt to put her at ease today. He'd even stood up to Fiona and promised things would change.

"Would you like to go up?"

"There is more?"

He nodded, and with a hand on her back, guided her up the makeshift ladder and into the bows of the tree. Wolf followed behind and helped her up onto a solid wooden landing rimmed with rails that hugged the structure, adding warmth and an invitation to come inside.

Wolf reached around her and swung open the arched

door, but not before she had a chance to see the exquisite detail etched into the dark surface. A dragon filled the scene, its scaled body and swirling tail nearly leapt from the carving with richness and life. Her gaze swept past the doorway inside.

"Go in," he encouraged.

She paused, as her stomach suddenly fluttered and fear froze her limbs as she surveyed the darkened interior.

Wolf must have sensed her sudden distress. He brushed past her. A moment later, shafts of golden sunlight spilled through the room, edging out the darkness and her fears.

Izzy stepped inside and paused yet again. Her gaze moved about the circular room, was pulled into it with a sense of awe and wonder. Never had she seen its like. Two chairs, a table, and two benches made from bent and highly polished tree branches were scattered about the room. The branches were artistically woven together to create high, arching backs and sturdy seats, worthy of a fairy king.

The wooden floors were smothered in thick fur pelts to keep out the chill of the night and add softness to the day. But most breathtaking of all was the ceiling. Branches had been woven together high overhead to create a tight shield against moody Scottish storms. On the smaller branches where there would have been leaves, drops of liquid color glittered in the afternoon sun.

Suspended as though floating on air were glass bulbs of green and gold and amber and red, sending prisms of light and color against every surface in the small room. The room breathed of life, of vitality, of creativity and warmth.

"You did this?" she asked, as a cacophony of discordant emotions skittered through her. "You created this beauty?"

He nodded, his gaze fixed on her face as though he were experiencing a similar joy as she was simply by watching her reaction to what he had done.

"How? Why?"

Again, he shrugged. "This is my home and my special place."

A pang of longing shot through Izzy. What would it be like to have a home, a family you cared about and who cared about you?

Did he offer her that now?

"It's beautiful." Such a bond was too much to hope for, too much of a risk to take. Reaching up, she brushed her fingers against one of the drops of color overhead. Hard and cool, yet filled with life. She never would have thought such a thing was possible if she hadn't seen it herself.

Perhaps other things are possible as well, a voice inside her challenged. *Tell him about yourself. Tell him about the trapped little girl who used to stare out the tower's arrow slits dreaming of something more from her life.* The words sat on the tip of her tongue, but they would not slide into speech. Exposing herself like that, laying herself open to his rejection, could be her undoing.

She wasn't willing to give him that much power over her. She turned to him. He watched her, his face puzzled, as though he, too, were assessing whether or not to confide in her.

"Isobel. I need to leave you on the morrow. I've avoided my duties today, which means they will be all the more pressing tomorrow."

"Might I come with you?"

"Nay," he said harshly, then softened his tone at her startled reaction. "I must leave to pursue a matter of honor with an enemy of mine."

A memory came forward. He'd whispered something in her ear while she'd lain in bed, suffering the poison's effects. What had he said? And suddenly she knew. He'd said something about her father, Lord Grange. "Must you go?" Fear for him motivated her bold words.

"You wish me to stay?" His brow rose in question.

Heat rose to her cheeks. "I merely meant . . . sometimes it is better to ignore one's enemies—"

"Grange is not a man to be ignored." A pulse beat in his suddenly clenched jaw.

She knew the truth of that statement. But her father was also dangerous and unpredictable, as her mother had always warned. Izzy swallowed hard. "It's just that . . . I know him. He—"

"It is up to me to put him in his place." Wolf's features hardened, and he gestured toward the door. "We should go."

She moved to the door before turning back to him. Nothing she could say would stop him from going except perhaps the truth. Could she tell him about her father, his enemy? Or would that knowledge make her his enemy as well? Unsettled by the thought, she moved down the wooden ladder. At the bottom she waited until he stood beside her. Regardless of how this time together had ended, these stolen moments had been magical for her, and she wanted to let him know that. "Thank you for sharing this with me." She nodded up at the tree. "I feel lucky to be one of the people you've shared your secret place with."

For a moment his features softened. "I've never shared it with anyone else—not even my family," he said, and a touch of surprise laced his words.

A strange tingle filled her at his admission. Her husband had shared a piece of himself with her that he had never revealed to anyone else before. That knowledge warmed her all the way back to the castle.

Lurking behind the trees, a shadowy figure watched Wolf and the girl climb out of the tree and hasten down the path back to the fortress beyond. Even as they vanished, an image stayed imprinted upon his mind. The look in the girl's eyes as she gazed at that bastard. It was a look he'd seen very few times in his life, but one he never mistook—passion, true and simple.

He clamped his fists around the crossbow in his hands, letting the pain focus him, control the anger that threatened to break free. "Damn you," he whispered, his voice as icy as his heart.

The girl was his to do with as he wished. A stinging pain pierced his heated rage. His hand throbbed beneath the viselike grip he held on his weapon. Droplets of crimson blood seeped through the seams of his fingers, fanning out across the back of his hand to fall upon the ground.

The man only smiled. There would be blood, all right, and plenty of it before he was through. The Black Wolf of Scotland would be the first to pay. Once he was out of the way, the girl would be easy prey.

He was tired of the failures of all the others he had employed to do his bidding. He'd take charge himself and see the deed done.

He'd take what he wanted, what he deserved. He'd

lived in the shadows for too long now. It was time to strike hard and fast. And this time no one would stand in his way.

No one.

Chapter Seventeen

Moonlight shimmered through the open window, casting a silvery glow about the room and across the woven rush mats spread about the laird's solar. Fiona followed the beam of moonlight with her fingers as it passed through the heavy night air and onto the coverlet of Wolf's bed. The lord and his new bride dined below.

Any moment now that would change. A few coins to the right servant would see that Wolf came up to the solar—alone. She smoothed the gold linen sheets with trembling fingers, waiting for the door to open, waiting for him to come back where he belonged. She did not want to think about where he had been today, or with whom. Fiona's hands slowly clenched into fists as a poisonous twist of jealousy curled inside.

A soft click sounded at the door and her heart thumped in her chest. The time had come. The door slowly opened. She disentangled her fingers from the sheets and draped her naked body into an enticing pose.

Silhouetted in the doorway, Wolf stopped. His gaze traveled slowly over her feet, up her leg, and across her abdomen and breast until he reached her face. His eyes were as dark as the depths of night. No passion lingered there as it once did. Instead, the harsh lines of his face spoke more loudly than words that he was not pleased with her.

"Dress yourself." His words were like ice.

She forced a nonchalant smile. "Funny, you used to tell me that after we satisfied our passion, not before." When she made no move to cover herself, he strode to the bedside and tossed a woolen blanket over her, shrouding the only weapon she had left in her arsenal.

"You might find her intriguing now, but mark my words, you'll tire of her after you've bedded her once. The girl has no more meat on her bones than her scrawny little fowl. What do you see in her?" she blurted out before she could pull back the angry words.

"She is my wife."

He said the words lightly, but she could read the warning in his eyes. She was treading on unsteady ground, yet she could not stop. "She is only yours on paper, Wolfie. I can offer you so much more. I will not deny that I had hoped to be your bride, but the idea of being your mistress holds a certain appeal as well." She threw back the blanket that covered her and slid one hand down the shapely arch of her hip and down to the creamy flesh of her thigh.

His gaze did not follow the motion. Nay, his gaze remained fixed on her face. "You will be neither, Fiona. I want you to leave."

Although not entirely unexpected, the reality of her situation sparked her anger anew. "How could you toss me aside after I gave you everything I had to offer a man?"

"I gave you protection, Fiona, when you had nowhere

else to turn. The rest was freely offered, as I recall. I made you no promises."

"I've been cheated." She leapt off the bed and rushed him with her fists raised, ready to strike.

He caught her wrists in his hands effortlessly, ceasing her assault. "Two knights await belowstairs to take you to your new home. I have arranged for you to have a cottage in the next village, as well as an income for the remainder of your days or until such a time that you decide to marry again."

Humiliation and rejection brought a flush to her cheeks. "You think you are done with me? That you can buy me off with pretty promises?" She struggled against his grip. He released her immediately.

"You know I shall be true to my word."

She knew that, all right. He would live up to his promises to her just as he lived up to every promise he had ever made. If only she had gotten a promise of marriage, or of faithfulness. But he'd never offered her such words, no matter how hard she had tried.

"What about the threat to my life? The poisoning? I won't be safe if I leave here."

Wolf's face remained hard. "We both know those apples were meant for Isobel." He paused. "Will you accept my offer and leave this castle tonight?"

"I do not stay where I am not wanted," she replied.

For a moment the anger faded from his gaze and she saw a familiar softness that brought a catch to her throat. "Fiona, you have so much to offer to the right man. But I am not that man."

Her throat tightened as she responded with a nod, then pulled the blanket he had offered her back up around her body.

"Dress," he said softly. "I will have Mistress Rowley pack your things. I shall await you belowstairs."

She nodded once more as he turned and left the room. She'd known this day was coming long ago, before Isobel had ever entered the castle walls. Fiona tucked the blanket around herself and stepped into the silvery rays of moonlight that forced their way through the glass windows.

She turned her face up into the light, hoping that the ethereal beams would somehow erase the sentimentality that washed over her now. With her previous protector, she had set up the scenario on the beach where Wolf had found her two years ago. She had known Wolf would be there and that his sympathetic heart would never allow him to leave her there. Through trickery she had come to this castle, but once ensconced in Wolf's household, she had allowed herself to hope for other things. None of those things were a reality now.

She had played all sides of the men in her life—Wolf, Lord Grange, and even the king—in an effort to get what she wanted. Yet none of those deceptions had brought her the kind of success she truly desired. Which left her only one choice: She had to follow through with her original plan. If she did not, she was as good as dead.

She released her hold on the blanket, letting it skim down her body until it came to rest upon the floor at her feet. Slowly, hesitantly, she reached for her discarded clothing. She knew what she had to do, and she would do it. Because above all else she knew what it took to survive in this cold, cruel world.

Deception and death. Those were the words that would guide her future now.

Fiona forced back tears. She straightened her garments and ran her trembling fingers through her tousled hair. She had always wanted something more from her life. Too bad she always took the wrong path toward that goal.

She had to do what must be done. What that turned her into, she would have to live with for the rest of her life.

Chapter Eighteen

Early the next morning, the great hall buzzed with activity. At the sound of voices, Izzy quickly dressed, then left the solar, where she had spent the night alone, hoping to catch a glimpse of her husband before he left. Wolf had informed her after they'd returned to the castle the night before that he would be gone with the morning light.

She knew from their conversation in the tree house that he intended to find Lord Grange. He did not say what he would do when he found the man, and at the time Izzy had been too stunned to ask for details. Now that she'd had time to think on the matter, she did not know which prospect frightened her more: the thought that he might find her father or that her father might find him.

Perhaps if he hadn't left yet, she could intervene. Racing down the stairs, she wondered what she could say. All night long she'd debated about telling him the truth about who she was. He'd opened himself up to her at the tree house. She owed him the same courtesy, regardless of the outcome.

"Where may I find my lord Wolf?" she asked a maid who passed by carrying a tray of freshly baked bread for the morning meal.

"He's gone, milady," she said with a deep curtsy. "He left at dawn."

Wordlessly, she motioned for the maid to rise, so startled by the show of respect that she could do nothing more. The maid offered Izzy a pleased smile before continuing on her way. Izzy sighed. So much for unburdening herself of the truth. As soon as he returned, she would tell him everything. Until then, however, she might as well learn something about the castle in which she now lived, or if she was truly honest about her feelings, something about the man she had married.

Because after yesterday, she could no longer believe he was the beast his name implied.

Suddenly restless and in need of answers, Izzy searched the room. A welcoming fire glowed in the hearth. Contented serving maids shuffled about the hearth, grinding grain into flour on one side of the big wooden trestle table. On the other end of the table, two elderly women kneaded already risen dough in preparation for baking. Other servants bustled to and fro, performing their daily duties, repairing tapestries, stocking wood near the hearth, and replenishing the barrels of ale for the next meal.

Several warriors sat at trestle tables farther away from the hearth engaged in a game of merrills. For a moment she found herself moving the three wooden pieces along with the players, mentally trying to place the markers in a row while blocking the opponent.

As the last peg slipped into the hole on the game board, a cheer went up. Izzy recognized the winner as Hiram, the disfigured warrior who had brought her bath when she'd first arrived. In this setting, he no longer appeared shy and uncertain. Among his peers, he commanded their attention as he moved his game piece across the board, exchanging ribald comments with the others. Roars of laughter followed each man's jibes, filling the large hall with a warmth and cheerfulness she had not expected to find.

The room's occupants acknowledged her presence with a nod as they continued in their work or play. She returned their greetings while trying to disguise her own discomfort. Never had she been so visible before, and she found the attention a little disconcerting. She had tried hard all her life to be no more than a mere shadow while around others. The lack of attention had suited her just fine.

But things were different now. It was her responsibility to do as Wolf had asked—and care for his people. But how? Izzy glanced about the immaculate chamber. Everyone in the hall had a job to perform or some way to contribute to the care and upkeep of the castle. Uncertainty crept over her. She had been trained by the MacDonalds as a servant, not as mistress of a castle. How would she ever find a way to help her husband here?

The thought had barely materialized when Brahan appeared at the bottom of the stairway. As soon as he saw her, he made his way toward her.

Nervously she moistened her lips. He was bound to ask her more questions about the necklace. How could she talk to him about something she didn't understand herself? Desperate to escape that conversation, Izzy scanned the room. That was when she saw him: Walter.

He sat alone at a table on the far side of the hall. A queer sensation tingled along the fine hairs of her arm. A sign? Was this how she could help Wolf? Ever since she'd first met Walter aboard the *Ategenos* she had sensed awkwardness in his interactions with her. He didn't like her, though she had no idea why.

Yet Wolf had specifically asked her to help Walter feel more comfortable in his new home. She knew Walter had been imprisoned—an experience she knew all too well.

She glanced behind her. Brahan had almost reached her. Perhaps she could help Walter in some small way. She hurried to the table where he sat. Whether Walter would accept her intervention or not, he would serve as a diversion from Brahan.

"Might I sit with you?" she asked in a calm, unhurried voice.

Walter looked across the table at her. She didn't miss the flash of resentment in his eyes. "I suppose I cannot stop you now that you are *mistress* of the castle."

As she sat, she allowed her gaze to move past Walter, to where Brahan leaned against the wall not twenty paces away. His casual pose said he would wait all day for her, yet his expression revealed his true haste.

Izzy turned back to Walter. "The hall seems very busy today," she said, trying to make conversation.

He frowned. "So it is." His breath smelled of ale.

Not the best circumstances under which to have a chat with the man, but she would not turn away from this opportunity. "Can we talk, Walter?"

"I doubt my brother would want me to talk to you."

"Why?"

"Because I have caused him enough trouble already." He thumped his fist on the table. His half-full mug of ale jumped at the violent attack, then clattered against the tabletop once more. All eyes turned her way. Warriors and servants stopped their tasks to appraise the situation. Brahan stepped away from the wall, heading toward her.

Izzy forced herself to remain calm. Neither of these men would get the best of her. She had dealt with angry and abusive men all her life. If she had to, she could handle Brahan's questions and Walter's anger. "I did not mean to disturb you, Walter," she said in a soothing tone. "You just looked like you could use some conversation."

"The very fact that you are in this castle disturbs me." He reached for his mug and took a long drink. "The fact that Wolf married you disturbs me even more." He set down the mug. His hand slipped from the table to rest at his belt. "And I hate that our father wants . . ."

A flash of pain entered his eyes before he looked away. "You have no idea how guilty I feel," he said.

Izzy frowned. "Guilty over what, Walter?"

His gaze lit on her once more. Instead of guilt, hatred hardened his eyes. His fingers left his belt, and before she could react, a dagger embedded in the wood a mere whisper from her fingers. She snatched them back against her chest. In the space of a heartbeat, Brahan, along with seven of the warriors, surrounded the table, each with their sword drawn.

"Move away from the table, Walter," Brahan said, his voice a deadly calm.

Izzy hugged her fingers to her chest in an effort to hide their sudden trembling. Eight long and lethal-looking swords pointed at the man opposite her. Walter merely sat back in his chair and hoisted his mug, as if he had not a care in the world.

The dagger before her vibrated with the force of Walter's blow. Perhaps she had been wrong about knowing how to deal with men such as Walter. Anger and aggression she was used to, violence she was not.

"What's going on here?" Mistress Rowley forced her way through the warriors surrounding the table. One look at the swords and her eyes widened in horror. "Put your weapons down."

Instantly, the whisper of metal sheathed in leather filled the silence that had crept over the hall.

"What is the meaning of all this?" Mistress Rowley continued.

"Walter attacked her," Brahan said, his voice low and dangerous.

Mistress Rowley's gaze flew to the dagger embedded in the wood. "Walter."

With a sound of disgust he shoved away from the table, his bench scraping heavily against the stone floor. "Nothing ever changes. No one tries to understand my side of the story." Walter kept his gaze fixed on Izzy's face as he backed away from the table. "You all jump to her defense. But what do we actually know about this girl? Who is she really? Wolf didn't bother to find out before he married her."

"We know all we need to know." Brahan straightened. "Wolf accepts her. And we do as well."

Walter's face became ragged and pale. "How unpleasant for you all. I hope you feel the same way when she brings disaster down upon all our heads." On those words he turned and left the room.

"Don't listen to him." Mistress Rowley patted Izzy's shoulder, trying to lend comfort.

The gesture brought no ease to the threat she'd felt at Walter's reaction. His words tumbled through her mind. Did he know who she was? Had he somehow fig-

ured out the secrets she carried? Why else would he act
as he did? He did not just dislike her—the man hated
her. She'd seen that barely contained emotion in his
eyes. And if he hated her, how would Wolf react when
he discovered that she was the daughter of his mortal
enemy?

Izzy clutched her hands, desperate to hide the tremor
that moved through her at the thought of Wolf learning
the truth from someone else.

But how could Walter know who she was? The attacks
on her life proved her father knew she lived, attacks her
mother prophesied would happen when he discovered
the truth. And yet, Walter's strange behavior made her
wonder if others knew her secrets as well.

"Away from the table, all of you." Mistress Rowley
shooed the warriors away with her hand. "Lady Isobel
has had a fright and needs to rest."

The warriors returned to their table and resumed
their game of merrills as though nothing extraordinary
had taken place. Brahan, however, remained beside her.

"He did not hurt you, did he?" Brahan took the seat
Walter had vacated.

"Nay." She forced herself to take several slow, even
breaths as she unfurled her hands and settled them in
her lap. "He scared me, nothing more."

"Why did he react that way toward you? Walter might
be rash and impulsive, but he's not usually violent."

"I was only trying to help." Eager to get away, Izzy
twisted in her seat, preparing to leave. Brahan's questions probed too deep.

His hand snapped out to grasp her wrist, stalling her.
Izzy gasped and flinched.

He immediately released her. Contrition shone in his
eyes. "I meant you no harm."

She rubbed her right wrist with her left hand. He had not hurt her other than to remind her of the restraints that used to bind her there. "You startled me. That is all." His brief nod told her he had accepted her explanation as the truth and she relaxed.

"I apologize for my earlier attempts to press you for answers. I let my own needs override my duty." Brahan paused and frowned, his frustration obvious. "I can sense there is something you're not telling me about that Stone around your neck."

"I've told you everything." Izzy's hand crept up to her necklace. At her touch, the usually cool Stone warmed. She dropped her gaze to the necklace. It glowed. A soft luminescence at first, then a brighter red. Curious and a little scared, she continued to stare at the bright light emanating from the Stone. Without prompting, an image filled her mind, and she saw herself standing on something dark and soft. The image sharpened until she saw a crossroad. One path led off into a woodland. A woman stood at a distance in the center of a dew-dampened road just outside the tree line. Wild and disheveled, her lined face contorted with pain, the woman beckoned Izzy forward.

She took a faltering step, then paused as the woman's face became clear. "Come down the path you were destined to follow," her mother's voice called.

Izzy took two hurried steps back and gazed down the other road. A hunched beast sat toward the side of the path. The animal appear tired, its fur damp and matted. It held up its head with pride, but it almost appeared weighted down by some heavy burden.

She studied its face. A beast's visage stared back at her, yet the look in his eyes made her gasp. Inky wells laced with pain. Excruciating pain. She noticed it then.

The trap that sank deep into its leg. A pool of blood gathered in the dusty soil beneath his body. He needed her help.

Without care for her own safety, she took two more steps forward. She came to a halt when the animal barred its teeth. "I want to help you," she called out in her mind.

A snarl rent the air, a warning. And still she moved forward. She couldn't help herself. The need to help the beast overcame all reason.

The image shifted in her mind. Gone was the straggly beast. In its place lay a man surrounded by the same pool of blood, the iron trap clamped around his booted leg.

He looked up, his dark gaze meeting her own.

Wolf.

She gasped and flinched away from the necklace. The vision ended.

Her mother—the visions—memories of the miseries of the tower crowded Izzy as she drew a short, sharp gasp of air. There had been the weeping, endless weeping, and the ramblings, and the visions that had left her mother prostrate for hours on end. And in all those hours of suffering, there had been too little knowledge imparted, too few lessons learned about the affliction her mother said Izzy would be doomed to share.

Brahan's face appeared before her. A frown turned down the corners of his mouth. "You had a vision." Brahan's sharp tone cut through the residual mistiness that shrouded her brain. "You are a seer."

"Nay." Izzy shuddered as a bone-numbing chill wracked her body. Her fingers tingled as though exposed to the icy winter winds. "It is not . . . possible." Her teeth chattered uncontrollably. Could he be right?

The chill in her hands seeped up her arms and into

her chest. She glanced at the hearth, wondering why the room had turned so cold. A roaring blaze rolled across the logs and peat piled on the grate. Despite the evidence of warmth, she shivered again, then forced herself to shrug off her chill. She had no time to figure out the mystery. "My lord Wolf is hurt."

"You know this from a vision?" Brahan asked with a frown.

Her heart thundered until it felt as though it would leap from her chest. "I saw something in my mind."

His gaze dropped to her chest. "The Stone you wear makes it possible."

Izzy clutched her waist with her hands as a chill swamped her. Her father had done this to Wolf. She gasped and jerked backward, nearly unseating herself with the force.

"My lady?" Brahan reached for her arm, offering a steady anchor for her to cling to.

"I must find Wolf."

"Where?"

"I have no idea. Only that he is in a forest somewhere." She twisted away from the table, then stood on legs that were less than steady. "He needs me." She didn't wait for Brahan's response. As quickly as she could, she headed toward the huge doorway at the opposite side of the hall.

When she reached the knights, she paused, then straightened as she assumed a great lady would. "Your lord and master needs your help. Come, follow me."

Without hesitation the men set their game aside and obeyed as though she commanded them every day. Once she knew they followed, Izzy didn't look back. She had to find Wolf. She had to protect him from her father.

Chapter Nineteen

Brahan stood, staring after the Lady Isobel as she hurried toward the castle door with seven strong knights in tow. He should follow, and yet he hesitated.

Mistress Rowley hastened to the table as Lady Isobel left. "Where is she headed?" The housekeeper wiped her flour-covered hands on her muslin apron. "The master will have our heads if she disappears for hours as she did yesterday, or worse yet, is harmed."

"She's had a vision," Brahan said with a mixture of displeasure and awe.

"How could you know that?" Mistress Rowley asked, untying the garment and placing it on the table, ready to follow her new mistress.

"She says Wolf is injured."

"Injured?" Mistress Rowley's eyes went wide. "Well then, what are you waiting for? If he is hurt, he needs your help."

"And what if she is wrong?"

Mistress Rowley's mouth thinned with displeasure.

"You said yourself she'd had a vision. Can you take the risk that she is wrong?"

"Nay," Brahan agreed. "I will follow her vision just as I would my own. We will know the truth if we find Wolf safe."

"Let us pray she is wrong then," Mistress Rowley said, lines of worry etched deeply into her face.

Brahan caught up with Isobel in the courtyard, where he heard her quietly command Hiram to help her into her saddle. A second horse stood empty at her side, and a legion of knights gathered behind the two horses.

"Where are you going?" Brahan asked as he came to a halt beside her, his mouth falling open in surprise at how quickly she'd managed to rally Wolf's troops.

"To find Wolf—to find my husband." She perched precariously upon the saddle, looking terribly uncomfortable. She shifted her weight back. Too far back. Off the saddle she slid. She hit the ground with a thump. The green damask of her gown tangled about her legs as she tried to stand. Briefly, Brahan caught a glimpse of a shapely calf.

His irritation shifted to amusement mixed with a bit of envy. Wolf might not have done such a bad thing by marrying the girl. A shapely and very appealing package lay beneath her voluminous gown.

Brahan extended his hand to her. "Milady."

She accepted his assistance and gained her feet. She batted at her gown as she approached her horse. "Please, help me up."

"You should stay here at the castle, where it is safe. The men and I can verify the truth of your vision for you."

She arched a brow, and for a moment he thought she might actually laugh. "Safe? Can you honestly say I am more protected behind these castle walls than I would be out there?" She pointed beyond the large wooden portcullis that remained closed.

He would like to have responded, aye, but he knew better. Already she'd been attacked twice since her arrival. "Nay."

A look of determination crept over her delicate features. "Then help me into the saddle and command the gates open."

The strength in her voice surprised him. Where had the timid and meek creature they had taken from the isle gone? The knights seemed to agree with her sentiments. They brought their horses into a tighter formation around her. They had gathered under her direction, but they awaited Brahan's nod of approval to make their next move.

"Do you know how to ride a horse?" Brahan asked.

"How difficult can it be? You sit upon the beast's back and hold on." A renewed spark of determination flashed in her eyes.

"How difficult, indeed," Brahan replied. He grasped her about the waist and tossed her into the saddle.

She settled herself in the center of the saddle and appeared every bit as uncomfortable as before. Brahan patted the edge of the saddle with his hand. "Place your hands here and 'hold on,' as you said. It will help you balance."

She did as he suggested and instantly appeared more at ease. "Much better, thank you."

Brahan mounted the horse beside her, inspired by her transformation. Her chin came up, her shoulders went back. Confidence and poise seemed to settle around her, regardless that this was only her second attempt at mounting a horse. She sat atop the beast as if she should be dressed in mail, brandishing a sword instead of her long, flowing gown. She wore no protection and carried no weapon.

With no thought for herself or her own safety, and for the sake of another, the girl from the isle had vanished, transformed into a woman with the spirit of a warrior. Wolf's warrior bride.

"Open the gates," Brahan shouted. At his command, the portcullis rose, and she urged her horse forward, heading toward the forest lands. The knights fell into formation around her and would protect her with their lives.

Brahan kept his senses on alert as they crept ever closer to Grange's land on the other side of the forest. Slender needles of sunlight pierced the boughs overhead, stabbing the earth with brilliant pinpricks. Beneath the horse's hooves crunched the remains of accumulated yew needles, their fragrance sharp and pungent.

He hadn't been back to this part of the forest for years. Not since he was a little boy, hiding from the men who had raided his village and murdered his kin. Memories of blood were everywhere, blood that had seeped into the ground from the dead long ago, their discarded weapons useless against the force of the attack. They were all dead—everyone he knew, everyone he loved. He had searched through the bodies until he'd found his mother's lifeless form.

The next thing he remembered, he'd woken up to a gentle touch. It hadn't been his mother's touch, or even the sharp prick of his enemy's sword, but an understanding, compassionate nudge. Wolf had found him there, alone among the dead, and had taken him away from the nightmare. The young boy had begged his own mother to offer Brahan shelter in her household.

Lady Marion had given him a job as squire to her son. She had incorporated a bedraggled orphan into her home right along with her other children. He and Wolf had been inseparable companions ever since.

"You're very quiet." Lady Isobel coerced her horse to fall in step beside him.

Brahan started. He shook off the memories, as he always did of those darker days in his early life. "Merely considering what you said about Wolf needing help."

"He does need our assistance. I know it."

"Your visions are that strong?"

"I have no desire for this talent. Only bad things come of such a skill." She turned toward him, her color high. "Even so, what I saw leaves no doubt in my mind. It is Wolf someone is trying to harm and not me." Fear filled her eyes.

"You do not wish to be a seer?"

She shook her head. "It is not the path I choose."

"We don't choose the path, milady. The path chooses us."

Lady Isobel stared at him. Her expression betrayed a momentary puzzlement, and then realization dawned and hot color flooded her cheeks. A slight mist came to her eyes. "You?"

"Aye, milady." An odd tension came to his throat at the relief he saw in her gaze.

He remembered what it had felt like the moment he realized what magic and what evil he held inside him. The turmoil of strange, unsettling, and frightening emotions mixed with the headiness of power. "The visions are both curse and gift."

"You know what it is like? To bear the burden?"

"Aye." He knew what it was like. The gift of sight had cost his family their lives. His whole village had suffered when his mother had foretold a future the receiver did not wish to hear.

He had learned through his mother that often it was best to leave the future untold. And yet, their very quest today could help save a man he cared about more than himself. If her visions kept Wolf safe, then that was worth any risk, or any price. He returned his gaze to Lady Isobel. "When you have your visions, does anything happen to you as a result?"

Fear crept back into her eyes. "What do you mean?"

He pointed to the white patch at his temple. "Whenever I use the Stone to foretell the future, I lose a bit of my essence. The whiteness of my hair indicates the cost to myself. So tell me, Lady Isobel, what do the visions drain from you?"

She looked down at the reins she clutched tightly in her fists. "I do not know." Her horse reared its head, protesting the tension against its mouth.

"Relax your grip and the horse will settle down." Brahan sensed she lied.

Lady Isobel did as directed and the horse calmed.

"Tell me the truth," Brahan challenged. "I might be able to help."

Her brow furrowed. "I do not know for myself. My mother paid for the visions with her sanity."

He frowned. "Explain yourself?"

She shook her head. "I've told you more than I should have already."

"Milady, your secrets are safe with me. For my lord's sake you must know I could never hurt you."

Her back went stiff. "My father said words very like those to my mother," she paused, "each time he struck her."

Brahan frowned. "Not all men treat women that way."

Her gaze remained fixed before her. "The risk is too great. I—" She pulled her horse to a stop. Just then, the bark of a dog cut through the air. Her horse pranced at the noise, which came from the other side of a rocky out-cropping that shielded their view of the forest beyond.

Brahan tensed, bracing to leap for her horse's halter, afraid that in her inexperience her horse might get away from her. But she managed to put just enough pressure on the reins to keep the animal in place.

The acrid scent of burning wood came to him, as did the sound of raucous laughter and coarse jests. He cursed himself for letting down his guard. He, a crea-ture of these very woods, had been so intent on discov-ering Lady Isobel's secrets that he'd inadvertently endangered them all.

Brahan came to a sudden, silent stop, signaling the oth-ers to do the same. He scanned the area. A curl of smoke floated up from a smoldering campfire just ahead. He searched for guards at the perimeter of the camp, finding none. All the men must be around the campfire, then.

"Stay here," he commanded as he slipped off his horse and crept forward. He peered over the rock, his body stiff with tension, every nerve stretched.

Half a dozen men lounged before the fire. They laughed uproariously and shouted suggestions to four bedraggled villagers, who scooted around a nearby tree, their legs bound by thick ropes. With unbound arms, they reached up, trying desperately to free a man who swung upside down from a stout tree branch, the chain of an iron trap clamped tightly about his left leg. The man's right leg was curled around the chain, absorbing the weight of his body, protecting his captured leg from being shredded by the trap.

Blood obscured the man's face, but Brahan still recognized his friend.

Anger heated his blood as his fingers gripped the hilt of his sword. Forcing his mind to go completely blank, Brahan reacted with what years of practice and repetition had taught him. His sword left its scabbard. He plunged over the rocky outcropping, killing two men before the others gained their feet.

The clashing of swords mixed with the frenzy of the horses' hooves as they met their enemies head-on. No more than a moment passed since the first stroke of the sword, but already the ground was red underfoot, the air was choked with dust and smoke. Horses reared, their shrieks of fear adding to the general chaos that erupted. Brahan slashed his sword, relieving his opponent of his life as he made his way to Wolf. A heartbeat later, Brahan released the pin on the trap. The villagers caught Wolf in their outstretched arms, gently lowering him to the ground.

What torture would the guards inflict upon him now? He would not reveal the information they wanted. No one would ever learn the location of the Seer's Stone from his lips. It was Brahan's secret, and his alone.

Wolf rolled onto his side. He pressed his cheek into the soft earth of the forest floor. The heady combination of musty leaves from last season and sweet mulch filled his nostrils. Blessed ground. The earth beneath him meant he no longer swung from the tree with the jaws of the metal trap lashing into his leg. His arms and legs tingled as the blood returned to his limbs.

"My lord." The words came softly.

Isobel? Impossible. He lifted his cheek and tried to

focus on the shape that came in and out of focus. He closed his eyes as a wave of nausea swept over him. His innocent bride would never come here. Only evil lurked in these woods.

A feather-soft touch caressed his cheek, startling him. How long had it been since he'd felt such tenderness?

His body shifted without his assistance, and he found himself on his back, staring up at the forest canopy overhead. Pinpricks of light forced their way through the trees, casting an eerie greenish-gold light that filled the space between sky and ground. Shadows moved about him. Most likely the guards, ready to further their torture. He tried to sit up, only to be pushed back against the earth. It startled him to find the hand that forced him back lingered on his chest. A delicate stroke moved to his arm, then down to his hand, twining about his fingers.

His mind played tricks on him. Unimaginable pleasure flowed through his fingers, like a warm salve against the pain. He coiled his fingers, trapping the sensation, never wanting to let it go.

In the next instant a lash of red-hot pain shot through his leg. He tensed, prepared to take whatever new torture they offered. But the pain ceased as quickly as it had come. His boot slid from his leg.

"His boot is mangled, and the flesh around the mouth of the trap is bruised. The skin is broken, but the muscle appears intact," a voice said from near his feet. A familiar voice. Brahan?

"What of the bone?" a softer voice queried. "Did it snap the bone?"

"Miraculously, nay."

"There is so much blood."

"I've seen worse and so has Wolf. The damage to his leg looks worse than it is. We need to get him home."

"My lord." Isobel's voice filled his mind. "You're safe." The voice sounded thick with emotion. "We are taking you away from here."

He struggled to will the darkness out of his mind, to see if it truly was Isobel who spoke to him, or some new trick. In the last hours of this torture, he'd discovered he could will his mind to do things when his body seemed to fail him. If he channeled all his energy into the effort of opening his eyes he might discover the truth. Slowly his lids lifted and his eyes focused on the face above him.

Dark eyes glittering with moist brilliance gazed down at him. Isobel's eyes. She looked scared, and another strange, darker emotion lingered there as well. He had seen that look somewhere else recently. He struggled to pull the memory into the front of his mind. If he could only remember where . . .

Her gaze fixed on his face and something connected. He saw Grange's image reflected there. He clenched his eyes shut, sure his mind failed him.

As if his own senses meant to prove him wrong, he became chillingly aware of the damp earth beneath him, the scent of decaying leaves that surrounded where he lay.

Why would he see Grange in Isobel's face? Was it some sort of sign, like the ones Brahan saw with the assistance of the Seer's Stone? Was there some sort of deception here? "How did you find me?" Wolf asked, turning toward where he had heard Brahan's voice.

"It was not I who found you. For that you can thank your wife."

"Isobel? But how? How could she know I was here?" Wolf turned back to the image he had seen. She was here. She was real. He searched her pale, drawn face. She looked as delicate as the most fragile blossom. And yet even the deadliest of nature's poisonous plants yielded flowers.

With an effort he forced the thought away. Nay, it was all the years of his father's deception that led his thoughts on such dark paths. He would not believe such things of Isobel. She could only be what she appeared.

He wanted to communicate his belief in her, yet he did not know exactly how to do so without scaring her further. He decided the simplest course of action was best. He brought her hand to his lips and pressed a light kiss there, squeezing her fingers gently.

A blush crept into her cheeks, warming her face, chasing away the fear. "We must get you home, my lord."

Her fingers slipped from his. "Isobel?" he forced the words from his dry, parched throat, the words sounding as though they belonged to someone else.

"Beside you, my lord. I'll stay beside you."

Despite the darkness that entered his mind he forced a slow smile. *Beside him.* He liked the sound of that. He would hold her to that promise, just as soon as he was able.

Chapter Twenty

Izzy watched the smile fade from Wolf's face. She eased his head into her lap, cradling him, sheltering him as much as she could. A groan escaped him at the movement. Tears sprang to her eyes at the knowledge that she continued to hurt him as her own father had done.

"I'll bandage his leg," Brahan said. "Then we will have to move him."

"He's lost so much blood," Izzy said, suddenly realizing that she knelt in soil made wet from her husband's blood.

"He is strong." Brahan tied his own shirt about Wolf's injured leg. Almost immediately, the saffron-colored linen sprouted a patch of red. But after a moment the seeping ceased as the bleeding stopped.

The shadows overhead shifted. Light filtered down through the trees, changing from gold to red. Sunset was upon them.

"We have to get him home before Grange or more of his henchmen appear."

Izzy knew the urgency they faced, and still she could not move. The light seemed to hold her in place. Dappled red and gold sparkled around Wolf's body, bathing him in a glow that was both ethereal and serene. "Give me a moment with him, please."

Brahan nodded. "I'll prepare the horses."

"My thanks," she replied as he moved away, leaving the two of them in silence. Izzy looked down at her husband, savoring the softness of his head in her lap, of the strange closeness that had been thrust upon them unknowingly by her father.

With trembling fingers, she brushed the grime and blood from his cheek. She'd never been the manner of girl who had fanciful wishes. Her life had been more focused on survival than anything else. And yet, at this moment, a wish bubbled up from the core of her being.

If only she could be trapped no more by fate, by her father, by her own fears. Perhaps then a real life would be possible. Maybe even a life with this man.

Izzy's gaze moved from Wolf's face to the trembling daylight as it slipped into night. An almost magical moment where the light of day faded and the darkness of evening pushed forward. Time stood still. Her heartbeat slowed. And anything seemed possible.

The fading sun caught and caressed his features, illuminating his usually dark face with light and tipping his lashes with gold. This man was no beast. Merely a man, caught in the same trap as she herself.

Would they ever find freedom?

A noise sounded behind her, breaking the stillness. "It's time to go, milady."

Brahan bent down beside her.

She nodded and released her hold on her husband. With the help of two of the other knights, he was lifted bodily onto a horse. Brahan mounted behind him, supporting his body with his own.

"Help our lady up on her horse," Brahan called back to the knights as he started the journey home.

"He's awake."

Izzy stopped raking the hen yard the next morning and turned to see Brahan leaning against the hen house. Over the objections of the other servants, she had insisted on setting the hen yard in order. Her fingers tightened on the rake. "Is he . . . well?" she asked, unable to keep the fear from her voice.

"If you mean did Lord Grange succeed in driving him mad while he tortured him, no, he did not." Brahan pushed away from the wall and came toward her. He stopped beside her and took the rake from her hands. She made an attempt to grab it back. He held the tool farther away, out of her reach. "My lord Wolf is strong. He's been through much in his life. His own father has tortured him in ways Grange could never conceive. I doubt Grange, or anyone else for that matter, could ever break him."

Relief moved through Izzy. Her father had not harmed her husband. This time. A queer twisting sensation centered in her belly. What would Grange do to Wolf when he learned that the man had married his daughter? She looked at Brahan, then looked quickly away. Had her father told Wolf of their connection? Did he know the truth of who he had married? "Did my lord talk to you about what happened?" she asked Brahan.

"So many questions." Brahan smiled. "Go ask him yourself."

She shook her head. She'd sat in the darkness next to his bed last night, but she had not seen him while he was awake and aware of her presence. She wasn't ready for that yet. Not until she could control the way her heart sped up each time he touched her, and not until she could find a way to tell him her secrets without him banishing her in return.

"Well, that's too bad for our lord Wolf then. Because as of this moment I will no longer be the messenger between you two. You are his wife, and he is your husband." Brahan frowned thoughtfully. "His injuries are not that severe. I suspect he will be up and walking by the morrow on that leg."

"That's too soon."

Brahan shrugged. "He's a fighter, as are you."

"A fighter?" Izzy averted her gaze to the neat and tidy ground she had raked since the sun first came up. Restless and uncertain how to help her husband, she had fallen back on old habits. Cleaning the hen yard had always cleared her thoughts when she had been on the isle. Yet this morning her thoughts were more confused than ever. "I do not see myself as such."

"You've changed, milady." Brahan paused. "Forgive me for speaking so boldly, but you are not the same woman we rescued from that isle. You are no longer the maiden trapped in a destiny of drudgery. You are the wife of a great warrior, with opportunities you have yet to even imagine, if you will only reach for what you want."

What did she want? The possibilities stirred inside her, and a smile came to her lips. The day Wolf had spent with her had made her feel as though she did have a purpose, as if her life and her abilities counted for something. The moments she'd spent with him had made her feel as if she had been asleep all her life and now, suddenly, she'd come fully awake.

She wanted more of the same. Her smile faltered. If only her secrets did not stand in her way.

Brahan frowned. "What is wrong? You appeared so radiant for just a moment."

"There are things that need to be said between Wolf and myself. Things I'm not certain he will understand."

"Wolf will respect you for telling him the truth." Brahan's gaze narrowed on her face, probing. "And believe me, he will learn the truth. The question is whether he will learn it from you or from someone else. Consider that."

Color rose in her cheeks. She had already considered that possibility. Would it be better for him to hear the truth of her birth from her, or from his enemy? And once he knew her secrets, what future could remain for them?

"Do you have so much to consider?" Brahan's voice broke through her thoughts.

"Nay." Izzy straightened at the sudden realization. She didn't have anything to consider. She had nothing to lose and everything to gain by divulging the truth to him.

The last traces of doubt vanished. Hope blossomed. "I must speak with Wolf." She started toward the gate when her gaze fell on Mistress Henny, sitting off to the side from the other hens in the yard.

She turned back to Brahan. "Will you help me?"

His brow lifted in surprise. "Name your pleasure and it shall be done."

"Feed the hens."

Surprise shifted to confusion on his brow. "You want me to feed the hens?"

"Aye. And do not set a separate place for Mistress Henny to eat as I have always done. If she is hungry, she must learn that it is time to come to the rest of the flock."

"As you wish, but you'll have to help me, for I know not what chickens . . . eat."

Before he could finish she strolled out of the hen yard, through the gate, and toward the castle, her face aglow with a smile so dazzling he had never seen its equal.

Brahan smiled himself as he watched her go. She had taken the bait he'd laid out before her. The straggly chicken of a girl they had picked up on St. Kilda was truly a warrior indeed.

Chapter Twenty-one

Izzy poised her hand to knock on the door of Wolf's solar. Should she knock? What if he were sleeping? Would he want to be disturbed?

A soft tap on the wood sent the already ajar door farther open. Odd. If he were sleeping, the door should have been closed. She opened the door a bit more. Instead of silence, the hum of voices greeted her. He was not alone.

She pushed the door fully open and peered inside. Several people blocked her way. A voice inside the room rose over the others, booming an echo up to the vaulted ceiling. "A message, milord. It bears his seal." The solemn tone was overridden by the sound of the bailiff. "Milord, what *will* you do about the poachers?"

Other voices joined in, one almost indistinguishable from the next in a cacophony of sound. "The menus. If he arrives as he threatens, then what shall we serve?" a shrill feminine voice piped in. "The tenant farmers want to know when they can expect their grain. The portions have been measured, but we need your approval to parcel things out."

Had her first instincts been correct? Wolf's home appeared to run smoothly, but did that efficiency come from the staff, or from the master himself leading everyone's way? Izzy stepped into the room, curious to know more. Morning light seeped through the stained-glass windows, bathing the room in a glorious splash of blue, green, and reddish gold, highlighting the close to twenty people who crowded next to Wolf's bedside.

"Please." His voice rose above them all. "For the love of God, silence!"

A hush fell over the room.

"The menus can wait. Give me the letter. The tenants may have their grain, whatever is their fair share. Set the poachers free with a warning that next time I will not be so merciful. I wish to hear no more. You may all leave."

"But, milord!" The cry rose up only to be silenced as quickly.

Izzy could not see the bed, but she could imagine the look Wolf directed at those who had invaded his private domain. A shiver tickled the nape of her neck at the thought. The crowd around his bed thinned and Izzy caught sight of him.

"*Isobel.*" His voice startled her. Was that a hint of pleasure she heard beneath his words? He sat upon his bed, leaning back against the headboard.

"Perhaps I should come back later." Izzy stood to the side as the others filtered from the room.

"Nonsense. I was hoping you would come."

She remained where she stood, uncertain what to do or say.

"Your people seem to rely on you for many things, my lord."

"Some need direction more than others."

She wanted to ask if she could be of some service. She did not know much about the operations of a castle, but she was capable of performing or overseeing many of the menial tasks involved in keeping a home. After all, that was her entire life on the isle once she'd been freed from the tower. The MacDonalds had seen to that. Yet she was sure doing the same sort of tasks for Wolf and his household would not feel as much of a burden. Still, she hesitated. First she had to tell him the truth of who she was. If by some miracle he wished her to remain, she would willingly offer her assistance.

"Come here, Isobel." His honeyed voice crept across the distance that separated them and propelled her forward.

"Do you ever rest, my lord?"

He frowned. "Need you address me so formally?"

She stopped two steps short of the bed. "Forgive me. It will take some time to get used to . . . everything."

He sat back against the headboard, his gaze assessing. Only a few days before she would have felt exposed by such a blatant perusal. Now, that unusual warmth curled in her stomach—as it always did when he drew near.

He held out his hand, wordlessly asking her to take the last two steps forward. She did, and surprised herself even more when she reached for his hand. "I am so glad you are feeling better today, Wolf." She said his name softly, adjusting to the feel of it on her lips. Her fingers seemed cold and clumsy as she joined her hand with his.

"I apologize that I was not more alert upon our return last evening. I did not realize until this morning that they had taken me to your bed," he said with an apologetic smile.

"It is your bed, not mine."

He grunted noncommittally. "Where did you sleep last night?"

Her gaze moved to the chair near the window.

"That will never do." He released her fingers and patted the empty space on the bed beside him. "Sit with me."

She clamped her fingers together in front of her in a futile effort to warm them. "I must speak with you."

He patted the bedside once more. "Then speak to me from here."

"It is best that I stay here." If an innocent touch could jumble her thoughts, what would sitting beside him do to addle her brain? She straightened, keeping her chin high. "You will not like what I have to say."

Wolf remained silent a moment before he patted the bed again. "Sit. You promised."

She shook her head. "I did no such—"

He caught her fingers with his. Warmth instantly returned. "You did. In the woods. You promised to be beside me." He offered her a wicked smile. "Your words." He patted the bed once more with his free hand.

Perhaps she could sit while she spoke with him. She had almost lowered herself to the bed when he stopped her.

"The other direction." He released her hand and pointed toward the foot board. "I want to look at you. Come, sit."

Drawn by his plea, she lowered herself to the bed.

"Still wearing that one green kirtle, I see," he said, his tone more assessing than accusing.

"It is all I have."

"Then we will have to remedy that soon."

She worried her hands in her lap. "There is no need, my lord."

"There is every need. You are my wife. I cannot have you wearing one dress for the whole of your life. It wouldn't be proper."

Before she could respond, he swished the hem of her skirt aside to reveal her practical woolen socks and sturdy slippers. "Now," he said as he sat forward and began sliding her slipper from her right foot, "you helped get that trap off my foot in the woods. Let me return the favor."

She tried to pull away her foot. "These are my slippers, not a trap."

"Traps come in many forms." His hand was warm and solid on her ankle.

She struggled against his gentle but firm grip. "I must speak with you, my lor—Wolf." She altered her words at his sharp look. "There are things you need to know about me. Like how I—"

"—like to relax." He took off her shoes and tossed them one by one onto the floor. Her stockings followed. He clasped her bare feet within his palms and lifted them onto his lap.

"Why must you constantly do things for others? Will you let no one do a thing for you instead?"

His hands stilled. "What do you mean?"

"You need some help around this castle," she stated boldly.

His expression became serious. "You are right."

"I am?"

"Aye. As my wife, you are now in charge of the running of the castle. You will oversee the staff." He smiled. "Do not look so frightened. Fiona is gone and Mistress

Rowley will assist you." He reached for a letter he'd set down beside him. "My father is coming to join us. A post-marital visit. I want you to prepare a feast and a pageant fit for a ki—" His words stalled and a seriousness she had not noted before came into his dark eyes. "I don't want to talk anymore."

She opened her mouth to protest, but he silenced her with a finger against her lips. "Not now, lass. We can discuss this later. I have other things on my mind."

"Other things? Oh." She drew a startled breath as he began rubbing his thumbs in little circles against her arches. She tried to keep her body stiff, but the sensual magic he worked on her feet made it impossible. Her muscles turned soft and she relaxed against the coverlet. "Oh," she sighed.

The shadows in his eyes disappeared, replaced by satisfaction as he continued. He compressed her heel, then slid his hand up the back of her ankle, only to repeat the motion over and over.

"Oh," she murmured again as her eyes drifted closed. If he kept this up, she would never be able to speak again, let alone tell him her darkest secrets.

He kneaded the balls of her feet, then with long, fluid movements worked the tension out of each one of her toes, dipping his fingers between each appendage, in delicious, sensual plunges. "How can anything feel so good?" she murmured, realizing too late that she had spoken her thoughts aloud.

She tried to pull her feet out of his grasp, but he held firm. "You helped me in the woods. It is only right I should return the favor."

He continued his smooth massage. One toe to the next. Until each felt special in turn. His touch a caress— so soft, so calming. She hated to end it with her next words, and yet she knew she must. "Lord . . . Lord Gr—" His name stuck in her throat at the thought of the pain and torment that monster had caused the man before her.

"I do not wish to speak of him. In fact, I do not want to know anything." Wolf slipped his hand along the length of her leg, from her ankle to her knee.

Izzy gasped at the riot of tingling that chased up her leg. The warmth in her stomach spread to her limbs like honey across a warm slice of bread.

His hand caressed the back of her thigh. A heaviness descended over his face. "I am burdened enough with responsibility, Isobel. Please be for me the one thing that is exactly as it appears. You are truly pure and innocent and unspoiled."

He could not be more wrong.

"I want you to be exactly what you are right here before me. Nothing else has to exist if we don't want it to." Never taking his gaze from hers, he sat forward until only a slight space separated his chest from her own.

He didn't want to know the truth. Why? Did he suspect it and fear it all the same?

She feared the truth but could not put it off. It was too important. "I—"

"Things can be simple between us, Isobel, if only we allow them to be." The expression in his dark eyes shifted from awareness to something more. Heat. It was the only word she could think of to describe the intensity in his gaze. Tendrils of that very same heat reached out to her, ensnaring her in its trap.

Slowly, carefully, he drew near her, his gaze never leaving her face. He lowered his mouth until she could feel his breath on her lips. As gentle as a breeze, his lips met hers. A simple touch and her body flooded with the same warmth she'd seen in his eyes. Her limbs felt weak, her mind numb, until all she could sense was him—his smell, his taste—spiced honey and mint. The combination as intoxicating as the feel of his hands on her cheeks, her neck.

She leaned into him, her hands crept up his torso to wrap about his shoulders. He trembled beneath her touch. She urged him forward, into her own body, hoarding the sensation of power she held over him.

The words she longed to put out before him shriveled, then died. He did not wish to know. And Lord help her, if he continued to kiss her like this, she would cease to care about anything at all.

His tongue moved against the seam of her lips. She opened to him and he delved within. Her eyelids fluttered closed as she give in to the overpowering assault. Weakness invaded and her body felt drugged, but this time from pleasure, not poison.

She skimmed her hands up his chest. His heart thundered beneath her palm, contradicting the slow intoxication of his kiss.

He made a sound, low and deep—a groan or laughter, she could not be certain—as his lips worked their way down her throat. His mouth against her flesh touched a note inside her, resonating, filling her with vibrations of heat and pleasure. He pulled back to loop a tendril of hair that had fallen over her shoulder about his finger.

He worked the strands of her hair with his thumb and fingers, caressing the fibers with the same gentleness he'd lavished on her skin. "Your hair is beautiful." His fingers moved higher and higher until he caressed the nape of her neck.

Madness. Passionate madness. Her body pulsed, then

ached where his touch met her skin. Startled by her thoughts, she pulled back, then stood. "I must go." Her voice shook, as did her limbs.

He came off the bed to stand somewhat unsteadily beside her. "Where will you go to escape this, Isobel? Am I not your husband? Are you not my wife?" He reached for her and brought her up against his chest.

"You should stay off your leg."

"I feel no pain now." He drew her toward him. She let herself be trapped as his lips found her neck, trailing kisses along the length down to her shoulder, and lower to the rise of her breasts.

She arched her neck, allowing her head to fall back ever so slightly at the riotous sensations he brought forth. Near him, in his arms, she felt wantonly bared, yet free, as if nothing but sensation stood between them. No lies, no deceit. Just one exquisite sensation chased by another, pooling deep inside her core as if preparing for something more.

And she knew what that something more would be. He'd said it himself. She was *his* wife. The reality of her situation seemed suddenly clear and the turmoil of doubts inside her shifted to a trembling, aching need.

"Nothing else has to exist for us right now except each other. A man and a woman in need of forgetfulness." He reached behind her and released the ties that pulled her gown tight against her chest. She drew a startled breath as he then pulled the garment up over her head, leaving her dressed in the sheer fabric of her shift that skimmed against her skin with the lightness of a lover's caress.

Wolf took a step back, but only far enough to draw his fine linen nightshirt off and toss it to the floor. She stared at him in helpless fascination. The dark hair thatching his chest looked soft and springy, and she felt a tingling in her hands. She wanted to touch him, to run her fingers through the downy softness she was certain she would find there, to explore the powerful muscles cording his chest and shoulders.

"Can you forget about everything that stands between us and just allow yourself to feel?"

She forgot everything as her gaze traveled down his chest to the tightness of his muscular abdomen, then down . . .

He stood naked before her, with his legs apart, blatantly aroused, the very essence of bold masculinity. She could not pull her gaze away, nor could she fill her lungs with air.

"What do you feel when you look at me?" he asked, his voice filled with as much vulnerability as there was confidence.

"Everything I should not." There was only chaos in what she felt. She was hot and dizzy and confused and excited. He had chosen her over Fiona.

"Come to me."

Only one step separated them, she would not have to go far, and still she hesitated. There would be no turning back if she took that one step. Had her mother not warned her of the insanity that would follow?

He took her right hand and raised it to his lips. He kissed her palm, his gaze never leaving hers. "I need you."

The simple words brought forth a sudden surge of tenderness that swept away the last of her reserve. Insanity seemed but a small price to pay for the pleasure that awaited.

She took a step forward. His arms came about her. Then the shift covering her body was gone, tossed aside along with his garments. Her nipples brushed the hair on his chest. She gasped at the sensation. His hands moved to her shoulders, her arms, her back, kneading her with a yearning tenderness, and an unbearable tension gripped her body.

In the next moment, he cradled her in his arms and gently nestled her onto the bed. He followed her down until he half-lay, half-knelt beside her. Before she had a chance to feel frightened, his lips found hers. Mind-numbing sensations flowed through her, making her long for things she did not yet understand.

His hands caressed her leg, her thigh, her midriff, and she lay open and exposed as she never had before. Only here, in his arms, she did not feel vulnerable. Instead she felt free—freed from the constraints that always had tethered her in place. Did he feel that way too? Was that why he had asked her to forget all else but this moment? So that he could find a moment of freedom from his oppressive responsibilities? And she could find freedom from her past?

Morning air rushed against her flesh, cooling her only briefly before the warmth of his hands covered her, warmed her, pulled her toward something more. She watched his face, watched the tensions ease from the corners of his eyes, yet another type of tautness took its place.

Bravely, she reached out and touched his chest. Her fingers coiled through the matting of hair she'd so ached to touch before. Her tentative exploration was met with a quick intake of breath, followed by a sound of pure pleasure. A groan, a sigh, a curse, a prayer, she could not tell precisely which.

His reaction spurred her to trace the outline of his hair down across his smooth abdomen, down further as the edges narrowed to a *V*. She paused, suddenly afraid to follow the hairline where it dipped closer to his manhood.

"You may touch me where you like, Isobel."

Could she be so bold?

"Between us, like this, there are no rules but pleasure. There is nothing to fear."

She drew her fingers back, hesitant.

He gave her a wicked smile. "Let me show you."

His hands skimmed across her waist, her abdomen. Where he touched, her body trembled, responding to him in a way she never imagined she could. He gave her no time for embarrassment. Nay, as his hands stroked her she could feel all reserve melt away, igniting a strange burning sensation between her thighs. As though reading her thoughts, his hand slid down her abdomen to the thatch of curls surrounding her womanhood. His fingers caressed, stroked, rubbing back and forth at the very entrance of her body.

She closed her eyes, arching up against his hand, wanting more, craving more, and yet she knew not what she searched for. Sensation after bewildering sensation tore through her as his fingers slipped inside the soft folds of her flesh. Her eyes flew open and she gave a little cry. She clutched at his hand, suddenly afraid. "It . . . hurts," she said, not knowing how else to describe what she felt.

He eased back but did not pull his hand away. "Describe what you feel." He gently, slowly entered her again. "What does this make you feel?"

She released his hand and relaxed, allowing the unfamiliar sensations to flow through her. "I feel warm. And I ache."

"So do I, my dear. That's how pleasure starts. A slow,

sweet ache that builds to so much more." His fingers delved deeper, his palm continuing his rhythmic caress.

Unbelievable ripples of feeling spread through every part of her body, intensifying that ache, shifting it to desire—desire that tore through her reserve and made her bold. She pressed against him, and the movement brought his fingers deeper inside. She shuddered and cried out—for what, she did not know. Something threatened out there on the edge of nothingness, something she wanted but didn't know how to reach.

The thought had barely formed when satisfaction exploded within her, bringing with it wave after wave of pure, physical rapture. She arched against him, until the waves of sensation settled, calmed. His hand moved to gently stroke her thighs.

Weak and shaken by overwhelming sensations, she watched him. Light from the room spread across his hard body, bathing him in hues of red and gold from the colored glass above. Her eyes riveted on his chest, which rose and fell with each ragged breath as though he, too, had experienced what he'd given to her. And yet tension lay there in his muscles as well. She reached up to touch his chest. His skin was damp and hot beneath her touch. His muscles tightened reflexively as she trailed her fingers down, down, until she stopped a finger's reach from his rampant arousal. Desire, so recently sated, pooled again, flooding her body with need.

"There is more if you are willing," he said as his gaze followed her own.

His voice was low, ragged, and filled with as much unbridled hope as raw vulnerability. Something inside her responded, flared, opened to new possibilities. Her hand cupped his cheek. He leaned into her touch, and a soft groan escaped his lips. A moment later his lips replaced his cheek, and he trailed kisses against her palm and down the length of her arm. "Unspoiled and pure," he murmured against her flesh.

She had no time to consider his words as he pressed her against the bed and moved between her thighs. His arousal nudged provocatively against the center of her womanhood. She gasped at the sensation and at the desire that flared so quickly inside her once more.

She reached up and pulled his head down to hers, capturing his lips in a hungry kiss. His hands moved down her shoulders, trembling as they moved across her flesh, urgent with a passionate need.

She arched against him in response to his touch. Tension coiled his muscles. A satisfied possessiveness flared in his dark gaze as he lowered his head once more and took the hard nub of her nipple deep into his mouth. He nipped and licked with deliberate slowness, playing with one nub and then the other until her body shook with need.

Her senses swirled and a heady intensity filled her. She wanted more. "Wolf—" was all she could say, unable to put into words what she felt deep in the center of her being.

His mouth once again found hers, sweet, urgent, and tender. Not breaking the kiss, he lifted her hips, bringing his manhood to the center of her being, poised for entrance, yet he held himself back.

"I want you," he breathed against her lips, sounding like a man in agony.

A rush of tenderness merged with her own desire, and she knew he waited for her to show her consent. She arched against him, wanting to be absorbed into his hard body, to join with him in this most intimate of ways, to burn with the same passion that hitched his breath in his throat.

On a groan, he pushed into her.

Pain tore through her, hot and swift. Her cry was smothered by his kiss as he eased farther inside her, then paused, poised above her as though he were afraid to move forward or back. Beads of sweat gleamed on his shoulders and chest. His hair fell across his brow, wild and untamed, yet he was no beast. Not now. He was only a man, mortal, exquisite, and joined with her.

She clamped her fingers around his arms, realizing she did not want to let him go. The thought filled her with wonder as the pain faded and she became aware only of a deep, rigid fullness.

His palms cupped her buttocks and held her against him, almost as though refusing to allow her retreat. Yet he waited, his gaze on her, his breathing ragged.

"I . . ." She tried to convey what she felt deep inside. "I . . . want you."

He released a low groan deep in his throat. He drew out and plunged forward. A hot shiver rippled across her flesh. He moved with raw, blinding sensuality, driving deeper and deeper, building that frantic urgency within her again.

He rocked her back and forth with each driving thrust and she reached to meet him, giving back what he tried to give her. Then it happened. A jolt of sensation blossomed, then ruptured, spilling over in wave after wave of pleasure. She tightened her legs around his hips and arched up. He thrust against her, accepting what she offered until a deep, body-wrenching shudder moved through him as his own pleasure peaked, then soared.

Silence settled over the room as he settled onto the bed beside her. His head rested against her shoulder while his hand continued to caress her abdomen, her ribs, her chest. "Sleep now," he murmured against her ear. His breath was warm, soothing.

Izzy sighed, utterly content. Gradually, her breathing slowed, and she could feel the tension ease from her body. Lush with the unfamiliar sensation of satisfaction, she drifted, allowing her mind to wander. In Wolf's arms, time and memory had no meaning. All that mattered was the fullness, the completion they'd just shared.

Her mind drifted, thoughts flitted through, disjointed, abstract, but no trace of insanity threatened. Izzy allowed herself a satisfied smile. Her mother had been wrong about joining with a man. Her mother had been wrong about many things.

Izzy's hand crept up to touch the necklace still fastened about her neck. Her fingers found the Stone, and she brushed her thumb over the polished surface. Perhaps it was possible to forget all the things that had brought them together, all the secrets that remained untold, and just live in the moment as he had encouraged her to do—to live a life of make-believe.

He looped his forearm about her waist, pulling her tight against his warm, solid body. She'd had enough of nightmarish times during her life in the tower and on the isle with the MacDonalds. Maybe this man and this life was her reward for those turbulent times. Or was this just a small respite from an even greater danger that threatened?

The thought had no sooner formed when a flash of white light darted through her mind. Her grip tightened on the Stone. She tried to pull her fingers away but instead found herself clinging to the necklace all the harder. The white light faded and a swirling vortex took its place.

A vision filled her mind.

Chapter Twenty-two

A splash of red appeared in Isobel's mind, followed by another splash of green, purple, and gold. Exotic colors blended together, twisting and turning. She tried to block the images, tried to fight the all-consuming power over her thoughts the images held.

She tensed and clenched her hands, her fists, every muscle tightened, but it was no use. The vision invaded until a clear image filled her mind's eye. She saw herself standing at a river's edge. Dirty brown water raged at her feet. White-tipped waves sprayed her with a fine mist. She wore her old ragged gown, the one Mistress Rowley had burned. The dress hung loose about her shoulders. What remained of the thin, wet fabric hung in loose strips that fell to her feet.

Behind her sat a wolf—the same wolf from her earlier vision, only this time his leg was healed. He watched her from a distance. His eyes were dark and as impenetrable as a sheet of ice on a cold winter's eve.

A chill invaded her. She tried to wrap her arms about her waist in an effort to retain what little heat remained inside her, but something pulled against her wrists. She tugged, harder this time, only to find her wrists were bound by manacles—just like the ones she had worn for years in the tower on the isle.

Water touched her bare toes. She flinched back, only to find herself surrounded by the current. The water tugged at her calves, then her knees. She tried to move, but her feet held fast, as if frozen by some force outside herself.

A rush of panic filled her. She looked back to where the beast sat. A shout left her lips, but her plea for help was carried away by the sound of the rushing water that now reached her waist.

The beast's features hardened and he loped away. *Secrets have a way of coming out. The knowledge of who you are will destroy you, destroy us,* a voice echoed all around her.

Confusion mixed with panic. The water seemed to rise higher and higher with each breath she drew. The current tugged at her flesh, brutal, unforgiving. It covered her head, pulling her down in its depths toward darkness, toward death. She had to get out. She had to live.

"Isobel." A voice broke through the darkness. "Isobel!"

"I am Isobel," she repeated to herself, trying to keep hold of herself and her reality. Something pushed at her arms. Her mind cleared. She sat up on Wolf's bed, clutched in his arms. "What . . . what happened?"

"I do not know," Wolf said, a frown darkening his face. "One moment you were here with me, the next you seemed miles away. You had a vision, didn't you?"

Isobel gazed hazily about the room, trying to gain control over the frantic beating of her heart. The water was gone. The chamber was bathed in muted light that filtered in through the stained glass windows. Dizzying relief soared through her, yet confusion lingered as well. "I have no wish for these skills."

Wolf reached for her necklace. "This Stone looks like Brahan's, except that the image carved onto its face is different, more rounded."

She might not want to be a seer, but she'd had another vision. That much she could not deny. And what did this vision tell her? That to continue her life as a lie would only end in death?

She shivered, not from Wolf's touch against her naked flesh, but from a chill that radiated deep from within her core. So cold. Had she ever been this cold?

He held her close against his bare chest, and she let him, not wanting to release the warmth and safety he offered. When she shivered against his shoulder, he pulled back and moved from the bed. He limped across the room to a short wooden chest and withdrew a fresh shirt and breeches for himself, then retrieved her shift and gown from the floor before returning to the bed. He draped the garments over her head and settled them around her body before he sat beside her once more. His gaze fixed on her face. "Are you warmer now?"

"Nay," she said truthfully. "This chill is worse than after my last . . ."

"Vision," he finished her sentence for her.

She cringed at the word. To acknowledge that she had visions meant she had to believe that what she saw could come true. He had asked her to withhold the truth from him. If she continued to do so, did that mean she would die?

There had to be another choice, something she didn't take into account. He brought his hand up to caress her shoulder, and she could feel the warmth of his flesh through the fabric of her gown. And still she shivered. Her body ached with a bone-chilling cold. Perhaps if she weren't so cold she might be able to think of something else, but her brain felt sluggish, incapable of rational thought.

Wolf's expression grew troubled. "When Brahan has a vision an increasing section of his hair turns white. Perhaps the same thing happens to you, except your sacrifice is your body's heat." Wolf tugged one of the blankets from the bed and wrapped it about her shoulders.

"If that is true," she said through her chattering teeth, "then I will surely freeze to death if another vision comes my way." She inhaled sharply, seizing a wild idea that came into her mind. With trembling hands she reached for her necklace, carefully avoiding the Stone. She untied the cord and slipped the treasure her mother had given her from her neck.

"What are you doing?"

"Without the necklace I can have no more visions." She reached for a small, intricately carved box on the bedside table, opened it, and slipped the necklace inside before closing it again.

"Will you do something for me?" she asked.

"Anything."

"Hide this from me. Put it where I will never find it."

"Whatever for?" He frowned but wrapped his fingers around the box.

"It has brought me nothing but misery all my life." She dropped her gaze, no longer able to look him in the eye, almost afraid that he would read the dark secrets she carried there. "My life here has changed all that. Please take it away."

He brought her gaze back to his with a finger beneath her chin. "If it is truly what you desire, then aye."

"Thank you." The words seemed so simple for the depth of emotion they contained. Taking the necklace away would stop the visions, and maybe even forestall

Wolf from discovering the truth about her past. If the Stone stayed away from her, perhaps the future she foresaw would, too. For now, it was her only option.

Despite the relief she felt, Isobel shivered violently. "If I can only find some way to get warm." She wrapped the blanket more tightly around her shoulders.

"Come with me. I know just the place."

Before she could speak, he set the box on the pillow, took her by the hand, and pulled her with him out of the chamber. Despite his limp, he set a steady pace, guiding her down the hallway and up the stairs to his private domain.

"Your leg," she said when she caught her breath at the top of the stairs.

"I think we have already proved my leg is fine."

Had she been capable of the warmth, she was certain her cheeks would have flamed scarlet. Instead, another chill wracked her body, nearly bringing her to her knees.

"Steady." He reached for her arm and offered her support before placing her hands against the doorjamb. "Use this to regain your bearing while I make a fire." He vanished into the darkness of the room.

Isobel stood at the doorway of Wolf's private tower chamber. Chill air surrounded her, engulfing her in what felt like a dark void where nothing and no one existed.

A light flared from within the small room and she could see him move toward the oddly shaped hearth in the corner. A spark from the flint leapt onto the kindling. A moment later, hungry flames lapped at the wood. Radiant warmth curled through the chamber, like fingers beckoning her forward, toward heat, toward life, toward him.

He stood next to the fire, his gaze now fully on her. "Come. The fire will warm you."

His eyes held dark, exotic mysteries and the curve of his lips was blatantly sensual. It gave her a queer, hot feeling in the pit of her stomach yet again. Before she could rationalize why she should not enter the small enclosed space, she found herself before him. Crisp morning air clung to him, making her head feel light, dizzy, euphoric. His very presence intoxicated her, robbing her of all logical thought. Near him, she did not feel the fear that usually followed when she entered a confined space.

"Are you warmer here?" he asked, his voice gentle, soothing.

A wave of heat tingled through her that had nothing to do with the fire. The heat from his body surrounded her. The muscles of her limbs felt heavy and weak, unable to support her own weight. She sagged.

"Easy now." His hand came out to support her. With his other hand, he reached out to caress her cheek, her throat. She inhaled sharply as a shiver ran through her.

Gently, he eased her to the floor until she sat upon his lap before the growing warmth of the fire. Shivers wracked her body even as the heat seeped into her bones. His arms came around her and he held her tight, allowing his own heat to mix with that of the fire, warming her.

Against his chest, she could hear the thump of his heart as the sound mixed with the pop and hiss of the wood. Her own heartbeat slowed, and a peaceful contentment wrapped itself around her. Is this what it felt like to be cared for, to be loved?

She tensed at the thought. He had shared his body

with her belowstairs, but he'd said nothing of love. How would he ever love her once he knew who and what she truly was? A different kind of chill filled her. She had to tell him the truth, whatever the consequences. This secret was too big to keep hidden a moment longer.

She drew a steadying breath, preparing to tell him, when her attention caught on a small sparkling object resting beneath the flames. She leaned in closer. It looked like a jewel, so clear, so pure, it might have been a drop of water frozen beneath the flames. "What is that?"

"It is a trace of my latest creation," he said, his voice suddenly soft, almost hesitant.

"You create diamonds?"

He smiled. Charm floated about him, light and effortless. The overbearing beast had vanished, replaced by a gentle man. "Nay, not diamonds, but something almost as precious. Would you like to see?"

She nodded, willing to put aside her own revelations for just a moment more. Besides, she was curious about what he would show her.

He set her off his lap, onto the floor, then moved to the table on the far side of the chamber. He mixed several different dry ingredients together in a small iron bowl that he then set in the flames in the oddly shaped hearth. He returned to the table, but Isobel could not pull her gaze from the powdered mixture that transformed into a pale green liquid beneath the intense heat of the flames.

"What is that?" she asked.

He returned to her side with a long metal pipe in one hand, a stool in the other. "Glass in its purest, unaltered form." He set the stool next to her, then sat. "Let me show you."

Isobel sat up on her knees, peering into the flames, watching as he placed the long, narrow pipe into the iron bowl and gathered the sticky liquid into a softly formed ball.

Heat poured from the hearth and a sharp scent filled the air. Isobel knew she should scoot back, but she couldn't move, so fascinated was she with the molten glass at the end of the metal pipe.

He slowly spun the metal rod with steady hands. All the while the molten mixture became more evenly shaped, almost round. He paused, and shifted his gaze to her. "Hold this a moment."

Before she could answer, he thrust the pipe into her hands. The tool was heavy, awkward, with all the weight on the end that hung above the flames. She stiffened her arms as the ball of glass drifted toward the ash-covered logs, desperate not to ruin his creation.

In a swift movement, he drew off his linen shirt and tossed it aside. The firelight danced across his chest, highlighting his corded muscles. The man was all power and strength. And he was her husband, and now her lover.

Isobel swallowed and moistened her lips, suddenly aware of just how warm the small chamber had become. As if proving her point, a small bead of sweat raced down her temple to fall upon her chest.

"The heat can be oppressive after a while. You should remove your dress as well." His words and the memory of what they'd just shared chased away the rest of her chill. Warmth invaded her limbs. Her fingers sagged. The pipe dipped. His hands came about hers, supporting the weight of the rod. "I'll take this now."

She slipped her fingers out from beneath his, suddenly feeling as though her clothes steamed on her body. Another drop of sweat trailed down her temple, then another. She would only continue to sweat if she remained as she was. Her decision made, she slipped the heavy kirtle over her head. A rush of coolness brushed her skin. Comfortable now, she returned her gaze to the unformed glass.

His gaze, however, remained on her. "Are you happy here with me, Isobel?"

Isobel. No one but her mother had called her by that name. Yet the more formal version of her name seemed right coming from him. So many things seemed right now that she was here with him, despite the fact they were forced to marry, despite the attempts on both of their lives. "Aye," she agreed. "I am." But would he be content with her once he learned her secrets? She pushed the thought aside. He had told her the past did not matter. Only the present had meaning, and the present was right here, right now.

With a satisfied nod he turned back to the fire. He set the mass of glass back into the flames, all the while turning the pipe with controlled and steady hands. "I am gathering the glass. I keep adding to the mass until I'm satisfied with the color and quantity."

He pulled the glass from the oven, then set his mouth to the pipe and blew. A bubble formed and grew as she watched in fascination. Molten glass mixed with his breath, taking shape into something that had not existed moments before. He drew his mouth away and handed the pipe to her. "Your turn."

The pipe was warm but not hot, as he thrust it into her hands. Hesitantly, she placed the pipe against her mouth and blew. Her breath stalled in her lungs, rushing back to fill her head. The shape remained unchanged beneath her assault.

He chuckled and rotated the pipe in her hands, not allowing the bubble to drift downward. "It is harder than it looks. Try again, and this time breathe from here." He placed his hand against her abdomen.

She inhaled sharply, and a shiver ran through her at the intimacy of his touch. The air in the room was suddenly charged not with heat but with a startling awareness. His hand splayed against the lightweight fabric of her shift and his eyes darkened.

"Blow," he instructed without moving his hand.

She inhaled deeply, feeling his touch even more intensely than before. Her breath came out, forceful but controlled. The bubble grew, giving birth to a shape that glistened as it caught the glow of the flames—transparent, fluid, timeless.

"Beautiful," he breathed as he slipped his fingers from her barely concealed flesh to once again grasp the rod. He set their creation on a stone block at the side of the hearth. He worked quickly, rolling the glass against the stone, using just the right amount of pressure to shape the glass into a ball. "If I were making a window, I would cut the end off the bulb and spin the rod in a circle, creating a flat, circular shape. But I want to form the glass instead, so it must be chilled with a block until it forms an outer skin."

As she stared at the glass bulb before her, her mind drifted back to the tree house he had shown her in the woods. "You created all those glass bulbs in the tree house," she said, her voice edged with awe.

He offered her a smile, and the darkness of the tower seemed to all but disappear. "Aye. I had to do something with them. They were starting to pile up around here." He turned back to his work, molding their creation into shape by pressing it against the stone. The tension that always seemed to pull at the corners of his eyes eased. A sense of calm surrounded him as his hands coaxed the glass from the realm of imagination into reality.

Her gaze moved from the glass up his arms to the muscles that rolled and flexed beneath his controlled movements. His arms gave evidence that this man was a warrior. Yet an artistic side lingered as well. So unlike other men she had known on the isle, who were loud and rough and only concerned with their own pleasure.

Yet Wolf had shown her something more. He had pleasured her quite thoroughly just a short time ago.

As though sensing her gaze, he turned to her—his dark eyes alive, and this time it was not from the reflection of the flames. "This creation is done," he said in a way that left her wondering what other creations he might still have in mind.

He stood and limped to the small window and swung open the slatted wood covering it. A ray of sunlight struck the pale green glass of the bulb they'd created, passed through it, bathing the room in a rainbow of color. Her gaze fixed on Wolf's face. "It's beautiful." A sense of wonder swept through her, lifting her up, until she felt as though she were sparkling with the same jewel-like brilliance as the light surrounding her.

"Beauty has many forms," he said as he moved to the hearth and picked up what looked like a small iron shovel. Carefully, he brushed the wood aside to scoop up a pile of red-hot coals that he then placed in a smaller oven above the hearth that she had not noticed before. He arranged the coals in a half circle, then placed the glass ball inside. With one hand on the rod, he reached for a long slender tool that looked like a file. She started when he struck the file against the blowpipe, breaking the seal. "The glass must cool slowly." He set the pipe and the file aside. "As the fire dies, the glass will anneal, slowly hardening."

"How did you learn this skill?" she asked quickly, seizing the new line of conversation as he stepped toward her.

"In Italy. From a master there."

"You go there often?" The light caught his face, revealing the broad, strong planes of his cheekbones, and illuminating the rich brown depths of his eyes. They were not black, but brown. Why had she never noticed that about him before?

"In the past, aye." He reached out to caress her throat. "I had no choice but to do as my father directed. But no longer. For now, I have every reason to want to stay here."

He trailed his hand against her long, slender neck. She turned into his touch, giving him total access to her silken flesh.

How things had changed for them since their first meeting. Something inside her had changed, strengthened. She no longer feared the darkness as she once did. The man before her had filled her life with light. Less than a week's time in his presence and in his castle had put years of tormented memories to rest.

He took her hand and brought it to his lips. "Isobel." The word was as much a caress as the feel of his lips against her flesh. "My father threatens to arrive within the next two days."

"So soon?" She dropped her gaze to their intertwined fingers, hiding the panic she knew reflected in her eyes.

He put a finger beneath her chin and drew her gaze back to his. "He is like any other father," he said softly, belying the flash of anger and resentment that darted across his features.

There was something he was not saying, a bit of the truth that he held back. Yet how could she press him for more? Not when she withheld her own secrets. She had to tell him the truth. Right here, right now. She tightened her fingers around his, afraid that if she released him, he would drift away from her forever. "Secrets should not be kept between two people who care about each other."

His face went pale. His features shuttered and he pulled his fingers from hers. At his withdrawal, a piece of her heart withered. She was losing him already, before she even uttered the truth.

He turned away to retrieve their clothing from the cool stone floor. "Your gown." His words were crisp, sharp, snapping like crystals of ice on a cold winter's morn.

With trembling hands, she accepted the garment and quickly slipped it over her head. Her fingers barely functioned as she struggled to gather the laces behind her back. His back to her, Wolf slipped into his shirt, then tucked the hem into the waistband of his breeches.

She abandoned her attempt to secure the laces. "Wolf," she said, his name catching in her throat as she forced herself to continue what she had begun. "There is something you need to know about me."

He twisted back to her. "About you?" His surprise clearly reflected in his gaze.

She hesitated, baffled by his reaction to her words. "It is not your father that concerns me. I mean, I do want to make a good impression, if you will but give me the chance." She grasped her wrists with her hands, her fingers digging painfully into the scars her past had created. If she were ever to have a future she must tell him her father's name. "My father . . . he is Lord G—"

"Forgive the intrusion." Brahan's deep voice called from the doorway.

Isobel forced back a groan at the untimely interruption. Their gazes locked for a brief, strained moment before Wolf turned away toward Brahan.

"You know better than to disturb me here." His tone was thick and low.

Brahan's large body filled the doorway, his expression anxious and determined. "I would not interrupt your privacy if the situation were not so urgent."

"What could be so important that you—"

"A kitchen maid is dead. Murdered outside in the chicken yard. The scouting party you sent to patrol the borders of your land has been attacked. Only one warrior returned alive, and he is badly injured, and . . ." he paused.

With each revelation an ache grew in her chest until the pressure threatened to smother her.

"What else?" Wolf's voice was hard, and the sound of it shivered across the back of her neck.

Brahan drew himself up as though preparing to defend himself against the anger he knew his next words would evoke. "Before the scouting party was attacked, they sighted your father's envoy at the border of your land. He will arrive before nightfall unless Grange's men get to him first."

Chapter Twenty-three

The moment Brahan mentioned Wolf's father, Isobel saw a shadow fall across his face. His features turned dark and dangerous. The softer side of her husband vanished. He grasped her arm and forced her toward Brahan. "Take her belowstairs to the solar." There was nothing malleable or soft in him now.

The breath stilled in her chest. The beast had returned.

"I must assemble the warriors to protect my father." A flash of fear—or was that challenge—sparked in the depths of Wolf's eyes. "Once the Lady Isobel is safely in the solar, join me, Brahan. We prepare for battle."

His gaze snapped to Isobel. "You will prepare things here for my father's arrival." His gaze left her face to travel down the length of her body. "Go to your chamber. I will see that Mistress Rowley and the castle seamstresses join you shortly. My wife will have more than one garment to wear before she makes her introduction to my father." He smiled cruelly.

Isobel took a stumbling step backward. Her heartbeat

sounded in her ears as she waited for that hot flash of anger in his eyes to pass.

"Isobel . . ." His voice became softer, more desperate. "We will continue this discussion later. For now, do as I ask. I need you to make things ready here, and that includes yourself."

"Aye." She forced out the word as the war between the need to unburden herself mixed with the sudden realization that her appearance embarrassed him. He wished to present a different type of wife to his father. Before she could respond, he whirled away and vanished from the tower.

"We best do as he bids." Brahan offered her his arm.

"How did the maid die, Brahan?" Isobel asked as he escorted her through the doorway.

"She took a crossbow bolt in the back out in the chicken yard."

"Nay." Isobel tensed and her heart skipped several beats. She knew exactly the girl Brahan spoke of. "The thin blond girl who, from a distance, resembles me." She spoke her thoughts aloud without meaning to as her mind whirled.

"That's not a coincidence, I fear." Brahan drew her down the stairs. "And neither is the fact that the warriors on patrol were attacked."

"And his father's arrival at the border of his land?"

At the bottom of the stairs, Brahan drew her toward the solar. "That is sheer bad luck."

Isobel entered the room and stared down at her hands, fingers lacing and unlacing, unable to focus her thoughts. "What do I do, Brahan? How do I help him?"

Brahan's forehead furrowed. "You wish to help him?"

"I would if I only knew how. He asked me to prepare

for his father's arrival. Yet I do not know where to start, or what to do exactly. I've never had any experience with a household of this size."

"He obviously thinks you are capable. I am impressed he asked you. He's never asked for help before." Brahan's frown deepened. "He likes control. But it's more than that. He feels a deep responsibility for all who live in this castle. And that responsibility sometimes makes his life a little unbearable."

He shook his head. "So many changes, and in such a short time. Perhaps one of us should see what the future holds for our lord with all these changes. That might be the best way to help him. Use your Stone to—" His gaze shot to her chest. "Where is your necklace?"

She pressed her fingers against her throat. They mourned the emptiness that greeted them, but she steeled herself against the response. "I won't allow the necklace and Stone to control my life."

Brahan's gaze narrowed. "You think you can toss away the Stone and find freedom from your gift? Ridding yourself of the Stone will only make matters worse. Where did you put it?"

Her gaze shot to the bed and the box where she'd hidden the necklace. "It's gone." The revelation surprised her, but she could not say she was sad. The farther the necklace and the Stone were from her, the better.

"Where is it?" A hint of panic laced his words.

"I don't know. And I truly don't care."

His features hardened. "You will care very soon. If you want to help my lord Wolf, get that necklace back, or the troubles around here will only become worse."

"That is not true. The Stone is not responsible for

these events, nor am I. I am well rid of it." Isobel moved to the windows, finding a sense of peace in the proximity of the vividly colored glass. "That Stone brought my mother and myself nothing but pain."

"You think you've suffered?" Brahan moved beside her, his gaze angry as he towered over her.

Isobel put her shoulders back, refusing to let him intimidate her.

"Perhaps your fate would have been even worse without the Stone. What did it do for your ancestors?"

The question startled her. "I do not know that there were others besides us."

"Then where did it come from?"

"All I know is that it was handed down through my mother's line."

"Mark my words, without it in your possession, things will only get worse around here. And aye, the events will be because of you."

"Nay—"

"Wolf's father will arrive shortly because of your marriage to him. The kitchen maid is dead because she resembled you—you said so yourself. And the attack on the warriors, well . . . I'm not certain how that all fits in, but I am convinced there is a connection."

She knew the connection. Her father had found her.

"Brahan, I should leave here. My presence has hurt too many people already." Even as she said the words, a twisting regret centered in her chest. She had finally found a moment of happiness in her life, only to lose it as quickly as it had come.

Brahan's expression grew dark. "You will not leave. Wolf has gone to a great deal of trouble at your expense. You will not abandon him now."

"Abandon him?"

"He asked you to help him prepare for his father. I suggest you focus on feasting and pleasure. You are here to stay. Get used to it." He gave her a reproachful glare.

He had misunderstood. She only wished to protect Wolf, not anger or harm him in any way. "I—"

"There you are, my dear," Mistress Rowley exclaimed as she whisked into the room, along with four other women carrying lengths of fabric and baskets filled to the brim with trimmings and thread. "We are going to create such wonderful gowns for you. The master bade us to spare no expense." She beamed at Isobel. "When we are through with you, you will look like a princess, you will."

Before she could voice her opinion on the matter, the women surrounded her, draping her body in muslin from her shoulder to her toes. "Where did all this fabric come from?" she asked.

" 'Tis fabric Fiona had purchased from the peddlers a fortnight ago. With the master gone, we hadn't the time to make up the gowns yet. Such a boon for you. The five of us are more than capable of creating a simple dress for you in no time at all," Mistress Rowley said with an affectionate smile.

"Our first task is to make a pattern that is specific to your body," the elder woman of the group spoke softly as she cinched the fabric tight against Isobel's waist. "Too thin, you are." She shook her head in disapproval as she pulled the fabric all the tighter.

"Please," Isobel protested. "There are other things I must do that are more important. A woman is dead. Her family is grieving."

The older woman scowled. "Martha and Bertie are

with them now. You are mistress here, milady, and you must look the part before you go to them."

Isobel shot Brahan a pleading glance as he backed toward the doorway. "I'll check on the family before I join my lord Wolf," he assured Isobel. A moment later he was gone, and she was all alone with five women who wanted nothing more than to transform her into something she was not.

It all happened so quickly. First she was draped with muslin, then a rich peach silk, a mauve velvet, a gold taffeta, a tawny linen, a reddish brown satin—a rich array of fabrics and colors that were so foreign to her that she could do nothing but stand with her arms held away from her sides in mute fascination and dismay.

A woman was dead because of her. A numbness crept inside her while chaos ensued around her. Fabrics were cut by one woman while another continued to drape her body. The rest of the small army of seamstresses sat near the stain-glass windows pulling their needles through the cloth. It seemed like only moments but was probably more like hours later that they dropped the finished garment over her head.

Mistress Rowley fussed with the hem before standing back to assess the finished product. She brought her fingers to her cheeks, covering the flush of pleasure that darkened them to pink. "You are a vision, my dear. A vision."

The other women stopped their sewing. Each smiled at Isobel in turn.

"Lovely," one said.

"Truly a sight to behold," the eldest seamstress added.

The youngest seamstress put her needle and thread down, then moved to the side of the room where the washstand stood. She picked up the rectangular looking glass that sat beside the water basin. "A princess, indeed." She held out the mirror to Isobel. "Take a look for yourself."

Isobel hesitated. She should attend the girl's family now, while she could. She took a step toward the door when she was caught by her image in the mirror. A simple velvet gown in a rich shade of mauve with no elaborate embroidery or trim draped her body. The tight sleeves came to her wrists; the line of the gown was straight and graceful, falling from a low, square neckline across her breast where the fabric was gathered with a brooch across the flat of her stomach. The rich mauve color made the warm tones in her skin glow golden, and the low neckline revealed the line of her throat and the swell of her breasts.

She looked sophisticated, regal, and so very unfamiliar to her own eyes.

"There be no denying you are the lady of the castle now," Mistress Rowley said with a satisfied sigh.

Isobel didn't feel like the lady of the castle, yet each day since she'd left the isle some part of her old self slipped away as a bold, confident person emerged. Even her own body seemed to be part of this transformation. Wolf's touch had awakened sensations of pleasure, anticipation, even desire, that she had never known she was capable of feeling. At the thought of his touch, her skin tingled, and she became more aware of the sensuous velvet that draped against the flesh at her arms and neckline.

She was no princess, but she was a Highland lass. And the Highlands bred only survivors with strong resolve and the need to fight for what they wanted. She would follow through with Wolf's request of her no matter how uncomfortable the idea made her. She would figure out how to manage this castle and how to prepare a feast, and she would embarrass him no more.

"Come, my dear." Mistress Rowley's voice intruded on her thoughts. "Let us go below and start the preparations for the k—" The ladies' needles stilled and their faces paled. Mistress Rowley's face, however, flushed scarlet. She fanned her cheeks with her hand. "Dear me, I'm all a flutter. Can't get over how pretty you look." She turned away, expecting Isobel to follow. "Our lord Wolf's father will be here soon. We've a feast to prepare."

Isobel hesitated. Before she did anything else, she had other, more important, tasks to perform. "Mistress Rowley?"

The woman paused and turn back around. Her brows rose in silent question.

"I want to do as Wolf bid, but before we do, I would like to attend the warrior who was injured, then pay a visit to the family of the girl who was . . ." Her words fumbled as a rise of emotion pressed against her throat. "The girl who was killed. I must pay my respects."

Instead of the censure she expected, Mistress Rowley nodded her head and smiled. "Now you not only look like mistress of the castle, you are acting like her as well. Come," she said as she held out her hand. "I will take you to them both."

Isobel accepted Mistress Rowley's outstretched hand, and feeling bolstered by the support, slipped from the room, heading down the stairs into the great hall and her new role as mistress of Duthus Castle.

Wolf sat atop his horse and studied the forest floor, searching for signs that Grange's men had moved through this area recently. No one else would be injured by his enemy. It was time to take a more direct approach.

There would be no more mysterious deaths, no more scouting parties besieged and tortured. There would be nothing at all left of Grange or his henchmen if he harmed one hair on his father's royal head. The king usually traveled in a secure entourage. But where Grange was concerned, no one was safe—especially the king.

Wolf shifted his gaze back to the men who followed him to battle. They were dressed in mail beneath their Stewart tartan, prepared for whatever might come their way. And now, after his last experience, Wolf knew what to look for. Grange's tactics had changed yet again. Now he used animal traps and pits dug into the forest floor to take his enemy unaware.

Wolf would not fall for that ploy again.

After two hours of searching, Wolf dismounted at the site where the injured warrior had said he and the others had been attacked. Wolf ran his hand across the freshly swept ground. The area had been cleared. Why? What was Grange up to this time?

An uneasiness settled inside him. They had found nothing during their search. No signs of any disturbed brush, no telltale marking on the ground. Even the area where he had been captured and found had been cleared of all traces.

He wasn't sure which disturbed him more, the thought that they could find nothing or the fact that Grange was going to a lot of trouble to make sure his steps could not be traced.

Wolf remounted. "To the ridge," he instructed his men. From there they would be able to see the southeastern border of his land, from which his father would most likely come to Duthus Castle.

"I don't like it." Brahan brought his horse alongside Wolf's.

"Neither do I." Wolf kept his eyes peeled on the territory ahead. He couldn't shake the feeling that something was wrong. "Tell the men to be alert and prepared for anything," he ordered Brahan.

Brahan nodded but did not fall back into the ranks. "I could help figure out what is to come." His hand strayed to the pouch at his side, where he kept the Seer's Stone. "It might save lives as well as time."

Wolf drew his gaze from the land for a moment to study his friend. Brahan's sincerity coiled the tension in Wolf's gut even tighter. "After the rise. If we do not see what we need to then, aye."

Wolf returned his gaze to the hill before them and prayed it would not come to that. While they needed answers, he hated placing either Brahan or Isobel in that kind of life-threatening danger.

Lives were at stake either way—the lives of his men, or the life of his friend.

Wolf did not like either possibility.

Chapter Twenty-four

Isobel had gone to lend comfort to the murdered girl's family that night. The next morning found her with them as well. She stood with her hands clasped together, trying to think of the right thing to say at the eulogy of Cherie, the unfortunate kitchen maid who had died merely because she resembled her mistress. No words could take away the family's pain, or help them find the peace they deserved.

The girl's mother and father stood to her right at the head of the wooden casket that had been placed atop a small dais at the front of the castle's small chapel. Their somber mood was at odds with the radiant splashes of color the morning sun forced through the wall of stained-glass panels. Gold, red, green, and purple rays of light scattered across the casket, changing it from a thing of death and destruction into a thing of beauty.

Isobel allowed a sad smile to chase across her features as the appropriate words suddenly filled her head. "Just as the light now touches her in death, may the light follow her into the beyond. May Cherie find peace in her eternal reward, and may her parents find comfort in the arms of their family." Isobel took the mother's chilled fingers in her own and sent the father a heartfelt gaze of condolence. "My lord Wolf and I consider you both, and all who live in this castle, our family."

Tears sprang up in the mother's eyes.

"That means the world to us, milady." The father nodded solemnly. He set a single lily atop the casket that harbored his daughter's body.

"We had such hopes for our dear Cherie. Of all our children, she showed the most promise." The mother dabbed at the tears as they rolled down her cheeks. "Only five days ago she was promoted to the kitchens. 'Twas Cherie's skill with herbs that they took notice of and moved her up from the scullery to serve the lord and his new lady."

A shiver of unease crept across the back of Isobel's neck. The girl had been promoted on the day of her own arrival at Duthus Castle? "Who made the decision to promote her?"

"Why, Mistress Fiona, of course. She was in charge of the kitchens before you arrived here."

Isobel's gaze moved back to the casket. Perhaps her father wasn't entirely to blame for all the events at the castle. She knew he was somehow involved. Did that mean he had help from one or more persons within the castle's walls?

Fiona had been in charge of the kitchens. Curious that both she and Fiona had been poisoned by food that came from a place Fiona oversaw, and most likely from a girl whom she herself had promoted.

Isobel's thoughts began to swirl. Perhaps the girl had not been murdered merely because she resembled the new mistress of the castle. Perhaps other things were at

play. It was a lead worth pursuing if she was to sort out
what had happened and who might be to blame for the
attacks on herself, Wolf, and now Cherie.

It was the only lead she had.

Now she just needed someone who knew the castle and
its residents to help her. And she knew just who to enlist.

Isobel offered the family a heartfelt farewell before
heading back to the great hall. At the doorway of that
chamber she paused. The great hall was empty save for
one man who sat near the massive hearth, a tankard of
ale in his hands. Most of the other warriors had gone
with Wolf.

Walter, however, remained behind. He and a small
contingent of men had been ordered to stay and protect her. Judging by the droop of his shoulders and the
frown that cut across his somber face, the decision did
not sit well with him.

Steadying her nerve, Isobel approached Wolf's brother.
There would be no one near to draw away his anger from
her this time. Regardless, she kept her stride steady. She
needed help, and he could assist her.

The pop and hiss of the fire were the only sounds in
the chamber. Usually they added a certain warmth and
coziness to the room, but not today. Today they seemed
out of place and unusually loud in the cavernous room.

"Walter?" she asked. He did not look up when she
reached his side.

He took a sip from his mug. "What do you want?"

"Might I sit down and have a word with you?"

He looked up then. "If you know what is good for
you, you will stay far away from me." The pulse at his
temple quickened. He set down his ale.

Refusing to give in to the nervousness that suddenly
swamped her, Isobel lowered herself onto a bench

across the table from him. "I need your help, Walter. I do not know who else I can trust."

"Don't trust me if you know what's good for you." Instead of anger, resignation hung in his words. "Go away from this place while you still can."

"There was a time when I wanted that desperately. But now things are different."

His gaze turned hard. "Why? Because the man bedded you? He's bedded many women in his day. Ask Fiona. He will eventually tire of you as he did of her. Then where will you be?"

A jolt of unease rocked her, but she did not force it away as she would have in the past. Perhaps Walter was right. Wolf had many reasons to turn away from her, especially once he discovered who she was.

Isobel pulled her shoulders back and met Walter's gaze without flinching. He had asked where she would be when Wolf tired of her. Obviously the man knew nothing about her past or where she had come from. Her current predicament was paradise compared to where she'd been. Even if Wolf tossed her out into the wilds of Scotland tomorrow, she would be better off than before. At least she'd be free. At least she'd determine her own destiny.

She knew her choices would be few as a woman alone in the world without connections or family. But she would survive. Isobel dropped her gaze to her wrists and the scars that remained there. She'd lived as little more than an animal before, and she could do so again. Fine clothing, lavish food, even a soft, warm bed were not necessary for her survival. Life in the tower had made her stronger than most women.

A surge of confidence filled her as she met his gaze once more. "Thank you, Walter, for helping me realize I don't need your assistance. I am capable of doing this on my own." As she stood, the bench scraped gently against the wood flooring, mixing with Walter's gasp of surprise.

"Good day." Before he could respond, she strode across the chamber, determined to find the killer. One way or another, she would find out who had killed Cherie. What she needed was a trap—along with irresistible bait.

And she knew just what bait to offer.

Herself.

Isobel headed for the long hallway at the far end of the great hall. She'd seen the warriors enter the room from here dressed in their armor and mail. If she wanted similar protection, the rooms on this side of the castle seemed a logical place to search. An ominous silence followed her as she hurried through the semidarkness. Few of Wolf's glass windows had been installed on this side of the castle.

She had no time to consider why as she came to the first doorway on her left. She pressed the handle down only to find it secured. The next door was also locked. She moved on to the door at the end of the hallway. The door here had a thick metal lock attached to the handle, yet it hung open, failing in its purpose to keep others from the room. Isobel pushed against the heavy wooden door. It swung open easily and she stepped inside.

Giant urns hung from hooks at both sides of the chamber, bathing the contents of the room in a rich, golden light. Everywhere she looked weaponry covered the walls from the wooden floor to the vaulted ceiling. The weapons were organized by kind in neat and tidy rows. Spears and lances, swords and daggers, bows and arrows, crossbows and bolts, maces, battle axes, and shields. The metallic surfaces captured the light from the flames, making the chamber feel more like a magical place than a storehouse of destruction.

Yet the empty spaces on the wall testified that Wolf and his men had left the castle fully armed—armed to defend and destroy. And judging by the broken lock on the door, Wolf was not the only one who had access to the weapons. Unease brought a tingle to the back of her neck. Again she pushed the sensation away. She had a purpose here. She would see it through, no matter what.

To both left and right, racks of mail and armor lined the walls. Isobel moved toward the mail and searched through the heavy garments until she found what she wanted.

"Perfect," she said with a touch of satisfaction as she held up the small mail shirt that was probably fashioned for a squire or other youth. "Now, to find a weapon I can actually use." She draped the mail shirt over her arm and slowly walked down the line of weaponry against the back wall. None of the weapons were anything she'd ever had experience with before.

She paused before the crossbows and bolts, eyeing the weapons with as much curiosity as revulsion. Twice now someone had attacked a member of the castle with this weapon. Whether she knew how to use it or not, this was the tool that would help ensnare the traitor in their midst.

Isobel hesitated, her fingers hovering above the weapon. Could she do something so bold? Only a week ago she would have retreated to the chicken yard for safety, yet now she challenged herself to do something more.

She lifted the crossbow and two bolts from the wall. She would do what she could, regardless of her own future. She had what she needed to set the trap, then wait for the killer to strike.

The sound of bagpipes filled the air with a skirling melody that left Wolf's emotions raw. He signaled his men to stop. The setting rays of the sun gilded the borderlands below the crag where he and his men assembled. Wolf scanned the area below, finding what he'd expected: his father's entourage. The report he'd had from the injured warrior had been limited but accurate.

Suspicion and anger replaced the distress that had driven Wolf from the castle and away from his bride. His father was not in danger. Nay, something else was at play here.

Wolf tensed, but even as he did the sound of the bagpipes worked their magic. It went deep inside him, pulling him back to an earlier day. He closed his eyes and let the music pulse through him. In his mind's eye he could see the land that stood before him. He could hear the sound of the clear, cold water that ran through the burns, the rivers that flowed through the cliffs and crags. He could hear the wind as it whipped over the lochs and across the grassy green knolls.

He loved the land as much as he loved his own freedom, and only his father knew that. Wolf opened his eyes and gazed at the watchfires that surrounded the encampment below. His father's troops gathered there, and by the look of things they were not heading to Duthus Castle anytime soon.

His father—Robert II of Scotland, a Scot, a Stewart, and the rightful king on the throne—had brought clansmen who supported him. The clan chiefs gathered around him, ready to defend, no doubt, against the only man who disputed his claim: Lord Henry Grange. The echoing of the pipes, the skirling melody told it all. It was the music of war.

"What does he want?" Brahan reined in his horse alongside Wolf's.

"My guess is to finally put an end to his battle against Grange and Grange's weak claim to the throne," Wolf replied.

"You guessed correctly," an unfamiliar voice replied.

Twisting in his saddle, Wolf saw a line of archers take position behind him and his men. Bows drawn and aimed to strike.

"Artemis."

The man bowed his head with a newfound arrogance. "You may address me as master of the realm." He stepped forward, holding his sword at a threatening angle. "I am the king's new favorite, Lieutenant of the Realm."

"A new title? A change in rank? My, who did you have to kill to receive such a promotion?" Wolf kept his tone casual, bored. He cared not a whit about the man or any of the reasons why he had been moved from such a lowly position in his father's court to one of extreme rank. Nay, what he did care about was time—stalling to buy more of it in order to get himself and his men out of their current predicament.

"The king would have a word with you," Artemis commanded, his sword at the ready. Arrows or swords, both would be lethal once unleashed.

The sound of the bagpipes faded into the distance, replaced by the creaking of leather as the horses shifted beneath the weight of Wolf's men. The tension in the air sharpened. Wolf could see from the corners of his eyes as his own men grasped the hilts of their swords, ready to fight at the slightest inclination of his head. Anger tightened Wolf's gut. "So it has all been a ploy to get me to come to his aid."

Artemis shrugged. "I do not presume to know what goes through the king's mind. He has summoned me to bring you to him, and that I shall do. We can do this peacefully, or more of your men can fall. Which is it to be?"

Mercilessly Wolf gripped the reins in his hands, the leather biting into his palms. "*He* killed and injured my warriors, not Grange."

"The king did what he had to do in order to bring you here." Artemis raised his sword to strike.

Wolf tensed as he darted a gaze to his left, to his right, searching for some way out. The horse beneath him sensed his mood: its flanks tightened, its nostrils flared. Damn his father for deceiving him again.

If it came to a battle, Wolf held the tactical advantage from atop his horse. But that would not protect his men from the arrow volleys.

Bile rose in his throat as he forced a bow of acquiescence. He signaled his men to stand down and to fall in behind him. "Shall we?" he stated more as a challenge than as consent as he maneuvered his horse purposefully down the slope toward the king's encampment.

This time his father had gone too far.

The night sky darkened with angry rain clouds, and flashes of lightning darted across the sky. A storm threatened both in the heavens above and here on the ground. Wolf tensed as he waited outside the tent, listening as the lieutenant announced his arrival. Footsteps sounded on the other side of the oiled cloth. The flap swished aside and a pale light spilled from within. "You may enter."

Wolf stepped inside the king's domain. The lieutenant followed him inside. Standing as guardian beside the doorway, he drew his sword.

Wolf turned to where his father sat in a sumptuous red velvet chair that appeared out of place amid the trappings of war. "What do you want?" He did not bother to disguise the anger he knew reflected in his voice.

"Your cooperation."

"Most men would just ask."

"I am not most men."

Wolf regarded the king in stony silence as he bit back another surge of disappointment. Would his father ever treat him as a beloved son, and not just as a vassal to do with as he pleased?

The king stood, relying heavily on his cane for support. "It is time to rid ourselves of Grange."

"You have tried that tack before without success."

The king lifted his chin as though scenting the air, a warrior, an animal assessing his prey. "I now hold the advantage." The oiled flap flew back and another warrior entered. He stopped at the doorway until the king waved a hand for him to approach. In his grasp he held a leather pouch. Wolf recognized it immediately.

Instant alarm creased his brow. "Where's Brahan?"

The king accepted the pouch with a frown. "So worried about your men. That is your weakness, you know."

Wolf's hand moved to the hilt of his sword. "What have you done to Brahan?"

"Stay your weapon. Your lieutenant is safe. For now." The king flipped open the pouch and pulled out Brahan's stone. He brought his gaze back to Wolf's. " 'Tis the Stewart half. Now where is the Balliol half of the Seer's Stone?"

Wolf stared at the broken piece of stone as if seeing it for the first time. Lord Grange had been after Brahan's stone, a stone his own father now held in his hand. The small white stone appeared broken, only part of what it should be. Wolf had never noticed that before. He could only stare at the object, and as he did another stone came to mind. Isobel's stone necklace was also small, white, and broken on one side. "What do you mean, the Balliol half?"

The king shook his head in disgust as he stroked the smooth surface of Brahan's stone. "Did your mother never tell you of the significance of this stone? Or why she chose you, of all her children, to gift the Stone to at her death?"

Wolf felt the hilt of his sword bite into his hand. The pain seemed to focus him as his emotions ran the gamut from anger at his father to grief over his mother. "Nay. She never told me anything other than that the Stone was meant to be used by a seer. Since our family has never had, nor wanted that ability, I passed the Stone to Brahan, whose family is famous for such talents."

"God's toes," the king growled. "That woman did you no favors, withholding the truth."

"My mother did what she thought was best." Wolf's voice was laced with steel as he drew his sword. No one, not even his father, could get away with slandering his mother or her memory.

Artemis lunged forward, positioning his body between Wolf and the king. "Withdraw your weapon or feel the thrust of mine."

Wolf held his position. He wasn't afraid to die. It seemed entirely appropriate that he should do so at his father's feet. Their blood connection only became an issue when it served his father's purposes, such as now. The man wanted something, and Wolf knew the king would never allow his vassal to die before that purpose was fulfilled.

"If you are both so determined to use your sword, then do so outside, while you are chasing down that scoundrel Grange," the king roared, his voice booming in the confines of the tent.

With a twist of his wrist, Wolf sheathed his weapon. He stepped past Artemis to stand beside his father. Wolf took the Stone from his father's grasp, studying it in greater detail than he ever had before. One side of the Stone was rounded and smooth. The other was blunt, rough. The symbol etched into the top had always looked complete before, yet now it looked segmented—as if it was only half of something more.

Wolf met his father's curious gaze. "What did you mean by the Balliol half of the Stone?"

"That Stone is incomplete. When the two families— the Balliols and the Stewarts—battled over the throne, the high chiefs divided the Stone and gave half to each family." The king swayed on his feet, as if the memory suddenly drained him of strength. He shuffled backward toward his chair. "I must sit."

He did look tired, and Wolf felt a moment's sympathy before he checked himself. It was probably just an act to gain sympathy. "Go on. Tired or not, you started this game. You'll see it out."

He did not argue, merely nodded.

"Both families were happy until they tried to use their half of the Stone. The visions were suddenly unpredictable, not as clear. And the seer who tried to use the Stone either died immediately or aged a number of years over the course of a few minutes. Fear set in, and instead of being desired, the Stones became reviled. Lesser members of the family took claim of each half of the Stone, since the need for their survival was not as great as those who stood in line for the throne."

Wolf prickled at the comment. As a bastard child of a king, he most definitely fit that role. Yet that was never the issue between him and his father. Acceptance had always been the key—often desired, but never fulfilled.

The king continued, unaware of the tension his words had caused. "I have always known where the Stewart half of the Stone resided, but only recently did I learn about the Balliol half. It had vanished for many years, until my spies discovered what part of the Balliol line it had been passed down to."

Wolf kept his gaze on his father. "And now you think I have that half of the Stone. Why? Why would I have the Stone? I'm no Balliol."

"Nay." The king smiled wickedly. "But your wife most certainly is."

His wife? Isobel? A Balliol? Rage, hot and hard, pounded through Wolf. "Damn you." He clenched his jaw against the vile words he longed to say. "My marriage to Isobel," he bit out. His father had used him for his own benefit and advancement again. A Balliol? Impossible. Or was it? What had she tried to tell him before he'd left?

The king shrugged. "It was necessary to bring me the other half of the Stone."

"Yet you thought nothing of me—or of Isobel—in your scheming."

The king's eyes narrowed. "You needed a wife. I gave you one. That the two houses of Scotland are united again seemed more important than your feelings on the subject."

Wolf crossed his arms over his chest. "Now the truth comes out."

"I did what I had to do."

"Why do you really want the Stone?" Wolf asked fiercely, concentrating his anger on the Stone instead of the deeper issue of exactly who he had married. He would think on that later.

A look of surprise crossed the king's face. "Because Grange wants it. He will use the Stone and its power against me."

"So you fight your fear by creating more fear. Is that right?"

The king's face hardened, as it always did when Wolf had pushed too far. "You know naught of what it is like to rule a country."

"Perhaps not. But I do know what it is like to have the respect and support of my men not through fear, only trust."

The king met Wolf's gaze with eyes as clear and cold as polished stone. "Then I *trust* you'll have no objection to using that connection with your men to run Grange through."

"You might have succeeded in bringing me here, but that does not mean you have my cooperation," Wolf replied.

"I'll have your cooperation, boy. Because if I don't, it will be your beautiful new bride who will pay for your foolhardiness."

Wolf tensed. "Isobel is safe within my castle. You cannot touch her there. You'll have to try another tack, Auld Blearie."

The king's face turned crimson at the mention of the much-despised name. "Safety is at best an illusion. Even now, as we speak, your bride is at risk."

Wolf's gut tightened. "You wouldn't—"

"I'll have your cooperation and that of your men in order to defeat my enemy."

"Who is it?" Wolf demanded with venomous force. "Who did you plant to deceive me?"

"That matters not."

"Who is it?" Wolf's hand snapped out. He grasped the king beneath the chin. The old man's clear eyes became suddenly watery beneath Wolf's assault.

"Release . . . me!"

Artemis surged forward, but Wolf stalled him with a look as sharp as his own blade. "Another step and he dies," Wolf threatened.

Artemis froze.

"Who deceived me?"

A cold and calculating look settled over the king's face. "You won't . . . hurt me. Or you would have . . . years ago."

Wolf clenched his jaw and considered tightening his grip on his father's throat. He had more than enough reasons to justify killing the man right here and now. Yet his fingers refused to cooperate, so he shook the man instead. "Tell me who has betrayed me. Or I might be forced to prove you wrong."

"Your . . . brother . . . Walter," the king choked out.

A terrible sense of disbelief and betrayal stole his anger, and Wolf snapped back his hand. "Walter would do no such thing. Not against me."

The king grasped his throat and coughed as he struggled to regain his breath. "He had as much of a choice . . . as you have now."

He had a choice. By God, he would not be his father's

vehicle any longer. "I was ready to go to war against Grange because I thought you were in danger. But now things have changed—I've changed. As much as I hate Grange, I will not make war against him simply because you will it."

"Aye." His father's mouth turned up in an angry grin, like a snake smiling. "You'll do that and more, because if you don't your bride will die."

"Not even you could be that cruel."

The king's smile broadened. "You've grown fond of the girl despite her lineage. Despite the darker secrets you have yet to learn."

A chill pulsed through him. What did his father mean? What darker secrets? Wolf pushed the thought away. It was only more manipulation. He should know better than to buy in to that type of ploy where his father was concerned. "You've no right to toy with Isobel's life as you've always toyed with mine."

"I'm the king. I can toy with her any way I like, but her health and welfare now depend on you." The king leaned in toward Wolf's face, relying heavily upon his cane for support. He snatched Brahan's Stone from Wolf's hands. "Which is it to be, *my son*—a war or a murder? You choose."

There was no choice. He would never allow his father to ruin Isobel's life. Not if he could stop the man. Fury welled up inside Wolf. Damn his father. "We will fight."

His father smiled. "A wise choice." With a wave of his hand, the guards came forward and placed black iron clamps on Wolf's wrists. "To ensure your further cooperation."

Wolf stiffened as the weight of the manacles tugged at the flesh of his wrists. "I want Brahan returned to me."

The king nodded at Artemis, who withdrew from the

tent with a bow. "We will attack at first light. With any luck, the storm will pass during the night."

Wolf turned his heated gaze on his father. The storm outside might dissipate over the next few hours, but the storm inside him would never recede. His father had pushed him too far this time for him to ever be quieted again.

Chapter Twenty-five

Wolf sat astride his horse at the head of his army, where all his men could see him. Behind him were Brahan and his personal guard—men whose hearts and loyalties he knew as well as his own, men he trusted above all others.

Behind them, in a line two abreast and stretching back thirty fold, was his army. His army, his men—men he had given a home to and trained. Men who were beaten down before they'd joined him. Men who were whole once more because of the second chance he'd offered.

His men cheered for him as he rode down their ranks, waving their swords, their shields, and their lances high into the air. The first light of dawn glinted off the long, sleek blades and polished steel. They were, every one of them, proud to be his men.

And he, in turn, was proud of them. They were good men, loyal men, men who did not deserve to die for the sake of his father's bitter revenge against Grange. But if he did not lead them to battle, Isobel would die.

His father's troops filed in behind Wolf's men, creating a wall of soldiers, some on horseback, others on foot, all armed and eager for the battle to begin. They positioned themselves atop a ridge. Below them, nestled in the valley, was Grange's camp. Smoke rising from the encampment gave evidence that the area was occupied, yet not a soul could be seen anywhere among the tents or near the watch fires.

That fact set Wolf's senses on edge. He'd tried to communicate his unease to Artemis, without success. Artemis wanted no interference. He'd made that point perfectly obvious when he'd released Wolf from his prison of iron this morn.

The horse beneath Wolf pranced and capered, sensing the tension of its rider. He laid a hand on the beast's neck to quiet it. So it sensed something was not quite right as well. Why didn't his father?

The man in question rode down the line of men, not evoking the same response from his troops that Wolf had garnered from his men. They treated the king with respect but nothing more. They awaited his orders to march on the encampment below with a weary patience and not with the thirst for triumph that was necessary in order to win the day.

Unease prickled the back of Wolf's neck. These men were not prepared to fight. To engage the enemy now would not result in a battle but a massacre.

Wolf shifted his gaze to his own men. They sat at attention, their bodies alert, waiting to react to his most subtle signal. He searched their faces. As he did, he felt the hand of destiny tighten around him. These men would willingly give their lives for him. But would he ask that of them all for the sake of one woman? A Balliol?

Isobel would die if they did not fight. Walter had orders to kill her. Or would he? Had their years apart changed them both so radically?

His chest tightened at the thought. Why hadn't his brother trusted him enough to tell him of their father's latest machinations? What could he possibly be threatening Walter with to make him turn against his own brother?

They'd both been manipulated. And now, with hindsight, Wolf recognized the signs. Walter's odd behavior and his immediate disapproval of Isobel now made sense. Their father had set up this whole elaborate plan prior to Walter's imprisonment. Isobel could only be saved if Walter disobeyed a king's command. Could his brother do it? Wolf clenched his hands into fists. He honestly did not know what Walter was capable of anymore—but he had to trust that Walter's loyalty to him would sway his actions over his father's command. Wolf grasped that hope like a lifeline in a stormy sea.

Wolf turned his attention back to the situation before him. How to evade a battle that was doomed to fail? If they fought, his men would die. Wolf unfurled his fists and stroked his horse's neck once more, this time quieting his own restlessness.

He would not endanger his men for no reason. And if he refused to fight? Would his father's troops turn on his own men? Would death await them either way? He slid his gaze to Brahan's and recognized at once the slight lift of his brow, the question in his gaze as he awaited a signal.

Wolf shook his head ever so slightly. Brahan instantly understood. Silently, through a series of speaking glances and imperceptible movements, the communiqué rippled down the line of men. Each understood, and with a hand on his sword awaited whatever orders came next.

The decision made, Wolf could feel the strength of his convictions flowing in his veins. His father's horse approached, and Wolf prepared himself for the worst.

"What have your scouts reported back to you about the encampment below?" Wolf asked.

The king brought his horse to a halt beside him. "I need no scouts to tell me it is Grange's men down there."

"Does it not seem odd to you that no one is about?"

"His men sleep late," the king's voice turned hard.

"Or they lie in wait to trap you where there is no way to retreat."

The king frowned. "This is my battle, and I have the advantage."

"Perhaps he's turned that advantage on you the same way you turned it on me. Will you take that risk with your men? I, for one, will not."

The king's face flushed red, and he maneuvered his horse closer. "You will fight because I say you will."

Wolf held his ground. "My men and I decline."

The king's face turned crimson. "Isobel will die."

At the king's declaration, a question burned on Wolf's tongue. "Why have me marry the girl only to kill her?"

"The girl's a pawn," the king replied with a snap. "*My* pawn, and one that I used to get you to do what I wanted."

"How dare you play with Isobel's life like that—like it has no worth, no value."

"I dare what I must. Now do as I ask."

Instead of the usual anger at his father, pity rushed forward, as did a sudden dawning realization. "I always assumed it was *I* who was the beast in our dealings together." He shook his head. "What a fool I was. How arrogant. You were the beast all along."

The king's face faded to white. His mouth worked as though trying to form words, yet no sound issued forth. But a moment later he appeared to regain his composure, and a spark lit his eyes once more. "Beast or not, it changes nothing. You will do what I say or Isobel will die."

Wolf's insides twisted into a painful knot. "Nay." He paused, taking a deep, fortifying breath. "I trust that Walter will follow his loyalties and not your command."

The king's gaze drilled Wolf. "You would risk treason and death to defy me?"

Wolf met his father's gaze with a firm resolve of his own. He would be manipulated no more. "Aye."

The king continued to watch him. The intensity seemed to fade from his father's eyes, to be replaced by something that might well have been admiration. "So, I am to believe you would rather risk all than fight for me?"

"I would risk my own death, Isobel's life, and the lives of my men to have freedom of choice."

"What greater deed could there be than to fight for your king?"

"To fight for the good of my country," Wolf said firmly.

"Are you a Scot or a Stewart?"

"I was both for a while."

"And now?"

"Don't make me choose between my country and my name."

His father's scowl returned. "That is a Stewart tartan you wear." His gaze moved past Wolf and down the line of his men. "Your men wear the Stewart tartan as well."

Wolf reached up and with a jerk of his hand unhooked the metal pin securing his tartan at his shoulder. With another jerk, he pulled the fabric free from his body and tossed the yards of tartan cloth in a heap on the ground. As it fell, he met his father's gaze squarely, a stare at long last fully unfettered.

The flurry of dozens of tartans sliding to the ground filled the air, and Wolf looked up to see every one of his men had also unbound themselves from the king until each man sat atop his horse wearing nothing but a long saffron shirt to cover his chest and thighs.

"Your tartans are returned to you, Your Grace." The chill morning air brushed against Wolf's flesh, but he did not feel the cold. Instead, a euphoric heat swirled in his veins at his newfound freedom. "My men and I will now take our leave."

"How do you expect to leave here unharmed? My men have you surrounded," his father asked in a low, silky voice.

"We ride." Wolf shifted his gaze to his men. They watched him alertly. With a slight jerk of his head, he signaled them to fall out. Turning their horses in unison, they moved forward into the line of the king's men. Without orders to stop them, the men moved aside, creating a path for them to pass through.

"If you leave me now, I will take back all that I have given you." The king's voice rang out over the shuffle of the horse's hooves upon the damp ground.

Wolf signaled his men to continue as he stopped and turned his horse about. "And what have you given me, Father? Apart from my own birth, you gave a bride you threatened to kill." Wolf marveled at how easy it was to talk about the thing that had always brought great pain to him before. It didn't matter any more—the bitterness of his childhood, the neglect, the manipulation he had endured all his adult life. Nothing mattered except freedom from further abuse.

"I gave you my name," the king said with contempt. "For a bastard son you could have done worse."

Wolf let the words that used to hurt him roll off his back. "It was a gift I never wanted and freely return." He turned his horse around to follow his men.

"Wait," the king commanded.

Despite his desire to keep going, Wolf stopped.

The king brought his horse close, so close his leg brushed up against Wolf's. For a moment, the king hunched over in his saddle as though he were suddenly too old and frail to continue.

On instinct, Wolf reached out to steady him.

The king nodded his thanks. "Retreat with your men, but be forewarned, when this battle is through, I will come after you. Of that you can be certain."

"I'll be waiting." Wolf urged his horse forward. And as he rode through the column created by the king's men, he felt something that hadn't been there before lodged inside his boot. He reached inside, and locating the irritation, drew it out.

The Stewart half of the Seer's Stone lay against the palm of his hand. His father must have slipped it in his boot when he had slumped down in his saddle. He had placed it there for a reason. What did it mean?

Was it some sort of treaty between them, or fuel for a future fire? Wolf slipped it back inside his boot with a mixture of irritation and resignation. No doubt his father would reveal the reason when it best suited him.

Eager to leave all thoughts of his father behind, he spurred his horse to a gallop until he took the lead of his men and hastened toward the mountainous path that would take them home.

"You are in a hurry to return," Brahan said as they reined their horses in at the base of the pass, allowing the tired animals a chance to regroup in front of the steep and narrow path.

Wolf scowled at the path before him. "It looks like our haste ends here." Last night's storm had left the passage wet and slippery. Regardless of his desire for speed, travel over the pass would be a slow and treacherous climb. "Going around the mountain will take us twice as long." The path before them was the only way across for a day's journey in either direction. "Tell the men that when the horses are rested we will take the pathway slow and easy. We can't risk injuring the horses."

"What if I told you there was yet another choice?"

Wolf narrowed his gaze on his friend. "You know another way across the mountain?"

Brahan nodded. "As a child, these woods and hills were my home. I heard stories from others about a passage through the mountain that only the goats were daft enough to use, and only when the path before us was as slick and deadly as the devil's own back."

Wolf watched as his men exchanged worried glances. The hills around them were steeped in superstition. He'd heard the rumors about the passage they were attempting to cross, saying the Creator had fashioned this mountainous range, with its sheer drops and deathly slopes, on a day He'd been in a horrible rage.

He'd heard rumors about the passage through the mountain as well—that only madmen traveled through the "Devil's Maw."

"Do you know where this passage is?" Wolf asked.

"Aye." Brahan nodded.

Wolf's gaze moved over his men once more, trying to gauge whether they were willing to take this additional risk. They all sat tall on their horses with no fear on their faces, communicating their agreement to follow wherever he led. "Then lead on."

The passage Brahan brought them to was not much more than a crevice slashed between two gnarled stone columns of overlapping rock that rose at least forty feet above them. The entrance was covered with brambles and thorn bushes so that it appeared no more than a gap in the mountainside that disappeared into the sheer cliffs below. It took the men several minutes to hack their way through the undergrowth to the opening.

The chasm was just wide enough to accommodate the breadth of a horse's flanks. The horses balked at entering the darkness, their nostrils dilating, their flanks quivering with undisguised fear.

"We need torches," Wolf said as he smoothed the gleaming neck of his own horse, trying to quiet it. He understood the animal's terror. He, too, had to fight back a strong revulsion at entering the black maw. But the entrance was all that stood between him and Isobel, and this was a chance he was willing to take.

He accepted a torch from one of his men and kicked his horse forward into the narrow passage. Torchlight illuminated the slime-covered rock ahead, and the air immediately thickened with smoke. Wolf could feel his eyes start to burn and tear until he passed the narrow entrance and the ceiling lifted, allowing a draft to suck the flames upward.

The horse beneath him quaked. Wolf urged the animal on into the dark void, illuminating the passage ahead with the golden glow of his torch as the others followed behind. Several times he felt the sides of his legs scrape against the walls of stone, but he kept pushing forward. Far better for his legs to suffer this abuse than his horse's flanks. As long as the beast did not fear getting stuck, they would make it through. Every step took him that much closer to Isobel. Balliol or not, she was his wife.

A hundred yards . . . The air grew heavy and the cloying scent of decay surrounded them as they moved deeper into the bowels of the mountain. Torchlight cast an eerie glow on the dark rock, making the fissures and outcroppings appear almost human one moment, gruesome and beastlike the next. A deathly silence fell over the men, and Wolf knew he must not have been alone in his imaginings. Only the shuffle of the petrified animals across the slick stone could be heard.

Two hundred yards . . . The tension in Wolf's shoulders and neck screamed for release. Pressure built in his chest. Time seemed to stretch forever before him— the darkness muting all senses to anything other than the stinging pain of his exposed skin, which felt as though it was being sliced into bloody strips.

Three hundred yards . . . four hundred . . . five. He stopped counting after a while, falling instead into the rhythm of his heart beating in his own ears. He strained to see in the darkness ahead of the torch's glow. When a spot of white appeared in the distance, he reasoned it must be his own fatigue playing tricks on his mind. Until the splash of white grew as they drew near, and the sky spilled color into the dark void of nothingness.

He paused between the darkness and the light. How would they know there was no trap set for them on the other side? An enemy could easily strike them down as they emerged from the maw.

"Wait here, and keep yourselves hidden," he ordered his men. "I want to make certain it is safe. If I do not return shortly, then do not expose yourselves."

Brahan frowned. "I should go."

Wolf set his jaw. "Protect the men. I shall return."

Before Brahan could argue the point, Wolf spurred his horse forward. As he passed through the mountainside and into the light, Wolf gave in to his urge to draw a deep, heather-scented breath of fresh air. Yet the relief he expected to feel escaped him. Instead, the sensation that something else hovered just out of reach stretched his nerves taut.

Methodically, he searched the outlying areas for danger. When he was certain the area was clear, he went back for his men. One by one they appeared through the passageway. Weariness and relief shadowed their faces and beads of perspiration hung upon their brows. Rivulets of blood ran down their legs as they did his own, proof that the mountain had not been kind to their exposed flesh. All eyes turned to Wolf, awaiting his orders.

No matter what his senses told him, his eyes gave evidence that his men needed a break. "We will rest a moment before we continue on." Wolf dismounted and encouraged his men to do the same.

The afternoon sun stretched high overhead, chasing away the last of the morning mist. Evidence that the storm had passed during the night. And still, he could not shake the sensation that something else was wrong. He tensed, his senses on alert, like a beast catching scent on the wind. What was it he sensed but could not identify?

After hobbling the horses in a grassy area where they could graze, Brahan came to join Wolf. "The men are grateful for the respite."

"The pass cut off half day's journey. They deserve it."

Brahan wiped the sweat from his brow with the back of his hand as he studied Wolf's face. "What's wrong?"

Wolf kept his eyes trained on the forest beyond. "I don't know exactly, but my senses tell me it's something dangerous and deadly."

Brahan's frown deepened. "I thought I was the visionary here."

Again, the eerie sensation crawled along the back of Wolf's neck, feeling like a deadly spider unleashed from its web. "It has to be Isobel."

"What makes you so certain?"

Wolf clenched his fists at his sides. "I am not certain of anything anymore except that Isobel needs me."

Brahan nodded. "I'll gather the men, and we will ride out." He turned away, but Wolf stalled him with a hand on his arm.

"Nay." Wolf shook his head. "Let them rest. I'll go alone."

Brahan's brow rose in question. "Is that wise?"

"Nay," Wolf said without guile. "But something in my gut tells me to leave, now."

"All right," Brahan agreed. "The men and I will follow as soon as we're able."

With each beat of his heart, the sensation of impending doom intensified until Wolf's nerves were stretched so tight, he wanted to lash out against the pain. "Until then," he called over his shoulder as he raced for his horse. He leapt onto the animal's back and pressed his heels to its sides. The animal sensed the urgency within its master and plunged through the meadow and into the forest.

Isobel.

Chapter Twenty-six

Walter knelt on the cold stone floor of the chapel and set his crossbow in front of him. For a long moment he merely knelt there, his hands clasped, staring blindly into the prisms of multicolored light that bathed the altar in hues of blue and green and red.

He had come here not for himself, but for his brother. He knew his brother much better than most, and he knew that the girl he must now kill had crept into the recesses of Wolf's much-protected heart.

His brother would never forgive such a betrayal.

Walter squeezed his eyes closed, twisting his hands together until pain radiated up his arms. Desperation and anger and fear all coiled together. So much pain, so much deception, so much blood would spill, and for what end?

Defying his father's orders would only bring certain death—his own. Yet obeying them would bring death as well. "I walk along the blade of a sword," he whispered into the soft silence. He bowed his head, sliding out of desperation and into prayer. He attempted to think of the words, trying without success to make his jaw move properly. It all made so little sense, to destroy a life only to gain another's obedience. Would the control their father held over them ever end?

"Help . . . me," Walter finally mouthed the words. He hoped the simple words would do, be heard, and a response sent.

He brought his hands up to cover his face, to physically hold back the eruption of emotion that threatened.

He needed a solution. He asked for help. He waited for a sign.

Isobel stood in the center of the dreary and desolate outer bailey, allowing her eyes to adjust to the heavy gloom of the late afternoon. Storm clouds gathered overhead again, as they had since Wolf left two days earlier. She lifted one shoulder in an attempt to adjust the heavy mail biting through her linen shift and into her flesh. She had put on the garment underneath her clothing as she had seen Wolf do. She wanted the protection to go unnoticed beneath her fine gown.

From deep inside she summoned the courage to see her ruse through. Isobel closed her eyes, and instead of focusing on what was to come, she allowed herself an indulgence in the here and now. She drew in the sweet scent of rain, of the damp earth, of the gorse and heather and granite hills beyond. Different smells than those on the isle she used to call home. Yet these scents crept deep inside. The newly discovered scents of home.

Her eyes snapped open. Someone threatened her home and the people she loved. She tightened her fingers around the crossbow in her hands, wishing she was twining her fingers with Wolf's instead.

She loved him. The realization tumbled through her at the same moment that another rumble of thunder shook the ground beneath her feet. The wind picked up and a chill crept across the bailey. Yet a warm, liquid, honeyed heat spread beneath her skin, warding off the cold.

She would do anything to keep what she had—a husband, a family, kin. And to make certain nothing else stood in her way, she needed to be honest with all of them. She had to tell Wolf and the others who she was. Even if that meant losing everything, she would tell him the truth the moment she saw him again.

If she ever saw him again.

Isobel forced the thought away as she moved through the bailey until she stood fifty paces from the open gate. She had to be strong—now more than ever. Whether the threat came from inside or outside the castle, this position would give her equal opportunity to defend herself while revealing who threatened her newfound kin.

Isobel drew her shoulders back, waiting. She had sent everyone else into the keep and made them vow to lock and brace the doors. Over their objections, she had persisted until they'd had no choice but to agree, securing their safety. She could place herself in harm's way, knowing that her kin were safe in Wolf's stronghold.

Her gaze fastened on the open gate. What would she do, how would she react when she saw her father face to face for the first time? Would she even recognize him?

A flash of lightning made her start. She gripped the crossbow in her hands, using it to center her nerves. Whether she recognized his face or not, she would recognize other aspects of him—his cruelty, his temper, his deviousness. Her mother had warned her often of those qualities.

Another rumble of thunder filled the bailey, sounding far away and right on top of her all at once. Again, a moment of unease worked its way into her thoughts. Nature's sounds would cover all noise. There would be no way to hear her opponent's approach.

Great black clouds choked the sky overhead, smothering what remained of the daylight, pitching the bailey in semidarkness. She should have brought a torch or a lantern, she realized too late.

Before her eyes could adjust to the dim light, she felt another's presence. To her right, something shifted in the grayness. Before she had a chance to respond, a tall, shadowy figure appeared not twenty paces from her.

On instinct, she brought the crossbow up to her chest. She had no time to measure the distance or aim with any skill. She released the bolt and hoped it would find its target.

And just as the bolt took flight, so did she. A force came at her from the right, knocking her off her feet. Her crossbow flew from her grasp as she hit the ground, hard. Pain reverberated up and down her side as the chain mail she wore dug into her flesh. A sea of yellow cloth covered her face as she struggled to fill her lungs, fighting a wave of dizziness.

A grunt of pain sounded off to her left. A sound that had not come from herself. Had her weapon found its target? She had to find out who it was. She tried to move, tried to crawl out from under the fabric that blinded her and the heaviness that trapped her against the ground, but she could not. Her lungs burned at the effort. She drew in one painful breath, then another.

As the dizziness receded from her brain, she realized the heaviness on her right side was not of her own making. Hesitantly, she reached out. Her hand connected with warm flesh. Isobel gasped, not expecting that.

"Quiet," a feminine voice hissed close to Isobel's ear. "Make a sound or move and you die."

The grunting off in the distance became a groan, then a low, unearthly howl that caused the hairs on the back of Isobel's neck to tingle. She lay still despite the pressure on her side that forced her elbow painfully into the rocky ground.

"I cannot do it!" a male voice cried out, and a single set of footsteps retreated from where she lay, heading back toward the keep. One of the villains was escaping; the other held her trapped. Isobel refused to acknowledge the tightness in her chest. Instead she gathered her strength and with a lunge, forced off the obstruction that held her down.

She scrambled to her feet, searching the ground for her crossbow. The grayness overhead plunged the bailey in shadow, making it difficult to see anything other than a second gray shape that also rose to its feet.

"I am no threat, you stupid girl. I've come to save your life. But even that will be impossible if you don't follow me."

"Fiona?"

"I am here to help."

Thunder rumbled all around them, charging the air with tension. "Why should I trust you?"

A flash of pale blue-gray light filled the sky and Isobel saw Fiona clearly, her face filled with remorse. "I've given you no reason to trust me. But I'm asking you to do it, nonetheless."

Isobel regarded her critically. "Who attacked me? You?"

"I suspect it was Walter."

"Walter? Why?"

Fiona shook her head. "I don't know. But I do know you are still in danger. There's no time to waste."

A low rumble of thunder sounded again, a slowly building sound, growing deeper, richer, more intense.

Isobel remained where she stood. "Did you kill the kitchen maid?"

"We don't have time for this." A flash of panic crossed Fiona's face. "Do you hear them now?"

Again, a rumble came from the distance, growing louder. "What?"

"The horses. His men are coming and they are coming for you."

Hoofbeats thundered just outside the castle gates. The gates she'd left open to invite her enemy inside. Her heartbeat thudded dully in Isobel's ears as she scanned the bailey searching for her weapon.

"Your crossbow will not help you this time, not against all those men."

Isobel knew Fiona was right. She had prepared herself to face one opponent, not many.

A flash of lightning cut through the darkness, followed immediately by the roll of thunder, drowning out the frightened cries of the animals and the shouts of the attackers. Approaching the gate, Isobel could see the shadows of men on horseback. They appeared like mystical creatures emerging from a void of nothingness.

"Lead on," Isobel replied. Her chances of escaping Fiona were far greater than escaping a dozen or more men.

Fiona turned and raced through the shadows to the southeast tower. Isobel followed. Once inside the circular stone building, Fiona shut and bolted the door before heading up the spiraling stone staircase. "This way."

A sense of impending danger made Isobel pause. She pressed her palm against the doorway, feeling the pulse of the thundering hoofbeats just beyond. Were they friend or foe? It was hard to tell one from the other anymore.

"Hurry," Fiona urged. A look of concern brought her finely etched brows together.

Isobel hitched up the hem of her gown and ran up the stairs. In the tower room above, Fiona retrieved a length of thick rope from near the arrow slits. "We will have to lower ourselves down over the curtain wall. It won't take them long to figure out you are not here. We must move quickly."

Again, a niggling sense of doubt plagued Isobel. "Who, Fiona? It won't take who long?"

"The men who want to kill you." She turned her back to Isobel, wrestling with the rope, trying to shift it to the doorway leading out to the wall walk. "Help me lift this rope."

Isobel remained where she stood. "I need answers before I go any farther."

Fiona's gaze moved to the stairwell. "That door will not hold them off for long once they discover you are missing. They will search everywhere."

"I'm willing to take that chance. Are you?"

Fiona released an irritated growl. "They are a group of mercenaries who know who you really are and want to make certain that you never have a chance to make a claim for the throne of Scotland. They were sent by the king to finish the job if Walter was unwilling or unable to kill you."

A cold chill crept down Isobel's spine. Fiona and now others knew the truth of her birth. How?

"The man who was your mother's caretaker revealed

your secret," Fiona explained, as if she'd read Isobel's thoughts.

The air in the tower room suddenly stilled. A tightness clenched Isobel's chest, spreading across her ribs. She tried to draw in a breath, but her lungs refused to cooperate. Darkness narrowed her view of the room. Fear gripped her, twisted inside her. On sheer will alone, she staggered to the arrow slits. Forcing her panic aside, she drew in a shuddering breath. She had to remain calm. She had to maintain reason.

Isobel clenched her right wrist with her left hand and massaged the abused flesh there, reminding herself that she was no longer a prisoner, would never be again, as long as she had strength and reason on her side. "I . . . I pose no threat to anyone."

Fiona's bitter laugh hung in the tension-filled air. "How could you possibly say that? You are a Balliol, married to a Stewart."

A stab of numbness returned. "What did you say?"

Fiona's gaze became hard. "You married a Stewart. The favored bastard son of our current king."

A whisper-soft silence hovered in the air as Isobel grappled with Fiona's words. The king's son. And suddenly it all made sense. Wolf's odd behavior in his secret lair, when she'd said there were secrets between them. She'd meant her own, but had he misinterpreted her words? Did his own guilt weigh as heavy on him as hers did on her?

And what about her secrets? Did he know who she was already? Or did that secret still hang between them, waiting to be revealed?

Isobel brought her gaze back to Fiona. "How do you know who I am?"

The hardness in Fiona's gaze vanished, and her

shoulders slumped. "I have done some terrible things in my life. Things I am not proud of. For years now, I have worked the three men in my life to my own advantage."

"Three men?" Isobel asked, uncertain of what any of this information had to do with her or her past.

Fiona's gaze shifted between the stairwell and the rope in her hands. "I will explain everything later. We must hurry."

Isobel folded her hands over her chest. "Explain now, Fiona, or I will go nowhere with you."

Fiona released a heavy sigh. "I have played Wolf against his father and Lord Grange for years."

"Lord Grange?" Isobel brought her fingers to her lips, trying to hold back the flood of emotion that threatened. "Why would you do that?"

Fiona shrugged. "I was protecting myself. I needed money. The reasons seemed good at the time." She turned away. "It doesn't matter now."

Isobel grabbed Fiona's arm. "How did you figure out who I really am?"

"I overhead Eldon MacDonald reveal your birth to Grange."

"And the king? How did he find out?"

"I sold him the information."

"Does Wolf know who I am?"

Fiona shook her head. "Nay. Wolf knows nothing of your parentage."

Relief washed over Isobel with such force that tears came to her eyes. "So it is my father who's trying to kill me and Wolf."

Fiona shook her head. "Your father wants you alive. Through you he intends to steal the throne from the Stewarts."

A numbness drifted through Isobel, weighing her

down, making it hard to focus her thoughts. "My father has been trying to kill Wolf, while his father has been trying to kill me." Their fathers had doomed them to disaster. As had the secrets they both withheld.

What about those secrets? Did she care who he had been born to, or what his surname was? Did it, in any way, change the man she had come to know and care about?

Nay. A warm flush of hope rose in her cheeks. Would he feel the same when she told him about her own father? Could there be hope for the future yet? Isobel squared her shoulders and moved to where the rope lay waiting. She would do whatever she had to do to see that they got the chance to at least try. Even if that meant going along with Fiona now. "Let's go."

Together, she and Fiona carried the rope to the wall walk. Isobel tied one end of the rope around the closest stone crenellation. "You go first," she said to Fiona once the knot had been tightly secured.

Fiona didn't argue. She grasped the rope and lowered herself over the wall. Isobel watched her descend. Knowing she could move faster without the heavy mail shirt obstructing her movements, Isobel drew the shirt off, then tossed it aside. As soon as Fiona's feet touched the ground, Isobel pulled herself up onto the edge of the castle wall. With her heartbeat thundering in her chest, she grasped the coarse rope between her hands and allowed her body to slide down the cool stone wall, not stopping for a moment to think about what she was doing or what might happen to them if they were caught.

When her booted toes touched the solid ground, she breathed a thankful sigh but did not give herself time to celebrate their success. The shelter of the trees was still far off in the distance. They would have to race across the open ground and pray that no one noticed their shadows fleeing over the wide-open space.

A twinge of fear threatened, but Isobel pushed it away. They had to keep going. "To the trees." She gathered the folds of her skirt in her hands and dashed across the open land.

In that moment, the clouds parted and the sun appeared, ripe and glistening above the trees, bathing the open ground and the forest beyond it in rays of yellow-gold light. The branches of the trees were etched against the grayness in an eerie relief, making the trees appear like the bones of ancient skeletons. Isobel's steps faltered. Were these ancient and gnarled works of nature guarding against trespassers, or would they protect two women fleeing death?

"Hurry!" Fiona called over her shoulder as she plunged into the edge of the tree line.

Isobel surged forward into the trees and kept running, stumbling over a fallen branch here, an exposed root there, until her eyes adjusted to the hazy darkness. The forest smelled of earth and decaying leaves, and the scent of rain hung in the air. Her breath came in short, sharp bursts as she continued to run.

Ahead, Fiona paused, hunched over, her hands on her knees, her breathing ragged. "Must . . . rest . . . a minute."

Flushed and fighting for breath, Isobel stopped as well, grateful for the slight reprieve. They were not out of danger yet and could little afford the precious seconds it would take to regain their breath. "We must . . . continue."

A shadow detached itself from the base of a nearby tree. "You've gone far enough for my purposes." The unfamiliar male voice had a deep, rich tone and was sinister enough to make Isobel shrink back into the shadows.

She heard a coarse chuckle as he moved forward. "Thank you, Lady Fiona. I could not have planned this better myself."

Fiona straightened. Her face was pale, her skin almost translucent where it stretched over her cheekbones. Fear glittered in her eyes as her gaze shifted between the man and Isobel. "I'll not hand her over to you."

"That wasn't part of our plan." The man's voice grew hard.

"Plans change," Fiona challenged.

Overhead, the afternoon sky yawned and errant rays of sunlight filtered down through the trees above, casting the world in a yellow glow once more. The man turned toward Isobel. At the first glimpse of his face, of his dark, penetrating eyes, her breath became trapped somewhere between her throat and her lungs. There was no mistaking those eyes, for she had seen a much gentler version in the reflection of her own face.

A brisk wind whistled through the forest, tugging at Isobel's unbound hair. Dread iced her skin as she stared at the one man she feared more than any other. Her father.

"Lord Grange," Isobel whispered into the cool afternoon air, not realizing she'd spoken his name aloud.

A slight curl came to his lips. "How quaint that a daughter should recognize her own father before they are even so much as introduced."

She knew him, all right—she knew his villainy, his deviousness, his treachery. She'd seen firsthand how he had destroyed her mother, what he'd done to Wolf in the forest, and how he'd used and abused his own men. But it didn't stop there. The reality of the situation hit Isobel like a cold, hard slap. She shifted her gaze to Fiona. "This was all a trap?"

"I didn't know," she cried, her voice filled with both contrition and fear. "I was trying to help you escape."

"Why, Fiona? Why would *you* want to help *me*? I still don't understand."

"Jealousy drove me to murder." Bitter, haunted pain in Fiona's eyes brought a catch to Isobel's throat. "How can I live with that? How can I live with the knowledge that I am a despicable person?" Fiona staggered forward. "Helping you meant there might be some hope for me. I want to change. You have to believe me."

Isobel didn't know what to believe anymore as her gaze moved between Fiona and her father.

Cynicism twisted Grange's expression. "Payments for services rendered is what you always got, Fiona. Your morals were never part of the bargain. Now step back. She's mine."

Like a deadly spider, her father skulked toward her.

"Stay back," Isobel warned. "Stay away from me."

"Or you'll do what? Scream?" He continued his slow crawl toward her. "Scream all you want. You are too far away for anyone to hear you."

In a flash, Isobel bent to the forest floor and came up with a large, pointed stick, a branch that had been left behind by a previous storm. "Stay where you are."

Grange paused, a dark look of displeasure cutting across his face. "You don't stand a chance against me."

"What do you plan to do with us?"

"That, my dear, depends entirely upon whether or not we can come to some kind of agreement."

"What kind of agreement?"

"I want something from you." His dark eyes narrowed. "You give it to me and then we will discuss the rest."

"I have nothing of importance." What kind of game was he playing at now?

"There you are wrong." He stretched out his hand, long and dark and as threatening as the rest of him. "Give me your half of the Seer's Stone."

"I have no such thing."

"Aye." His bottomless black eyes became darker. "You do." In his other hand, he held up a small white stone bound in a clasp and strung from a leather cord. It was the necklace her mother had given her so many years ago. "You recognize this?"

Her hands inched up toward her chest where the necklace used to reside. "How did you get that?"

His gaze shot to Fiona. "Fiona has been a useful spy and thief." He returned his gaze to Isobel. "Now I want the other half. I'm sure once I have you, your husband will give it to me."

"Why would you need both?" she stalled. She had to think of some way to escape. She would never allow him to use her as bait to trap her husband.

"I want the Stones reunited. Only then will the house of Balliol rule Scotland once more."

"You are not a Balliol." She tightened trembling fingers around the stick.

A terrifying grin pulled at the corner of his mouth. "But I married one, which gives me certain rights and privileges. If I possess both halves of the Stone, I can control events that will guarantee my succession to the throne. Now, come here."

The stick stood as the only barrier between them— one pointed stick between reason and the insane. Her mother had always claimed he was mad. Isobel had always hoped that assessment was more a fabrication of her mother's own insanity, but she saw clearly now it was not.

As he crept closer, a flash of steel glittered from beneath the folds of his tunic. Isobel stared into his bottomless dark eyes. No reason reflected there, only a twisted obsession haunted his gaze.

He lunged forward, sending the knife slashing toward Isobel's face. She brought up the stick to block his arm, then spun to the side, narrowly escaping the attack. He turned and came at her again, but this time Fiona launched herself at him. A howl of displeasure echoed in the trees as he flung up his arms to protect his face from the threat of clawing nails. Instead of deflecting the attack, as Isobel expected, his fist slammed into Fiona's temple. The blow snapped her head to one side with enough force to send her sprawling backward onto the ground.

She lay silent against the dark earth.

He crept closer, his knife extended, searching for an opening to strike. If she were going to do it, it must be done now. Her grasp tightened on her stick and she drew a shaky breath. An instant later her feet flew over the thickly padded forest floor. She avoided fallen trees and overgrown roots that grasped at her ankles and shredded the hem of her gown as she raced past.

Slashes of sunlight filtered through the branches above, guiding her way. Even so, footsteps pounded behind her, growing closer with each frantic beat of her heart. Isobel prayed for more speed. Fear scalded the back of her throat, and the wind brought tears to her eyes.

She had to outrun him. The land dipped and twisted as she surged forward, tearing through the dense ferns and saplings and scattering any number of sleeping creatures from beneath the dense underbrush. She headed northward. There was a path there; Wolf had shown it to her the other day.

No matter what direction she tried, angry footsteps echoed behind her, gaining speed. Her feet plunged into the brook, sending a spray of water up her legs and weighing down the hem of her skirt. Isobel tossed her stick aside and grasped handfuls of heavy, water-soaked fabric, determined to pick up her speed despite the slippery creek bed.

She leapt up the small embankment, anticipating the secure feel of solid ground beneath her feet, only to find herself jerked backward cruelly, into her father's chest.

She twisted in his arms, trying to break free. Her hair obscured her vision, but she could imagine his dark features leering down at her. "Let me go."

His only response was a low, chilling laugh.

Isobel screamed.

Chapter Twenty-seven

"Isobel!"

The roar of Wolf's voice died away. His entire body ached with fatigue and tension, every muscle afire as he sprang from his horse and bolted toward the keep. The night's storm had passed, leaving the bailey damp and boggy. But instead of the fresh newness one might expect the breeze to carry after a storm, a desperate chill hung in the air.

With more force than necessary, Wolf threw open the massive door to the keep, startling those inside as it reverberated off the stone wall behind it. The warriors he'd left behind sat at benches in the chamber, their faces grim.

Mistress Rowley and several other servants bent over a pallet set by the hearth. Wolf could not see who lay there, but the blood-soaked cloth near the bedside told him all he needed to know. Wolf looked to his men. "Who attacked?"

Hiram stood, pushing away from the table to join his master. "The king's own men."

Wolf fought to stay calm as his thoughts flicked back

to Grange's empty encampment. Another trap. They had drawn him away from his own people, leaving them vulnerable to attack. "How many are injured or dead?"

"Only one injury, my lord Wolf." Hiram's gaze dropped to the floor.

Wolf's heart stopped. "Isobel."

"Nay, 'tis Walter."

"Where is Isobel?"

Regret twisted Hiram's scarred face. "No one knows. She forced us all to lock ourselves in the keep. The last we saw of her, she walked out of here with a crossbow in her hands."

"And no one went after her?" Wolf clenched his hands into fists, fighting the trembling that threatened.

"Walter followed on her heels. We all assumed he would stop her. Then when we heard a howl coming from outside, we immediately went to arms." Hiram stared down at his hands, folding and unfolding them as he spoke. "By the time we made our way to the bailey, the king's men were gone, as was the Lady Isobel."

"Where is Walter?" Wolf asked.

Hiram pointed to the pallet by the hearth. "He lives, but he was badly injured by a crossbow bolt that narrowly missed his heart."

If Walter had been injured, did that mean that he'd failed in his attempt to kill Isobel? Wolf strode to Walter's side. He drew his dagger with a trembling hand as he bent down beside his straw pallet and pressed the tip of the weapon against the curve of Walter's chin. "Traitor."

Walter's gaze remained fixed off in the distance. "One who deserves to die," he replied, his misery obvious.

"You don't deny that you betrayed me."

"Father threatened *your* life if I did not kill her. I had no choice."

"Everyone has a choice, Walter. Sometimes you just have to look for the options." Wolf sheathed his weapon as his anger diffused.

"I couldn't let him kill you after all you have done for me."

"Our father is not all-powerful. He is just a man," Wolf ground out.

"He's a king." Walter's jaw clenched through a shudder of pain.

"Aye, but that doesn't make him God."

Walter swallowed with difficulty as his fingers crept up to the blood-soaked bandage that covered his chest. "Nay. God is more merciful," he said softly. A plea for forgiveness lingered in his eyes. "I could not shoot her."

"Where is she?"

Walter shrugged, then gasped in pain at the movement. "I located her in the bailey before the others attacked. She opened the portcullis and just stood there in front of the gates as if she were waiting for something."

Or someone.

A chill rippled across Wolf's flesh. Had Isobel betrayed him as well? Was she working for his father? How could that be, if the man had gone to so much effort to ensure Walter's cooperation in killing the girl? Even so, suspicion roared through him. Why would she leave the gates open? Why would she just wait there, alone?

Wolf shoved a hand through his hair, hoping to bring clarity to his thoughts. But only more questions lingered. The attacks had been on her life. Or were they? Perhaps they truly had been directed at him the whole time, and not her, as he'd assumed. Had she willingly poisoned herself to throw him off her trail? Why would she do that?

A wave of raw emotion crashed over him, and he closed his eyes against it, searching his memory for facts, for things she might have said or done that would confirm his suspicions.

In his mind's eye he saw Isobel in the crofter's cottage when they'd first met, looking desolate, alone, and in need of a champion. He pictured her sitting at the edge of the pond, her feet tucked primly beneath the hem of her gown. When her gaze had touched him that day it had been filled with tenderness and a sincere desire to help him. And he knew in his heart that what he'd seen there had been the truth and not some act.

And when they'd made love for the first time. . . . Wolf opened his eyes and met Walter's remorseful gaze. He knew with each trembling touch of her hands upon his flesh that she cared for him—and a part of him had come back to life that day. A part of him that he'd thought his father had crushed out of him long ago. He'd trusted her then, and he trusted her now.

"There had to be a reason she left the gates open." Wolf narrowed his gaze on his brother. There had to be another explanation. "I need to ask you something else and I will tolerate nothing but the truth."

Walter nodded.

"Did you at any time try to harm Isobel or myself?"

"My only attempt was in the bailey." His words rang with sincerity. "Although I knew of my mission since the moment we arrived on St. Kilda. Why do you think I have been so angry since our return here? I knew I would have to separate you from what you'd come to care about—all for the sake of our father."

"Did he tell you why he wanted her dead?"

Walter shook his head. "I never asked. I thought it was just one more way for him to control our lives."

"He controls me no longer."

Walter's eyes widened. "What have you done?" He struggled to sit up, but a fit of coughing forced him back against the pallet, gasping for breath.

"I made a choice. One that might well cost me my life." Wolf stood, anxious to find his wife and learn the truth from her own lips. "I need to find Isobel."

Walter struggled to sit up once more. "You—" Spasms of coughing wracked his body. He cried out in agony as he collapsed against his makeshift bed.

Wolf snatched up the neatly folded tartan and black leather tunic that lay near Walter's side and quickly put them on. "Rest. You'll need it. For I still haven't decided what is to be your fate." Without waiting for a response, he strode out of the great hall and into the courtyard. He had to find Isobel; nothing else mattered more than that.

Walter had last seen her out in the bailey. It seemed as good a place as any to begin his search.

"Isobel."

He strode through the inner bailey until he found himself standing before the hen yard. "Isobel," he called again, listening for a reply, but there was only the furious squawking of the chickens as they pecked the ground in search of food. Mistress Henny stopped her grazing to peer up at him ever so briefly before settling back into her newfound routine.

Isobel had adapted to her routine at the castle as well. She'd taken up the challenge of preparing the meals each day, as well as ensuring that they had ample supplies of food and cloth in the storerooms. She had even taken up the drying of herbs from the garden to mix into medicines so that his kinsmen would have only the best care if the need arose. She had been given no choice in their marriage, but she'd done everything a wife should do. If she were only here as a spy, would she have done those things?

There was no denying that she had deceived him. But would the knowledge that she was a Balliol have stopped him from touching her that very first time on the isle? He had taken one look into those bottomless eyes of hers and imagined seeing a plea there . . . a plea to be taken, to be held, to be loved.

And yet something his father had said lingered at the edge of Wolf's thoughts. The man had hinted that there was more about Isobel he did not know, something his father had not revealed.

Wolf shook off the thought with disgust. His father could not be trusted. Nay, he had to keep his faith in Isobel. With a purposeful stride, he left the hen yard, heading for the outer bailey.

"Isobel?"

The slight morning breeze snatched his voice and carried it across the open space as he strode to the outer bailey, where Walter had seen her last. He walked the length of the bailey before he paused near the large castle gate. Where could she be?

He saw something on the ground—a somewhat battered crossbow. He picked it up. The one Isobel had carried? Wolf stood and turned back toward the keep.

"Wolf?"

He stopped and swung back toward the closed portcullis at the sound of a familiar voice. Fiona clutched the iron bars between her delicate fingers, looking as though the very act of standing upright was more than she could bear. Her yellow velvet gown was torn and filthy, her hair a wild tangle of grime and leaves. A gash surrounded by an angry blue bruise marred her temple.

"Fiona?" He signaled to the tower guards to raise the portcullis. The grinding of metal filled the air as the gate rose slowly upward.

Fiona released her grip on the bars and swayed on her feet, though she remained upright. When the bars cleared a path, he moved to stand before her. "What happened?"

Her blank gaze focused on his face and fear rooted in his chest. "He took her away."

"He took who?" he asked, already knowing what she would say.

"Isobel." Tears streamed down her cheeks. "Grange has her."

Every fiber of his being became alert. "Where?"

"I do not know." Her tears came all the harder now, as she fell to her knees. "I tried to help her. You have to believe me."

Fear and confusion twisted inside him. He didn't know what to believe. He stared off into the distant trees. Was this just another trap? Or did Grange truly have his wife? If so, where Walter had failed, Grange could easily succeed.

Emotion forged by fear and something else he still refused to acknowledge beat against his breastbone, demanding to be heard. He'd kept it prisoner for too long, refused to acknowledge its importance in his life, denied its softness, its power . . . its effect on every breath he drew.

"I must find her," he vowed.

Fiona nodded as she slumped forward. Wolf caught her as she slid into unconsciousness. He lifted her into his arms with a curse and carried her limp body back to the keep. Any information she might have would remain untapped. Once inside the hall, he deposited Fiona on a nearby pallet.

Isobel could be anywhere. And if she were with Grange, he had no time to waste. Brahan and the others would return to the castle soon and would help him search the forest for his wife. But soon he might be too late for Isobel. He needed to do something now.

He hurried toward the stables. With a fresh horse and a little luck he would find her. He secured a horse and leapt onto the animal's back. As he did, a stab of pain shot through his left leg, and he remembered what his father had slipped inside his boot. He reached for the Stone, clasping it between two fingers.

If only Brahan were here. He could use the Stone to locate Isobel. Wolf rolled the Stone's smooth surface between his fingers. What was it his father had said? His own family had had the ability to see into the future at one time with the help of the Seer's Stone. That only half the Stone remained was why Brahan's visions had never been very clear or predictable. Yet some of those visions had been true.

But at what cost to Brahan? Wolf pictured the streak of white hair that marked Brahan's temple—a visual reminder of the drain each vision had upon his life's essence. And Isobel . . . she experienced periods of desperate cold after each of her visions. Again, a token paid for the use of the Stone.

Wolf cupped the Stone in his palm, then held it against his own forehead. Using the broken Stone to foretell the future came with a toll—a toll he would willingly pay if it helped him find his wife. The time for caution had passed. It was time to be reckless, to take risks as he had taken last night against his own father, to trust what his heart told him.

He closed his eyes and cleared his thoughts. "Show me Isobel," he whispered into the wind.

Chapter Twenty-eight

Grange's hand cracked across Isobel's cheek with such force she flew backward and hit the forest floor. She gasped, trying to catch a breath.

"Where's your husband and that Stone?"

"I don't know." Isobel shook her head, trying to clear it of fear as well as the ringing pain of Grange's blow to her cheek.

"Don't lie to me." He bent down and effortlessly lifted her onto her feet. "I'll get that Stone one way or another." His voice was misleadingly gentle.

"You already have the one my mother—" Agony rocked her as Grange struck her again.

"I need them both to get what I want."

The forest whirled, then blurred before Isobel's eyes. "I'll never help you."

He struck her again.

She swayed on her feet. She would never reveal the knowledge about Wolf or the Stone. What could he possibly do that would be worse than what he'd already done to her mother and herself? "I'd rather die than help y—"

Pain exploded against the back of her eyes, and she hurtled down into a welcome darkness.

"Come on, wake up. My patience grows thin. You've been unconscious for the better part of the day."

Isobel slowly opened her eyes to find Grange gazing down at her.

"Very good. You are awake. I had feared I had done you some grievous physical injury. That would never do. I need you awake and able to interpret."

"Interpret what?" she whispered past the dryness in her throat. As her vision cleared she stared above her, realizing with a surge of panic that the colorful canopy overhead was not the filigreed lacing of tree branches, but the dappled glass canopy of Wolf's tree house. She tried to sit up, yet could not because her wrists and ankles were bound to the floorboards.

A prisoner once more.

Early evening light crept through the windows, casting a deep golden glow about the room and reminding her of the time she had come here with Wolf. She clung to the good memories. She had to, or she would be overwhelmed by the terror and despair closing in around her.

Grange smoothed back the hair from her temple. "Poor little dear. You're frightened."

She forced back a shiver, refusing to give him the satisfaction. He wanted her fear; she could see that knowledge in his expression. Her fear gave him power over her. And she would never give in.

"You should be scared." He trailed his fingertips over

her bruised cheek, leaving pain in their wake. "Until you give me what I want, I will not stop." He reversed his caress over her cheekbone, pressing more firmly this time. She bit back a cry of agony.

"Now, let us get back to the matter at hand, shall we?" He sat back on his heels and studied her. "Where can I find your husband and his half of the Stone? And do not lie to me this time."

"I don't know where he is. That's the truth." She struggled against her bonds, allowing her fury to burn what remained of her despair. "Only a seer could tell you such a thing," she snapped at him, realizing a moment too late what it was she had said.

A glint entered his dark eyes. "I couldn't agree more." He reached into his tunic and withdrew her half of the Stone. "I have wondered if you possess the same abilities your mother once claimed she did."

Isobel couldn't speak. Her throat refused to function as he knelt beside her. She instinctively began to struggle against the bonds holding her tight against the floor. He leaned in closer, pressing the Stone into her forehead. "Where is the other half of the Stone?"

Isobel shuddered and closed her eyes, holding back the tears that threatened to spill over onto her cheeks. She was alone and helpless, and nothing she could do would stop her father from using her in this way.

She opened her eyes on a gasp as he pressed the Stone cruelly into her flesh. His cool, unfeeling gaze searched her own, watching her fear, feeding on it.

Isobel forced herself to look beyond him, at the colored spheres of glass that dotted the ceiling. Wolf's creations. The light glinted off the glass, sending prisms of color dancing on the walls of the room.

In the light she found comfort; Wolf was here with her.

Her eyelids drifted closed, yet the colors remained. Red mixed with orange, green mixed with blue, until a palate of color and light surrounded her mind and she felt no fear.

"Where is the missing half of the Stone?" Grange's voice intruded into her thoughts. "Tell me what you see."

A shiver wracked her body as the edges of her mind faded and an image appeared. The warmth of her flesh seeped from her with each pulse of her heart. Her skin tingled with a thousand pinpricks. Numbness settled into her limbs.

The image strode toward her framed by a smattering of trees in the distance. Nay, the image did not stride toward her, he ran. The lean lines of his body extended and contracted with the grace and strength of a wild beast.

A frigid chill washed over her, slowing her breathing, draining the life from her limbs. She relaxed into the vision, no longer able to fight the drain of the Stone's forces on her body, her mind, or her soul.

The image of the beast sharpened. His long, dark shape elongated and became upright, until he ran on two legs—powerful legs encased in black leather boots that failed to conceal sinuous muscle.

Chain mail lay beneath a black leather tunic that covered his upper body. Over that, he was dressed in a tartan in the new design she had helped the weaver create. The scabbard at his waist held a long and lethal sword. A warrior, not a beast, drew ever closer in her mind.

Wolf.

A burst of light flashed in the room. Despite the bone-crushing chill that immobilized her, Isobel turned toward it. Wolf filled the doorway, his broad frame slashing the beam of sunlight into hazy, dust-laden streamers. With what remained of her rational mind, Isobel marveled at how lifelike her visions had become. The smell of bay soap and mint, and a distinctive male fragrance she remembered as Wolf's own touched her senses, evoking a smile. Even the scent of him transcended time and space to bring her comfort.

She released a satisfied sigh, no longer afraid of the place the vision had taken her. Perhaps her mind knew she needed to see this man more than she needed to reveal the location of Brahan's stone.

"Is this what you seek?" Wolf's voice sounded from the doorway. The image held up his fingers, revealing a small white stone.

"The other half of the Seer's Stone." The pressure on her head lessened. A soft thunk sounded close to her ear, and pinpricks of warmth replaced the numbing chill. Grange scrambled to his feet. A wild gleam flashed in his eyes.

"Set her free and it is yours."

Her mind, her body hung suspended somewhere in the room, yet not quite all there either. This was no vision. Wolf had come for her.

"You are safe, Isobel." The cloudiness that had gripped her mind receded as Wolf's voice filled the room.

He moved, shifting the play of shadows and light, hiding his features in a wreath of darkness. Yet her senses told her what she could not see—a quaver sounded in his voice and tension hung suspended in the room. He cared for her, whether he'd spoken the words or not.

"Give me the Stone, and then you can have the girl," Grange said, drinking in the sight of the Seer's Stone.

"Cut her free."

"Give me the Stone."

A muscle jerked in Wolf's jaw. "Take it." He tossed the Stone high into the air. Grange made a wild leap for his treasure. Wolf dove toward the ground. He rolled effortlessly across the floor and came to his feet wielding a dagger. He slashed the bindings at her feet and wrists.

Familiar dark eyes glittered with brilliance as he gazed down at her. "You came for me."

"I promised to protect you." He drew her to her feet, then released her immediately, positioning his body in front of hers, shielding her from Grange.

Her legs were shaky and weak, and it took all her effort to remain standing. Warmth centered in her belly, chasing away the chill from her vision.

"Now that you have what you want, leave." Wolf's voice was as sharp as the steel of his blade.

Grange had caught the Stone and now twisted back around. The light from the open doorway behind him glinted off his ready sword. "I'll not leave until I have everything I want." His gaze moved past Wolf to Isobel. "The Stone does me little good without a seer."

Wolf raised his sword, every instinct tuned to the danger, every muscle in his body tensed.

"That sword will do you no good. My men have you surrounded." Grange preened. "You played right into my trap."

Isobel stepped back to the open window and glanced below. True to his word, Grange's troops surrounded the base of the tree. Her heart leapt.

"To leave here alive, you'll have to go through me and my men." Grange's eyes blazed hatred.

"Then so be it."

Isobel dimly heard their conversation. All her thoughts focused on how to keep her husband alive. She scanned the room, hoping against hope that she'd see something she had missed before—a weapon, a means of escape, something, anything to help their situation. Nothing came to her. The only weapon she had at her disposal was herself and her abilities.

She stepped around Wolf. "I will go with you, wherever you desire, if you promise to leave this man unharmed."

Wolf reached for her, trying once again to shield her with his body. But she spun away, moving closer to her father. There was no way he could fight his way out of this one. She would rather sacrifice herself than force him into a futile battle.

Isobel gasped when Grange snagged her by the hair. He jerked her head back, painfully, so that her neck arched. The room swirled before her eyes. He brought the tip of his sword to flirt with the pale curve of her neck. What had she done?

"Unwise, my dear. You've left your husband nothing to bargain with."

"Release her." Wolf lunged forward.

Grange swung. Wolf swerved to the side, barely escaping the full impact of Grange's blow. The blade sliced through Wolf's tunic but could not penetrate the mail beneath.

"Not another step, you Stewart bastard." Grange retreated, pulling a bruised and battered Isobel with him. "Drop your sword or she will die."

"Since it is my family you so despise, release her and take me instead." Wolf met her gaze, allowed his feelings to show in his eyes. He no longer wanted to shield from her what he felt in his heart.

Her eyes filled with tears.

"Why would you feel so strongly about protecting my daughter?"

Grange's words chilled the nape of his neck. "Your daughter?" His gaze shot to Isobel's. "Is this true?"

Isobel's bruised face went pale. "I wanted to tell you," she whispered. "I tried to, but—"

An evil smile creased Grange's face as he jerked her head back so violently that her words turned into a painful moan. "The secret's out."

Wolf's body tightened. Grange's child. His father had shackled him to his enemy's offspring. One last ploy for control.

Isobel twisted toward him, despite her agony. Her gaze filled with sadness, and in that instant she looked older and wiser than he'd ever seen her look before. He wanted to wipe that wisdom from her eyes.

"My offer stands. Trade her for me."

"I think not."

"Then release her, and I will give you safe passage."

Grange only laughed, the sound low and ugly. "Did you forget it is *I* who have *you* surrounded?"

There was a sound outside, one that could have been easily mistaken for thunder. "Do you?" Wolf asked with confidence.

Grange regarded him in stony silence. He dragged Isobel backward and peered out the open doorway. Wolf could not see what was happening below, but he heard the roar of a battle cry. "You have both pieces of the Seer's Stone." Wolf took two steps closer to Isobel.

Grange's eyes glittered—with madness or the fear of a cornered animal? "I want it all, everything you Stewarts have. I want the throne, the lands, everything you possess." His gaze dropped to Isobel. "Aye, even her. Do you think she means nothing to me?"

Wolf took another step forward but stopped when Grange jerked Isobel's head back again.

"I can see how much she means to you by the way you treat her now."

Grange growled an obscenity and waved his sword in the air. He ranted about his plans to kill Wolf, the king, and all the Stewart heirs until no one stood in the way of the Balliols' return to the throne. Mad ideas. Impossible ideas. But Grange believed them, postulating with such abandon that he forgot about his grasp on Isobel.

From across the distance, Isobel met Wolf's gaze. Her eyes filled with remorse, then determination.

Wolf frowned. Grange was too dangerous, too unpredictable for her to try something on her own. But before he could stop her she rammed her elbow into Grange's stomach.

With a grunt of pain, Grange released her hair, but before she could run, he grasped her. "Betrayer!" he cried as he ruthlessly shook her. "You'd choose him over your own father."

Grange shuffled backward until he and Isobel were framed by the door. "Just like your mother you are." Grange pushed Isobel through the open doorway and into the nothingness beyond.

Her scream died beneath Wolf's roar of outraged pain. He charged, his sword slashing with the violence that pounded in his chest.

Wolf allowed his grief to fuel blow after blow. With an upswing of his sword, the glass globes that hung down from the ceiling crashed to the floor. Soon the crunch of broken glass mixed with the clang of steel, creating a cacophony of violent sound. Yet none of it dulled the memory of Isobel's death cry.

Chapter Twenty-nine

Wolf charged his enemy, giving him no time to do more than defend each stroke. He would avenge Isobel's death. Justice would be served.

Pain and remorse burned in Wolf's chest, but he forced it deep inside. There would be time for grief later, a whole lifetime. What he needed now was a clear head and a steady sword if he was to put an end to Grange's grasp on all the people he loved—Isobel, Walter, his men.

What he did now, he did for them. He circled the room, searching for an opening. But Grange skittered like a spider as he dodged and ducked the blade. There was no predicting this madman.

Grange's sword thrusts darted here and there with no rationality or form. Wolf focused on Grange's eyes. His eyes would signal his next move. But only a terrible emptiness dwelled there, attesting to the madness that had taken over his soul.

Mad or sane, Grange had taken away the one woman Wolf had ever allowed to touch his heart. Her own father had killed her. With a renewed vigor, Wolf pressed his attack. Steel shrieked down steel as Wolf hooked Grange's sword with his own. With a twist, he tore the pommel from Grange's hand and sent the weapon flying. The sword arched through the air, shattering the glass bulbs suspended above. Wolf raised his sword, prepared to run his enemy through when the madman threw back his head with a keen of anguish.

Wolf stood rooted in place, watching a dark, malicious stain blossom high on Grange's chest. His eyes rolled upward into his head, then he collapsed forward. A long and lethal shard of green glass protruded from his back.

Behind him stood Isobel. Her face was ashen and marred with streaks of red. Her hands were covered with blood.

Sweet, dizzying relief stole through Wolf. "Isobel. How is it possible?" He sheathed his sword, knowing by the roar of victory below that his men had defeated Grange's army.

Her bloody fingers curled around what remained of her shredded skirt. "My gown caught on the tree. It gave me a moment to cling to a branch." The fabric of her gown sifted through her fingers. "I pulled myself up, and then I . . ."

He drew her into his arms. He gently trailed his finger over the purple welt on her cheek and closed his eyes, gathering her close enough to feel her heart beating against his own. "It's over."

"I was so frightened." She buried her head into the curve of his shoulder.

"Aye, Grange can be a terrifying enemy."

"Nay." She drew back but would not look him in the eye. "I was so frightened of what would happen once you learned the truth about me. That you wouldn't want me."

He angled her face toward his. Tears slipped down her cheeks and he brushed them away with his thumbs. "You are my wife." Cupping her cheeks with strong, secure hands, he pressed his lips to hers for a brief, heartfelt kiss.

"What happens now?" she asked, her voice tremulous. They both turned to look at the sprawled form of Lord Henry Grange.

Wolf stepped away from her to retrieve Grange's fallen sword, then handed it to Isobel. "The battle is not yet won against Grange's men."

Isobel accepted the weapon, her grasp firm on the hilt. "I will do all I can to help."

He nodded his approval and guided her to the stairs. "I'll go first to cover your descent." A moment later he leaped to the ground, prepared to fight. But the battle had ended. What remained of Grange's men had been rounded up as prisoners. Their weapons lay in a pile at the base of the tree.

"Stay here," Wolf instructed Isobel. He climbed back up into the tree house, then appeared a moment later with Grange's body slung over his shoulder. He deposited his enemy's corpse at the feet of his men and drew his sword. "Grange is dead."

A ripple of shocked disbelief spread through the men. "Grange's lands and all his possessions now belong to me as a spoil of war and by virtue of my marriage to his only child," Wolf declared.

All eyes turned to Isobel. Wolf's breath caught in his chest at the sight of her. She was magnificent, despite being covered in blood and her gown in tatters. A fire in her eyes said she would never be defeated. She was every inch the avenging queen. Wolf had to force his gaze away from the awe-inspiring sight of her in order to deal with what was yet undone.

"I offer you a choice for your future. You may either disband and go your own ways with a promise to never attack me or my people again, swear fealty to your king and follow me back to my castle, or if you continue your hostilities, you will die."

Murmurs spread through the troops as they broke up into smaller units to discuss their options. After several moments, two men, most likely the lieutenants of the groups, came forward.

"We choose to disband," one man said.

"Then go, but vow to me that you will travel far beyond these hills and vales."

"Agreed," they both said in unison before they turned away from the crowd and, taking six other men with them, walked into the woods.

The others remained. Three other men stepped forward. "If you agree to provide us with shelter and food, we will serve you, my lord," the elder of the three men said.

Wolf sheathed his weapon, grateful that no more blood would be spilt this day. "Then swear fealty to your king and help me tend the wounded and bury the dead."

One by one the men stepped forward and knelt before him before swearing their obedience. When they had all pledged their vow, they got to work. As the men worked, Isobel stepped beside him. "How did you know your men would come?"

Wolf reached into the folds of his tartan, producing Isobel's half of the Stone as well as the piece his father had given him. He held them out to her on the flat of his palm. "You and Brahan are not the only ones who can see into the future."

Isobel's gaze clung to his face, searching. "Your hair—" With a gasp she reached up, and with trembling fingers, brushed a lock at his temple. "A streak of white in a sea of midnight."

"A battle mark. Nothing more." He shrugged as he curled his fingers around hers.

She turned her gaze to his, and Wolf saw the pain in her eyes. "I am sorry."

"For what?"

"For endangering you and your men all because of . . . him." She swallowed roughly, and it took an almost physical effort not to try to ease her hurt with his hands, or silence her with a kiss. She needed this moment to say these things if she were ever to be free of Grange's hold on her life. He understood that need since he'd experienced the same himself with his own father. "The death and destruction he caused can never be repaid," she finally said.

Wolf reached up and laid his hand against her cheek. "Then do what you can to repair and rebuild by staying with me always as my wife and mistress to my people."

She turned her face into his hand and kissed his palm. "I'll stay."

He had just heard pledges from twenty men. Yet this vow from Isobel meant more to him than any other. The sincerity in her eyes reflected what was in her heart. "The others can finish here. Let's get you home." He led her to his horse and placed her on the animal's back before he swung up behind her. He rearranged the folds of his tartan around her bare legs so that they were both wrapped with the warmth his body offered.

As they set off for home, she settled back against his chest. He folded his arms around her. For a brief, blissful moment, he indulged in their newfound happiness. But in the span of a heartbeat reality returned. "I will hold you to another promise you made, Isobel."

She gazed up at him, a spark of challenge in her eyes. "What promise is that?"

"That you will stay at the castle, no matter what."

The teasing vanished from her gaze, replaced by fear. "What do you mean?"

She would know what he meant soon enough. For now, he wanted to live in the moment. "What kind of husband would I be if I didn't want to keep you safe?" He pressed a kiss to her lips, then pulled back to see the fear vanish from her gaze. An urgent hunger took its place.

Wolf smiled and set his heels against his horse's sides, spurring the animal into greater speed.

"Are we in a hurry?" she teased.

"We are if you don't want me to seduce you right here on the back of this horse."

As soon as they entered the inner courtyard of Duthus Castle, Wolf dismounted, scooped his wife into his arms, and carried her inside.

Upon their return to the castle, Wolf had stopped by Walter's bedside and been informed that his brother would survive his injuries. Relieved by the news, and encouraged by his staff to see to his own needs, Wolf had escorted Isobel upstairs to the solar.

Wolf knelt by the hearth, adding a log to the flames. He and Isobel had both bathed the last of the grime and blood from their skin. The remnants from their last battle with Grange were gone.

Firelight cast a glow over the room, gilding Isobel's soft curves in gold. The reflection of the flames danced provocatively over her breasts, her thighs, on down to her delicate and enticing feet. His wife, his Isobel. She was a survivor. She'd already survived her early years of torment, of abuse and misuse at the hands of the Mac-Donalds and her own father. And now . . . he would ask her to survive once more.

He would ask her to keep going after he was gone.

It seemed such a cruel twist of fate that his own father had finally given him a gift so precious as Isobel only to destroy that gift in the end.

An aching emptiness filled his chest. He'd never really thought about dying before. It was always something that happened to other people. Wolf forced his thoughts to still. He did not want to waste these moments on such dark ponderings. He wanted to revel in the softness of his wife for as long as he would have her.

As though sensing his need for her touch, Isobel held out her hand. When he joined her at the bedside, she pulled him down beside her. He shifted his body until he cradled her in his arms.

An amber-gold light caressed her skin. But even the firelight could not conceal the bruise on her cheek. Gazing upon her, he felt heavy inside, weighed down and full of grief at what she had suffered at the hands of her own father.

He brushed her hair away from her cheek with a feather-light touch, then leaned down to gently kiss her battered flesh. Sympathy and guilt assaulted him in an overwhelming tide, deluging his thoughts, drowning his voice until he could only say, "I love you."

He whispered the words over and over against her skin as he kissed her throat, her shoulders, her arm.

At her hands he paused and sat back. He nestled her hands, with all their gashes and cuts, between his fingers. Slowly, gently, with all the love in his heart, he kissed each wound. They were united in their pain, bound together in their love. He hoped, he prayed his affection would act as a salve and ease the trauma she had suffered.

She ceased his ministrations, placing a finger beneath his chin, bringing his gaze back to hers. A light mist of tears shone in her eyes. "Never in my darkest times in the tower did I believe my destiny would lead me to you. I feared I would die there alongside my mother. At times I prayed I would."

A tear rolled from her lashes onto her cheek. "I have no idea what I ever did to deserve you, but I am so very grateful." She tunneled her fingers through his hair with its new white streak. "I love you."

He caressed her cheek with his thumb, brushing away her tear, before placing a kiss to her eyes, her forehead, her nose, and finally her lips, softening them, taking away her pain. *She loved him.* Exquisite satisfaction filled him as the words echoed in his mind.

"You take away my fears," Isobel whispered against his lips. "You make me whole."

He laid her head against the pillow, her golden hair lying like a halo about her beautiful features. They completed each other, just like the two halves of the Seer's Stone. The Balliol half and the Stewart half, reunited.

Wolf buried his face in her hair and gently kissed her neck, hiding from Isobel the tension, the anger building inside him. He had finally found a woman who loved him for who he was, a woman who saw into his own heart. He breathed deeply, etching her scent of heather into his memory, storing her essence for that moment when the noose would tighten about his neck.

He lay there, allowing her strength to flow into him, until his anger faded and he became keenly aware of the soft pulse of her heart so near his own. He tilted his head back, gazing into her face. Desire shot through him so intensely that a groan tremored through his chest.

Her eyes widened and her lips parted. He stared at her mouth, aching to taste her. He caught her lips. She tasted of warm sunshine and sweet naïveté, as heady a brew as known to man. Against him, she was like a fragile white lily, supple and pliant, adapting and bending as she always did to survive.

Her breath played on his mouth, and she murmured something as he slid his hands down the satin skin at her sides, molding her flesh to his rampant arousal.

With a quick intake of air, she released his lips. Desire dilated her eyes. And something more—a look that said she trusted him, loved him, desired him above all else.

Nothing in his life had prepared him for that look. Nothing. Not her sweet surrender or the heady yearning in her eyes. Beneath his hands, her skin was on fire, burning with her need for him to touch her. And touch her he did.

He trailed his fingers up the delicate curve of her hips, her waist, and to her breasts, circling her nipples, urging them to taut peaks. He heard her soft moan of desire, felt a responding echo within himself, inflaming his passion all the more.

He replaced his fingers with his tongue. His mouth fastened on first one breast, then the other, licking, nipping, teasing. Continuing his assault, he kissed the valley between her breasts and dipped lower, to her waist, her belly, her navel, and lower still, until he kissed the softness between her thighs.

She tensed in surprise, but he allowed her time to adjust to his presence there, until the heat spreading through him also spread through her with his hot, wet kisses. He continued to gently stroke her until she was unable to control either her broken moans or her trembling.

He circled her with his tongue, then pushed inside her. She thrust against him in response, wanting more, and he could feel the tension building inside her, growing tighter and tighter with each thrust and circle of his tongue. Then, on a broken cry, she arched against him, erupted, surrendering to the dark, whirling pleasure he'd created.

For a moment he backed away, and she reached for him with hungry hands, urging him upward, over her body. She rose up to meet him, kissing the sensitive flesh of his chest, his shoulder, his mouth. "I want you so much. Please . . ." she murmured passionately against him.

In answer to her plea, he urged her back against the bedding and with a groan of capitulation parted her thighs. He tangled his hands in the silken cloud of her golden hair, then cradled her head, drawing her mouth to his once more. "Isobel . . . my love."

Her lips parted in unconscious provocation. And he accepted what she offered. With one quick thrust he entered her slick core, his mouth crushing hers, absorbing the sigh of ecstasy that twined in their breath.

Warmth and fullness. Deep. So deep. He thrust inside her, never wanting to let her go. In and out, he continued to stroke her, holding himself back, wanting her pleasure to soar again before he joined her in that dark and magical place.

She locked her legs around his hips and rocked with him, until the very essence of her being—her feel, her taste, her scent—merged with his own. Until there was no telling where she ended and he began.

Unable to hold himself back a moment longer, he guided her hips, thrusting hard, surrendering himself to her hot, wet sweetness, wishing the moment could last forever. But he knew it could not.

He remained deep inside her, until their breathing returned to normal and the beat of her heart slowed to a steady, even rate. He rose up on his elbows and looked down into her face, memorizing every detail of her passion-filled face before he rolled onto his back, taking her with him, pulling her against his side. She nuzzled against his chest. He lay back and gazed deeply into her dark brown eyes. Why did it take his father's command to bring him to this woman? He should have been searching the seas for her from Brahan's first vision of a fair-haired maiden. They had wasted so much time apart, living lives that were only half-complete.

She turned toward him, and instantly her passion faded at the look on his troubled face. "What's wrong?"

With one finger, he swept the dampened tendrils of her hair back from her face, then leaned down and kissed her with great gentleness. "I must ask you to do something for me without question or argument."

A flicker of unease crossed her face. "That would depend upon what you asked."

She sensed something was not right and he would no

longer hide the truth from her. "I want you to lead my people when I am gone." The raw ache returned to his chest.

"Gone?" Her face drained of color until only two rosy spots remained high on her cheeks.

He steeled himself against his need to comfort her. "It won't be long now before my father's guard comes for me."

"Why?" She looked at him then, as she had never looked at him before, her face a study of conflicting emotions.

"I've committed treason against the king."

She sat up, taking the bedsheet with her. "He's your father."

"You know."

She nodded. "Fiona told me."

"Then there are no more secrets between us." He offered her a sad smile as he sat up beside her. "My father is very much like your own. It matters not that we are blood. He will come for me, of that there is no doubt." He took her hand, fingering the jeweled ring he had placed there during their marriage ceremony. "When I gave this to you, I had no idea what you would come to mean to me. Let this ring always remind you of how special you are, how much I love you."

"They will hang you?"

"Aye." He closed his eyes against the sudden jarring of his heart. "The king is on his way to do just that."

"Let us go away. We can go to a remote isle where your father will never find us. I lived that way once; I would willingly do so again if it kept you safe."

He opened his eyes. "Isobel . . ." Desperate to remain strong, he stiffened. He heard the misery in her voice, and he would not add to her pain by making her believe they had options they did not. "I cannot run from this. If I do, the king will punish my people instead. He'll put a torch to everything I hold dear. And I couldn't live with myself if that happened."

"There is nothing I can say to persuade you?"

He shook his head.

Her resignation mirrored his own as she brought a trembling hand up to cradle his cheek. "How can I help?"

"When my father arrives, he will strip me of my lands, essentially taking this castle away from you and all who live here." Before she could comment, he continued, "I have a plan, and if it is successful, you will be allowed to stay for what remains of your life. You and Walter will take care of my people."

"And if your plan is not successful?"

Wolf drew a deep, shuddering breath. "It will succeed because there is no other way I can peacefully leave this world."

"We could go—"

"There is no other choice. Promise me you'll do as I ask and see this through."

"I'll do as you asked and care for your people."

"Thank you, Isobel."

She leaned toward him once more and brushed her lips against his. She lingered there, with their lips barely touching, and in that moment he felt it—the poignancy of her passion and her love. Such innocent seduction would have worked to keep him by her side if only he could stay. But as much as he longed to remain coiled beside her, wrapped in her warmth and her love, he could not.

Destiny had other plans. "I must go."

* * *

Isobel twisted the bedsheets in her hands. She brought the linen to her chest, praying the action would keep her heart from shattering as she watched her husband gather his clothing. In the silence of the chamber all the joy, the peace, the sense of belonging she had been feeling since her arrival at Duthus Castle vanished.

As he slipped a fresh linen shirt over his head, the pain and numbness receded and anger took its place. Not anger at Wolf—anger over their inability to find peace or happiness in the lives they had been given.

"I must leave you now." He fastened his newly woven tartan about himself, then secured his sword at his side. "There are a few more things I must settle before the king arrives."

Placing a final kiss on her lips, Wolf left the room, so ridden by his own inner turmoil that he did not see the shudder that swept through her body as she curled her fists in the bedsheets.

Wolf might think he had no other option except to sacrifice himself for his people. But he was wrong. Isobel pushed off the bed and strode to the armoire. She pulled the closest garment over her head and quickly brushed her hair.

He had things to attend to before his father arrived.

And so did she.

Chapter Thirty

It seemed to take an eternity before Brahan and the men arrived back at Duthus Castle, but when they did, Wolf was waiting.

Leaden clouds hung in the late afternoon sky, and a soft drizzle settled across the outer bailey as Brahan and the other warriors crossed over the drawbridge and into the castle grounds. Brahan broke away from the other men, who headed for the stables. He brought his horse to a stop near Wolf. "Why are you out here waiting for me in the rain instead of warm and snuggled against your bride? Trouble in paradise so soon?"

"I need to speak with you."

"About your father?" Brahan dismounted and handed the reins of his horse to a waiting stablehand. "We sighted him and his army heading this way. They should reach the castle by nightfall."

"I know."

Brahan frowned. "You know?" His gaze narrowed on the small tuft of white at the side of Wolf's temple. "You used the Stone."

He nodded.

"What else did you see?" Brahan's gaze moved beyond Wolf to the keep.

"My own death by hang—"

"Nay, that shall not be," Brahan cut in with sudden violence. "Not everything you see with the Stone is the truth. You should know that well."

"The Stone helped me find Isobel. It foretold your arrival at the same location as Isobel. It showed Grange's death at my hands. . . ." He paused, considering.

"What is it?" Brahan asked.

"I didn't kill Grange. Isobel did."

The tension in Brahan's face relaxed, and the corner of his mouth pulled up in a half smile. "As I said, things do not always happen as they are shown. Isobel affected the course of that vision. The course of the future is already altered because of that one thing. The future you saw no longer exists."

Wolf shook his head. "Perhaps. But you said so yourself, my father heads here now. So some part of the future I saw still exists. Which means I have to assume the worst and take care of certain things before he arrives here for me."

"We will go to battle." Brahan turned back toward the men. "I shall have them ready before he arrives."

Wolf caught Brahan's arm, halting him. "No more fighting."

Brahan's eyes widened. "You will not fight even to save yourself?"

"I will not fight him any longer." Wolf released his hold on Brahan. "I am not afraid to die."

"He has hurt you in so many ways over the years." Brahan's voice was low, barely discernible. "Don't let him hurt you any more. Consider that you might not be thinking clearly."

Wolf clenched his fists at his sides. "There is so much more at risk now. So many more people for him to hurt."

"Isobel."

"And you. And Walter. And anyone he thinks he can use to control my actions. I cannot allow that to happen again. Do you understand?"

Brahan nodded as he looked off into the distance. "I don't like it. . . ."

"Thank you, Brahan." Relief rushed through Wolf. "I must ask something else of you as well."

Brahan's eyes glittered moistly as his gaze slid back to Wolf's. "I would do anything for you if it kept you here with us."

For a moment, Wolf's resolve faltered, until he remembered all that was at stake. "Take half the men and half the servants from Duthus Castle and go to Grange's castle. Send half his men and half his servants here."

"Why?"

"Crichton Castle will soon be yours. I have drawn up papers for the king to sign, giving you the castle, the lands, and a title as repayment for your years of service to Scotland."

"The king will never agree to that."

"Aye, he will. I intend to make him an offer he can't refuse."

"You'll give him your life."

"That's what he's wanted for years."

Brahan remained silent, his gaze on Wolf. A myriad of emotions passed over his features—disbelief, anger, hope, and finally acceptance—until, with a sigh, he ran a hand wearily through his hair. "As you wish."

"Brahan MacGregor, I wish things could be different, but that is not to be. I need you and the others behind me if I am to leave Isobel with any sort of peace."

"There is no sanity in what you ask or what you do now, but I will do as you ask because you are my friend."

Wolf nodded his thanks, unable to find the words to express his true gratitude.

"When do I leave for this castle?"

"On the morrow," Wolf said. "All should be finished by then."

Brahan's gaze sharpened. "Don't make it easy for your father."

"Nothing between us has ever been easy. Why would my own death be any different?"

"I don't like it," Brahan repeated, his spine as rigid and unbending as the steely look in his eyes. He turned and strode toward the stable to vanish a moment later into the crowd of men who had served Wolf so well.

One task accomplished. Two remained yet undone.

Wolf did not have to go looking for Fiona. Instead, she found him.

The paleness of her face told him something was terribly wrong. "What is it?" he asked.

"Are you not angry with me?"

"In truth, aye."

Red spots of color came to her otherwise pale and bruised cheeks.

"You've hurt so many people. I still don't understand why."

"I needed the security Grange's money would give me."

Wolf felt a moment's anger, but he pushed it away. He needed to keep his self-command in tact, to deal with her quickly and move on. "So you became a spy and a murderess."

Regret lingered in her eyes as she took a step closer. "I'm not proud of what I've become." Only a hair's breadth separated them now. He grasped her arms and set her away, but not before she reached for his sword, pulling the weapon free of its scabbard with a whoosh of sound.

He reached for her, but she stepped away, out of his grasp. "Give me the sword, Fiona."

"I will give it to you if you promise to use it." Her gaze held a challenge.

"Against my father?" he asked.

She turned the weapon's hilt toward him. "On me. Take my life as a penance for all the bad I have done to you, to Isobel, to that poor serving girl, and everyone else who has crossed my path in the last score of years. Cut me down, I beg you. I deserve no less."

She forced the weapon into his outstretched hand, then dropped to her knees, exposing the length of her neck to him. "I beg you to make it quick and clean."

"Get up," he demanded, his tone harsh.

She twisted toward him. He saw her face. Saw her eyes. Saw in every aspect of her body the regret that pulsed through her. He also saw grief. "Do it!" she shouted up at him, then choked out a sob.

Wolf allowed the sword to slide from his fingers. It clattered against the ground as he bent down beside Fiona. On hands and knees, he reached for her slack fingers. "I will not release you from your own guilt through death."

He could see the burden of her guilt press down upon her, feel it in the shudder that coursed through her body as tears rolled down her cheeks. "I cannot live—" she sobbed, "with what I've done."

"Aye, you can, and you will." He reached down and wiped the tears from her cheeks with his thumb. "If you want to make something good of yourself from the bad, I will give you that chance, but it will not be in death."

"How do I find that redemption?" She sat back, staring up at him with a glimmer of hope in her eyes. "What can I do?"

He offered her his hand and pulled her to her feet. "Go to Crichton Castle with Brahan. Help him establish order among Grange's people. You will have ample opportunity to find forgiveness as you train the servants in the proper running of a home."

She looked skeptical. "That is not enough to make up for all the harm I've caused. I deserve to die."

"Your death will serve no purpose other than to end your pain. Going with Brahan is a start at redemption, Fiona. The rest you will discover along the way."

"What makes you think Grange's people will listen to me?"

Wolf allowed himself a grin. "They probably won't at first. But that will be the challenge, won't it?" More seriously, he added, "Brahan will need your help. Don't disappoint him, and don't disappoint me."

She nodded. "All right. I accept your challenge."

"Very well. You will leave for the castle with the others on the morrow. Prepare yourself." Without waiting for a response, Wolf retrieved his sword and headed back to the keep.

Two tasks done. One left.

"Walter." Wolf stood at the door of the chapel, as amazed as he was curious at the sight before him. His brother knelt before the altar, his freshly shaven head bent in prayer. His garb had changed as well. He'd exchanged his tartan for a monk's robe.

"What are you doing?" Wolf entered the chapel.

"Praying for the salvation of my soul." Walter's eyes were shut and his head rested against his folded hands.

Wolf knelt beside him. "Why now, when there have been so many other opportunities throughout the years?"

"Something you said." Walter's voice sounded tight and almost raw, as though he spoke through a wall of restrained emotion.

"When have I ever said anything that affected you one way or another?"

Walter's head snapped up. His eyes filled with pain and remorse. "You said I needed to stop letting Father control me. You told me to look for the options in my life." His gaze slid away from Wolf's to embrace the cross that hung above the altar. "I have searched for peace for so long, I hardly recognized it when I finally found it right here in this chapel."

Wolf frowned, confused by his brother's words. "Are you seeking forgiveness, Walter? Because if you are, I forgive you."

"I need so much more than your forgiveness. I need salvation." Walter returned to his prayers, but not before Wolf caught the determination and passion in Walter's gaze.

"What if I offered you a chance to put that determination into service?"

"How?" Walter's gaze remained fixed on the cross.

"Stay here at the castle and serve my people, serve Isobel. The king will arrive soon, and I will be charged with treason. Everything will be taken from me, unless you agree to step up and assume it all."

"I will be punished as well, for failing to kill your wife."

"You followed father's command. How were you to know that Isobel would be the one to stop you with that bolt to your chest? You've done your duty."

Walter shook his head. "He will never agree."

"He will by the time I am through. Now, will you commit to guiding my people? You may focus on their spiritual journeys, if that is what you choose."

Walter's gaze moved back to Wolf's and filled with disbelief. "You would trust me to do that? Me?"

Wolf smiled. "Only you."

"Why?"

He shrugged. "Who better to understand and guide those who stumble in life than someone who has stumbled as well?"

"I will need training."

"Father MacMurphy will train you. I'll make certain of that."

Walter's face brightened. "I won't disappoint you."

"Nay," Wolf agreed. "I don't believe you will." He stood, then headed out the door. All his tasks were now complete. All that remained was to wait until his father arrived.

At the thought his heartbeat faltered. He was tempted to go back to the chamber he shared with Isobel and spend the last few moments of his freedom losing himself in her sweetness.

He started down the hallway to the solar before he forced his feet to stop. He gripped the stone wall for strength, for support. If he went to her now, it would make it that much harder to leave her when the time came. With an effort, he turned around, heading instead for the great hall.

He still needed to speak with Mistress Rowley. With

any luck he would find her there. If not, he would go to the lists and work out his aggressions at the end of a sword.

Wolf found Mistress Rowley in the hall near the hearth, tending to the needs of the warriors who had battled against Grange's men.

"How are they?" Wolf asked as he approached.

"They are well," she whispered, "but they'd be better if they knew their lord would be with them to support them for years to come." She stood, stepping away from the warrior who slept on the pallet near the hearth's warmth.

Word of his father's arrival had spread quickly. "I cannot stop the king from coming for me."

Mistress Rowley stood before him, her hands perched on her hips. "Even in their battered condition, many of them want to fight on your behalf."

"No more fighting."

"Why?" Mistress Rowley's voice held a hint of desperation. "You've fought him all your life. Why stop now?"

"Because the man finally did something good for me. He gave me Isobel."

Mistress Rowley shook her head in dismay. "He threatened to kill her. He tried a time or two, as I recall." She leaned in closer, her gaze narrowing on his face. "Not that you have to explain yourself to me, my lord Wolf, but you had better if I'm to explain your reasons to her once you're gone."

Blood pounded at his temples. Why did they all have to make this so hard? Did they not see he had no other choice? The king would rise again and again, like a bloody Phoenix, until he killed them all. "If I fight him, he still controls me and Isobel. If I don't, at least she'll be free."

"Free for what?" Mistress Rowley pulled back, her eyes wide. "Free to mourn your loss every day of the rest of her life?" She shook her head in disbelief. "That girl loves you. Truly loves you. Do you know what a gift that is?"

Wolf allowed her words to sweep over him with all their sweet, shattering power. Aye, he knew what a gift Isobel's love was. In the wake of his joy, an emptiness settled inside him, threatening to consume him with its intensity. He clenched his teeth against the pain. He would not trade a moment of the time they'd spent wrapped in each other's arms, of the secret smiles, the heartfelt words they had shared in order to extinguish his anguish now. *He loved her.* He loved her enough to keep her safe and at peace.

He released a long, shuddering breath. "I cannot, I will not turn away from my destiny." He twisted away and strode across the hall when the door to the keep swung open. A clarion's call proceeded his father's entrance into the chamber.

"Well, what have you to say for yourself?" King Robert II asked as he strolled into the chamber, followed by two guards. The nearly empty room suddenly filled with people. They entered from the doorway behind the king, from the inner doors leading from other sections of the castle, and from the stairs above, until it seemed as though all the castle's residents lined the stone walls. All the residents except one—Isobel.

Wolf tried to mask the eviscerating pain that lanced through him at that moment. No amount of misuse on his father's part, or torture on Grange's, could equal the turmoil that made his legs weak and left his insides gutted. He longed to see her one last time. But such a thing was not to be. He did not blame her.

The king strode forward and as he did, his subjects bowed, casting their gazes to the ground as the man passed them by. All except Wolf. His spine felt suddenly rigid and unbending. If his father wanted him to bow, he could strike him down at the knees.

The king scowled, anger clotting his cheeks with high color. "You challenged my authority in the battle with Grange."

"Aye." His body felt numbed, dulled, as though nothing this man said could hurt him anymore.

"I could have you hanged for such an offense."

"I expected you might."

"You've left me few options, boy." The king searched his face. What did he search for? Regret? Remorse?

"I know." Wolf hardened his gaze until he was certain it was not only cool but as cold as ice—the kind of ice that burns.

His father flinched at the effect. "You've left me no option but to have you arrested for treason."

Wolf nodded. "And I will go willingly if you sign these two deeds." He motioned toward the table near the hearth. "One will bestow Grange's castle as well as a title upon Brahan for his service to Scotland. The other allows my lands to pass to Walter and Isobel jointly upon my death."

A deep frown etched across the king's face. "Why would I sign either of those?"

Wolf allowed himself a small smile. "Because I saved your life when I refused to fight. My treason served you well. If we had charged into battle as you had planned, you would be dead. Grange set up an ambush. By not engaging in that battle, I saved your life and kept your reputation."

The king's face paled. "You have no proof of that."

Wolf looked beyond the king and signaled for one of Grange's former lieutenants to come forward. He offered the king a bow.

"Angus, recount for the king what you told me."

" 'Tis true, Your Grace. Grange would have killed you. We were all there, hiding, waiting to trap you in the valley below. It would have been a massacre. When Wolf left with his men, you also withdrew. We never attacked because you held the advantage by virtue of the terrain."

The king waved a dismissive hand in the air. "That is hearsay. No one here will testify that is the truth."

"Aye, but they will," Wolf countered. "Grange's men who returned with me signed a statement claiming that as the truth—a statement that I have since sent to the Bishop of Cromarty for safekeeping should you go back on your word after my death."

"Damn you, boy."

"Aye, I have been damned for years by you. Now sign the deeds."

With a growl of displeasure, the king stepped up to the table. After dipping the quill in ink, he placed his signature on each deed.

The king's mouth compressed. " 'Tis done, and we can proceed with what I came here to do." He nodded to the two guards who had followed him inside. They strode forward, one on each side of Wolf, and bound his hands behind his back.

One of the guards stepped back and in a loud voice proclaimed, "Douglas Moraer Stewart, you are hereby charged with treason against the crown."

Chapter Thirty-one

The charge of treason hung in the air of the great hall when the door burst open, the heavy wood crashing against the stone wall behind it. The flame of the torches bent and flickered as the wind from outside wafted through the chamber. In the doorway, silhouetted against the red and orange fingers of sunset, mounted upon the largest stallion in the castle's stable, was Isobel.

Yet it wasn't Isobel. At least not the woman Wolf had left in the bedchamber only a short time earlier. This Isobel had fire in her eyes as she rode the horse into the chamber. The clatter of hooves on the stone flooring brought all the noise in the room to a hushed silence.

Isobel's chin came up as she drew near, dressed in chain mail from head to toe, topped by a surcoat, leather cross-garters over boots, and leather gloves. Golden locks spilled from beneath her coif and across her shoulders, softening her otherwise fearsome features. She appeared every inch the warrior's bride.

Mighty, dangerous, magnificent. At the sight of her, a curious warmth centered in Wolf's chest.

The soft hum of whispered conversation hovered in the room. Light from the setting sun streamed through the high, rectangular windows overhead and caressed her features, limning her cheeks with yellow-gold light and tipping her lashes in gold.

"What is the meaning of this?" the king roared with disbelief, bringing the room to silence.

"Isobel?" Wolf stared at her as she sat atop the beast, almost not believing the vision before him.

"Isobel? So your bride managed to survive. She must be clever." The king's tone softened. "Explain yourself, girl."

Isobel and the beast moved forward as one. "I was asked by the lord of the castle to oversee his people. I am doing just that." Her bearing was strong and proud, yet her voice held a strange intensity. Uncertainty?

The scrape of metal against leather sounded as she drew her sword from the scabbard at her side. She clutched the weapon with as firm a death grip as he'd ever seen in the course of battle.

At the sight of her sword, the king's brows pulled down. "What is it that you want?"

She brought the horse to a stop before the king and dismounted. "I have come to bargain. Since you intend to relieve me of my first husband, I demand you replace him with a second."

An unexpected tightness seized Wolf's chest.

"Put the sword away and we might discuss the matter," the king suggested.

"Unbind Wolf's hands and I will consider it." Her tone was firm.

The king nodded, and the guard slashed the bindings at Wolf's wrists.

Isobel sheathed her sword.

The king's bearing relaxed. "Who exactly did you have in mind as this replacement? Or am I to choose for you once again?"

She strode forward with a slight swagger to her step. A warrior's stride. "Oh, I have someone in mind, Your Grace."

That brought a frown to Wolf's face. "Who?" he asked before he could hold the question back.

She did not look at him, only the king. "I choose Douglas Moraer . . . *Black* as my spouse."

"Such a man does not exist." The king looked dubious.

"He does if you create him," Isobel challenged. "You want retribution for Wolf's treason? Very well. Destroy the man who disobeyed you, then give him life once more. As a father, can you do anything less?"

The king blinked, then laughed. "You're a clever girl."

Her gaze strayed to Wolf's then, and he saw all the love, all the bravery, all the fear of her actions that lay just beneath the surface of her facade. And he loved her all the more.

"What you ask is impossible," the king replied. "One woman's wishes cannot change the laws of a country."

She brought her shoulders back, her gaze spanning the other occupants in the room. "It is not only my wishes that you should consider here. There are others who will stand behind this man."

Brahan stepped up to stand beside Isobel. "I would."

Walter came forward as well. "As would I."

A paralysis seized Wolf's limbs as he watched his people step forward, one by one, each placing themselves at risk by vowing their support. Their collective voices echoed through the room, falling away until there was only silence.

"You are the king." Isobel's mouth took on a faint, wry curve. "You make the law. You also have the power to override it. All these people are your subjects. You have the power to make them beholden to you, or turn them against you. The decision is yours."

The king narrowed his gaze on her, yet not in anger. Respect and gratitude reflected in his father's eyes. "Nay, the decision is no longer mine, milady. You have seen to that."

He turned to Wolf. "Kneel," he said, without the harshness that usually followed his instructions to his son.

Wolf's chest ached, not at his father's actions, but at the show of affection by his people. Regardless of his past, they respected him, cared for him, were willing to fight for his life. A surge of emotion welled inside him, robbing him of speech as he knelt upon the floor.

The king reached for Isobel's sword, drawing it from the scabbard in a single, swift stroke. He placed the flat of the blade against Wolf's shoulder. "I declare before this assembly that Douglas Moraer Stewart, the man also known as the Black Wolf of Scotland, exists no more. From this moment forth, you shall be known as Douglas Black, guardian of the Seer's Stone." The king lifted the sword from his shoulder and handed it back to Isobel. "Guard him well, milady. And love him as he deserves to be loved."

"With pleasure, Your Grace." Tears shimmered in her eyes, and one of them raced unheeded down her smooth cheek. "With pleasure."

Wolf swallowed back the emotion that pulled at his

throat and met his father's gaze. Unable to do anything more, he nodded. His father's head dipped with an air of regal authority before he turned and left the room.

A touch on Wolf's sleeve brought his gaze back to Isobel. "You are free of him, Douglas, just as I am free of my father."

"Say that again," he said, his voice thick.

"You are free—"

"My name, say my name."

"Douglas."

He allowed himself a small smile. "On your lips it sounds right, but it will take some getting used to."

"We have the rest of our lives to practice," she said, her voice as passionate as her gaze.

He caught her hand. Her fingers twisted with his as she lowered herself to kneel beside him, her gaze level with his. "You fought for me, my warrior bride."

She bit her lip, trying to hide a sudden wayward smile. "Not in a real battle."

Her smile hit him like an errant ray of sunlight, warming his insides and bringing sensation back to his limbs. "In the battle for my life, for my freedom." He reached up and removed the chain mail coif from her head. "And for my heart."

Her fingers found his again and slid between them. "I love you."

The sweetness of her words warmed him, and he leaned close to brush the corner of her mouth with his lips. "Isobel," he whispered.

She met his lips with a sudden greedy recklessness, both innocent and ardent. The silence of the hall shattered with a frenzy of applause and cheers.

"I relinquish your lips for now, Lady Isobel," he whispered against her cheek. "But I promise a more thorough expression of my gratitude when we are once again alone." He stood, then drew her up beside him.

She nestled against him, her gaze searching the smiling faces of their people. The merry and spirited strains of a *rotundellas* broke through the noise of the chamber, evoking another hearty round of cheers as everyone assembled for the round dance.

Douglas grasped Isobel's hand and pulled her into the circle, but the others thought differently and thrust them into the center of the ring. Isobel held on to her husband's hands as he twirled her about. Laughter bubbled up in her throat, and she felt almost too breathless to release it.

Isobel slowed her steps as the sun's setting rays burst through the windows overhead, bathing the chamber in hues of gold, crimson, and orange. The light through the windows illuminated the castle just as the man before her illuminated her heart.

"What are you thinking about?" Douglas asked as his hands cupped her cheeks and he tilted her face up to look into his eyes.

"Glass . . . and stones." Her mind was whirling as if she were still dancing just from the look of love in his eyes. "What did you do with the two halves of the Seer's Stone? You are now their guardian. How will you keep them safe?"

"Curious that you should mention those two things— glass and stone—in the same sentence." He tipped up her head to the ceiling, to what must have been a thousand glass bulbs that hung suspended overhead. Each brilliantly colored bulb caught and scattered the light from the giant torches that hung from the walls, bathing the room in a profusion of prismatic light. "The best place to hide things is in plain view of everyone."

Her gaze snapped back to his. Had he encased the stones in a sea of glass and added them to the rest of the decorations? "You didn't."

"I did."

"But will the stones still hold the same power, encased as they are in glass?" she whispered.

"Who needs a Seer's Stone? If I want to know the future, all I have to do is look into your eyes." He smiled then, his expression far lighter than she'd ever seen it, free of the shadows of his past, free of obligations, free of duty, filled only with love and joy and anticipation of the future ahead.

She smiled in return as the light of the colored globes highlighted his dark hair with its one streak of white. "The future looks very bright, indeed!"

An Afterword
from the Author

As is the case with much of fiction, a little fact and a little fantasy went in to creating *Warrior's Bride*.

The original idea for the story emerged while researching Scottish tartans, when I read a story about a woman named Lady Grange. In 1725, Lady Grange was kidnapped by her husband, who wished to be rid of her, and his friend Lord Lovat, who wrongly assumed she knew too many political secrets about the Jacobites. They took her to the Isle of St. Kilda, where she was imprisoned for more than six years.

Even though it was common knowledge that Lord Lovat, along with her husband, had engineered the kidnapping, no inquiry into the extraordinary circumstances was ever made, and long before any rescue attempt, she died of neglect and loneliness.

Desiring justice, even through the pages of fiction, for Lady Grange, I gave her a daughter to see this through and to make the lonely days of isolation not seem so despairing.

The destiny stone featured in this book was also a real

stone that did not have a name. As legend has it, a seventeenth-century visionary named Cùinneach Odhar (Kenneth MacKenzie, from Uig on Skye), who was referred to as the Brahan seer, used a small white divination stone to foretell the future. The stone was passed on to him from his mother, who had acquired it from a Viking princess.

With the pebble pressed against his eye, Cùinneach foretold everything from outbreaks of measles in the village to the building of the Caledonian Canal, the Clearances, and World War II. His visions brought him widespread fame, but it also resulted in his untimely death when the Countess of Seaforth summoned him after her husband was late from a trip to France. Reluctantly, he told the countess that he saw her husband in the arms of another woman. At this, she flew into a rage and ordered him to be thrown headfirst into a barrel of boiling tar.

Before his execution, which took place near Brahan Castle on Chanonry Point, Cùinneach made his last prediction: When a deaf and dumb earl inherited the estate, the Seaforth line would end. His prediction finally came true in 1815 when the last earl, who was indeed a deaf mute, died.

I chose to take the brutal end for this unfortunate seer and turn his fate around. I changed his name to Brahan MacGregor and gave him the gift of sight with the use of the Seer's Stone.

One last historical note: Robert II, King of Scotland, sired twenty-four children with four different women, two of whom were his mistresses, two of whom were his wives. I chose to give him an additional child with his mistress Marion Cardney for the purposes of this story.

That the Black Wolf of Scotland, Isobel, or Brahan

never existed in history is a fact. It was my goal, within the pages of *Warrior's Bride*, to give these characters and the real people their creation issued from a chance to find a happy and more fulfilling end to their own personal stories.